MW01531838

To Vernon

Lost Between Two Lives

Philip W. Mancil

Phil M

$ Creative Arts & Sciences House
West Melbourne, Florida USA

Copyright © 2013 by Philip W. Mancil.

All rights reserved.

☝ Creative Arts & Sciences House
$ West Melbourne, Florida USA

ISBN 978-0-9829729-9-1

Current Printing: 3

Printed in the United States of America

Library of Congress Control Number: 2012956082

Special thanks to:

Berniece Rabe Tryand for her constant encouragement,

Susan Mancil Morgan for her endless hours of editing; I couldn't have done it without her,

Jill Mancil Nelson my technology wizard,

Aaron Mancil for his support,

My wife Elizabeth Mancil for keeping me focused,

Rusty Allred for making it happen,

And of course all the readers who kept me on track.

To
Craig Huls

Sometimes we wonder if we were born at the wrong time or place, or if life has cheated us out of what could have been. Then through chance and circumstance, it quietly disentangles itself and we find our true destiny. - Heinrich Müller

Chapter 1

May, 1945 Roquefort, Ohio

Jimmy, the Western Union messenger stopped, stood outside Parker's Drug Store, and gathered his thoughts before stepping in. He knew people dreaded a visit from the Western Union since the war had begun. This time would be no different except he was delivering it to Cathy Strauss. He had been 'in love' with her since he was in the ninth grade and she was a senior. She was a cheerleader for the football team and was dating David Strauss, football hero extraordinaire. Their life was perfect. Now things had changed. They were married and, while David was still a hero, this time he was an army hero and ... "missing in action" for the past eighteen months. Jimmy did not want to go in. He knew what these telegrams usually meant and didn't want to hurt Cathy.

The bell on the door jingled when he stepped in. As he began to look around, the shopping patrons stopped what they were doing and watched his movements. He hated this part of his job. Everyone kept an eye on the "messenger of death" as he stepped in, knowing someone would feel pain. The two women in one of the booths across from the soda fountain were no different. Catherine Strauss began to pale when the messenger caught her eye and started her way. Tears had already formed in her eyes when he stopped in front of her booth.

1

He reached into his pouch and pulled out a telegram. "I'm sorry to interrupt you this way Cathy, but I was sure you would want this as soon as possible."

Tears were streaming down her face and her hand shook as she reached into her coin purse and pulled out a dime.

"That's not necessary," he said with a quiver in his voice.

"Yes it is," she said. "Thanks for finding me Jimmy."

She sat and stared at the envelope for a moment. Passing it over to her friend, Ann Marie, she said, "Would you open it for me? I can't do it."

The room had become quiet and all eyes were turned their way. Some of the women had retrieved handkerchiefs from their purses as tears filled their eyes. The men looked grim.

With tears in her own eyes, Ann Marie gently took the telegram from Catherine.

She got as far as the first line, "THE WAR DEPARTMENT" and caught her breath. Catherine began to cry. Ann Marie read on:

"CAPTAIN DAVID STRAUSS, MD LIBERATED FROM STALAG 21 (STOP) CRITICALLY WOUNDED BUT STABLE (STOP) TRANSFERRED TO HOSPITAL IN LONDON (STOP)"

"He's not dead!" she shouted. "Injured and transferred to a London hospital!"

The people in the room began to cheer and applaud. Even Jimmy had a smile on his face and a tear in his eye.

Catherine looked up. "What?"

Pulling the telegram from Ann Marie's hand she read it and began to cry. "He IS alive!" Reading it again, she said, "What happened to him? They don't say anything except that he is critically wounded. What should we do?"

Ann Marie took Catherine's hands in hers and laughing said, "At least he's alive. Let's take this to Papa Strauss; he'll know what to do."

A slight frown crossed Catherine's brow. "I'd almost rather talk to Hitler," then smiling she said, "Come to think of it, I'd talk to the Devil himself if it meant getting David back, so this should be easy. For once, I'm glad we have Papa. Let's go!"

Chapter 2

Several days earlier - Stalag 21 near Barth, Germany

Captain David Strauss, MD, US Army, and Major Heinrich Müller, MD, Army of the 3rd Reich, were sitting around the battered wooden desk in their small office off the main infirmary area of the POW camp where they had served for the last eighteen months, one as prisoner, and the other as camp doctor. They had talked so often in here during the past year and a half that it was like home. There was a bottle of *Asbach Uralt*, the closest thing that Germans had to French cognac, in front of them.

"I hear the Russians are going to be the ones allowed to 'liberate' the camp. They're doing some vicious things to German officers. You've seen the butcher jobs they've done. I wouldn't be much of a surgeon without hands. I'm not sure what to do," said Heinrich.

"My father can pull some strings and get you to the states if we can get you out of here alive. Since the kommandant has said you are free to leave maybe you can make it to the American lines. I hear they're not far. I can write a letter telling the Americans who you are. That could help, that is... if you live long enough to talk. I don't know how touchy they are right now. All the letters in the world won't help, if you're dead!"

"I've thought about that. Maybe I should take my chances here, David my friend. Now let's finish this bottle off and get some rest. We have a big day ahead of us. You go home; I'll probably wind up in Russia. I don't speak

4

Russian yet, that'll be a good challenge for me," said Heinrich with both a sense of humor and trepidation in his voice.

David looked at his friend and smiled. "As for me, I'm not sure which would be worse at this point, my wife or the Russians."

"That bad, huh," said Heinrich.

"Ohhh yeah," he said with a knowing look. "When I left, I was glad to leave. Between her and Papa, I was getting torn apart. If Papa wanted something, she wanted just the opposite. What she really wanted was for me to defy Papa." Giving his head a slight negative shake he said, "It's just not in me. I considered it respect; she said he was running my life. The last thing she told me when I left home was, 'If you live through all this, I hope you come back a man. If you can't be a real man, don't bother to come back at all.'"

Heinrich smiled, "I'm sure she didn't mean it, she was probably just angry."

"If you had seen her eyes, you'd change your mind."

Changing to more pleasant thoughts, they continued to talk of old times until the morning sky began to glow.

"*Skoal,*" Heinrich said as he and David clinked glasses and drained the last of the Asbach.

David gave him a weak smile. "Well, it won't be long, the fighting is getting closer. I expect they will be here in less than an hour."

Just then explosions began to rock the compound. The walls of the infirmary shook and the roof caved in, as they took a direct hit. Heinrich was down with blood running into his eyes. When he tried to move he couldn't. He pushed rubble from off his body then tried to stand. There was something wrong with his leg, it wouldn't work. *David, where is David?* Heinrich looked everywhere until he got a glimpse of a once white lab coat. *Over there, he's under all of that rubble. I've got to get him out.*

He wiped the blood from his eyes with the back of his hand as he pulled himself to his friend. He rose up on one arm and began to pull boards off David. As soon as he got him clear, he checked his pulse. His own heart began to race with fear.

No! Not you! Dear God, why? Why must the good ones die? He helped so many. I had nothing to live for; he had everything!

Heinrich sat there not knowing if he could go on. The building rocked again as the room next door collapsed. For some strange reason, he wanted to live. Summoning all the strength he could muster, he managed to get to a half-standing position and started for the door. As he did, an idea formed in his mind. He went back to his friend and lifted his dog tags from around his neck. Replacing them with his own he said, "Thanks for this last favor, dear friend, maybe the Russians will have to find other entertainment."

If I can get to the Americans, and safely away from the Russians, I will tell them what I have done. I'll take American punishment over Russian justice anytime.

Heinrich worked his way back to the door, but as he stepped out, another shell hit the building and it collapsed. He tried to crawl, but his legs wouldn't work. *Maybe I can pull myself,* he thought. His arms wouldn't work either. *Strange, maybe I'm dead. I can't feel a thing.* Then... everything faded to black.

He regained consciousness briefly when the stretcher he was on bumped the side of the ambulance.

"Careful with this one," a voice said. "We have a genuine hero here."

"Hero? Who is he?" said another voice.

"I can't believe it, but this is Captain David Strauss, hero of the battle at Isernia."

"What happened at Isernia?"

"Man, it was headlines in the *Stars and Stripes*! Don't you read the paper?" He shook his head in dismay. "Well anyway, he was a doctor at a forward aid station near

Isernia, Italy when the Germans began to overrun their position. The colonel ordered a withdrawal but there were no vehicles to carry out the worst of the wounded so they had to abandon them. That is everyone but Captain Strauss. He refused to leave and stayed behind to care for his men. They were never heard from again. No one knew what happened to'em, whether the Germans shot'em or took'em away."

At the same time another body was discovered by others at the destroyed infirmary. "Here's another one. Get that stretcher over here."

"Does he have dog tags?"

"Yes, Major Heinrich Müller, He's a kraut."

"Load him in that ambulance over there."

David was unconscious, but nightmares were going through his head. He saw Catherine's face once again as she said, "If you can't be a real man, don't bother to come back." Next he had the dream he had so many times before, the death train.

Chapter 3

Eighteen months earlier in Italy aboard "The Death Train"

Even with his years of experience, the powerful stench of death and decay in the rickety cattle car was something David could not get used to. Taking a break from tending the wounded, he stood resting his back and knees with his nose pressed up against an opening in the slatted door. *What am I doing here? I should have left with the others.* He was so tired. His back hurt and his legs ached. In fact, he didn't know if there was a spot on his body that didn't hurt. *I had no idea it would be this bad. I wonder if I'll ever sleep again...*

Fortunately, the German officer in charge of their capture had been a humane man. The soldiers had wanted to shoot the wounded but the commanding officer would have none of it. David was aware of this because he understood and spoke German with native skill. His parents had immigrated to America from Germany in 1910 prior to the outbreak of WWI. German was the language of choice in their home when visitors were not present so English was actually his second language. He decided to keep this knowledge to himself as long as possible

He turned and looked at his ragtag group. *I can't believe I'm doing this.* He shook his head. *I just wanted to help these guys, but riding on a death train for two weeks was not what I had in mind. That lieutenant was right; all I seem to be doing is holding their hands and watching them die.*

At least Papa will be happy. That is, if I survive this mess. 'Be a hero, and I'll make you President.' Well, I don't want to be President, Governor, or dog catcher! All I want is to make it home alive and be with Catherine and little David. Who am I kidding? I probably won't have a wife when I get home. He turned back to look outside. *My life is so messed up. My father wants one thing, and Catherine wants another. No one seems to care what I want.*

He was brought back to reality as a GI tapped him on the shoulder.

"Captain, I think you need to check on Sgt. Hall. He's in a great deal of pain."

"He's not going to make it corporal. I've done what I can and we're out of morphine. Just stay with him and console him as best you can. I need to see to the living and those that still have a chance. I'm sorry but that's where we are."

"Yes, sir, I'm sorry sir. This has gotta be tough on you. I hope you know we appreciate your coming with us. We know you didn't have to do it."

"Yes I did corporal! And there will be no more of that. You give Sgt. Hall all the comfort you can. No water, though. That will only prolong his death and you may need the water yourself before this trip is over."

"I understand, sir."

He touched the corporal on the shoulder and the young man hobbled back on his makeshift crutch to care for his friend. Corporal Eckstein had lost his leg above the knee and been forced to stay with the group now on the train.

Returning to changing dressings and giving aid and comfort as best he could, he thought that if they had been cattle the conditions in the car would have been far superior. He had pleaded for water at the last stop, but the Nazi guards told him he would have to wait.

A short time later the corporal found David again and said sadly: "Sgt. Hall's gone; we need to move him in with the rest. Do you want to come for the service sir?"

"Yes, gather the men and thank you corporal. I know you and Hall were close. Would you like to conduct the service?"

"No sir, Hall would want you to do that, he had a lot of respect for you. Besides, I don't think I could do it captain." He turned, dropped his head, and began gathering those who were able to get around the body. The boxcar rocked along towards its destination as those who were conscious heard the sweet sounds of 'Amazing Grace'. Even the Nazis were calm during these brief memorial services. David said a few words about the resurrection and the bravery of those who gave all in defense of family and country. A prayer was given and then the body was reverently stacked with the rest of those who had lost their last battle. David thought to himself with pride that a priest in the finest cathedral in New York could not have done a better job than this ragtag group of men as they said goodbye to yet another of their comrades.

As dusk approached, they rolled to a stop on a siding off the main track. David felt certain they were at their destination. He called the men to gather around as best they could.

"Okay men. We are likely at the camp. Watch out for one another as best you can. I know that many of you are scared. That's understandable. The best advice I can give you now, is don't show fear. When you walk, stand proud. You are American soldiers. You did not surrender; you were taken prisoner because you were wounded. Do not let them think they have won. That will be all and God bless us all."

Just then the doors were unlocked and thrown open with a loud clang.

"Achtung - schnell aussteigen!"

Those who were still able helped those who couldn't make it on their own. Others simply did their best to get off the train as rapidly as they could. The dead were left at the end of the car where the Germans began to unload them onto wooden pushcarts. Fortunately David had already collected the dog tags from the dead. They were off-loaded and wheeled down the tracks to a pit about 100 yards away. There the bodies were dumped with no pretense of

10

ceremony. A prisoner stood by to shovel lime over the bodies, all under the careful watch of armed German guards. Seeing this, David reflected back on the crude memorial services that had been held for each man after he died. He knew that the families of these men would be grateful.

The camp was about a half-mile hike from the rail station. The guards kept hurrying the men along as though they were going to be late for supper. Whenever one of the men would fall, if he didn't immediately get up, the guards would kick him or strike him with a rifle butt. The other men began to rescue their comrades as soon as they fell. The walk seemed to take forever and he felt that it was the longest half-mile he had ever traveled.

Upon seeing the camp his first impression was death. He was terrified. His stomach wrenched and he almost threw up. He wasn't sure if he had ever been that scared before. The only thing that kept him from running was his responsibility to his men. Like it or not, he was the senior officer and the men depended on him. He had come this far and he would not quit now.

Light... There was light everywhere, glaring sterile lights. Darkness had fallen and the contrast was blinding. He had not seen this much light since the war had started, but felt certain that it would prohibit bombings as it would be obvious to any pilot that this was not a military target.

The compound was large with a perimeter surrounded by two fences topped with coiled barbed wire. They were spaced about fifteen feet apart with vicious guard dogs roaming between. Inside the compound, barracks were arranged in rows along three sides. They stood off the ground about three feet on brick pillars so there was a clear view beneath each building. David could see that no one would be tunneling beneath those buildings. The front door of each barrack opened onto a common area where he was sure the men would stand in formation for roll call each morning. No hint of grass was present in the frozen mud. At the two back corners of the compound were community latrines with showers, and left of the front gate was a building with *Krankenhaus* written on a sign over the door with a red cross on it. With his knowledge of German, he knew that this was the camp infirmary. A warehouse type building stood beside the infirmary. On the right side of the gate was a well kept building that must be the office and quarters. Next to this were two nice looking barracks that probably housed the guards. These buildings had the only lawn in the compound. A guard tower with a spotlight constantly scanning the area stood over each corner of the compound. In front of the kommandant's office was a raised platform that would allow guards or the kommandant to dominate the area when the men were standing in formation. It was obvious to David that this compound was laid out by someone with experience in crowd control, as there were few places a person could be outside the barracks without being under surveillance. Looking around, his heart sank as he realized that this could be the extent of his world until the war ended or he died.

When they had all arrived the men were assembled in formation in the common area. The new group totaled close to two hundred when those from all the boxcars were combined. They were arbitrarily divided into three groups. The ten Negroes amongst them were separated from the rest and moved to the front. David was taken to an area behind the podium to meet the kommandant.

Seeing David's rank, the camp commander approached him. In impeccable Oxford English he said, "Captain, I am Colonel Baumgartner. After I address you and your men, you will be fed and then assigned to barracks for the night. We will make arrangements for our doctor to work with you tomorrow to look after your needs as best we can. We are not blessed with a lot here, but we have some modicum of compassion and will do what we can. It would appear that you alone are unwounded?"

"Yes, sir, I am a doctor and chose to remain with these men when our group was ordered to retreat. We have several who need surgery, but that was impossible on the train."

"Admirable Captain, you Americans are a loyal people. There will be no surgery tonight. You will be able to meet with our camp physician Major Heinrich Müller in the morning and he will make recommendations to me. We have some access to the hospital in Barth if there is something that cannot be handled at this facility. You will find Major Müller a most excellent surgeon. Now if you will rejoin the prisoners I will make my welcoming remarks. David walked around the podium and took his place at the front of the group. When the preparations were complete, the kommandant stepped to the podium flanked by two soldiers. His boots shined like glass as he briskly walked up the steps. He wore a steel gray uniform with the insignia of a colonel and carried a riding crop tucked under his right arm. As he stepped up to speak, David couldn't help but notice the two spotlights mounted on the building behind him. They were blinding in intensity and placed his body in shadow. He wondered if the colonel had been in the theater before the war. The effect was amazing. The colonel seemed all-powerful with the light appearing to radiate from his body. He took the riding crop and began to lightly tap it into the palm of his left hand.

Speaking in his clipped, precise, Oxford English, he said, "Let me be the first to welcome you to your new home at Stalag 21. For some of you it will be your last home, for others not. It all depends on you. I am Colonel Baumgartner, your kommandant. I do not wish to be here. I wish to be at the front with other soldiers fighting for the cause of the Third Reich. If you had not been cowards and surrendered, I would be fighting for our cause. Instead, I am a babysitter. Do not think you have come to a luxury hotel or resort, you have not!" He slapped the crop hard into his left hand. "You will earn your keep. There will be no malingering while you are here. Those found malingering will be severely punished.

"Sergeant Wagner, on my right, is in charge of camp personnel administration. He has been ordered to give leadership training to the blacks in the camp who will then be assigned to each of the barracks as barracks administrators. Their responsibilities will include maintaining discipline in each of the barracks. They are to report any damage to the facilities to Sergeant Wagner. If there are any attempts to escape, the barracks

13

administrator is to report it. If infractions are not reported, the barracks administrator will be punished as if he had been the one to cause the infraction himself. Anyone caught trying to escape will be punished and the barracks administrator will be punished as well, for not maintaining proper discipline. The only way for the barracks administrator not to be punished is for him to stop the infraction before it occurs, or to report it as soon as he is aware of it. I am sure that when this war is over, we will have helped to elevate and educate the blacks that have been put in our charge.

"On my left is Corporal Rothenberger. The Corporal is our camp disciplinarian. You will find him fair, but stern. The corporal comes from a long line of fine soldiers, and the Third Reich is pleased to have his services. He has been told to watch for malingering. When you malinger, you take food from the mouths of the German widows and orphans. We do not want any of you to think you are here for a free ride. The corporal will provide quick and decisive punishment for any who does not want to work or provide for the welfare of the camp. Please, look at him as a friend. As long as you work hard and do your part, I am sure you will learn to respect him, and you will understand his desire to help you.

"I am glad that we have had this opportunity to explain our rules. I hope your stay at Stalag 21 will be a pleasant one. It is entirely up to you. Good night!" Then he turned to the sergeant, and barked orders in German. David understood more than he wanted to. "Sergeant Wagner, get these men into their barracks. Provide soup, bread, and water to them for tonight. See that Corporal Rothenberger is kept under control. We will evaluate the survivors in the morning. There is no point in wasting medicine on those who are about to die anyway."

"*JaWohl!*" The sergeant saluted, then organized the Americans and marched them off to the barracks. The other prisoners assisted those who could not walk.

David made a cursory inspection of the barracks and soon discovered that there was no running water. The only clean space in the camp was the area the Germans had set up as a token infirmary to show the Red Cross that the prisoners were indeed receiving "humane" treatment.

Chapter 4

That night David stayed in the infirmary on a cot that had been set up by the camp guards. The next morning as promised, he met with Major Heinrich Müller, the officer in charge of medical care at the camp. Since the Major spoke exceptionally good English, he didn't see any reason to reveal his own knowledge of the German language.

They immediately went to work assessing the needs of the wounded that had just arrived. The next eighteen hours were spent in surgery trying to save the lives of those in the poorest condition. It made David sick to realize that if they had been given proper drugs on the train, many limbs would have been saved, as well as lives. Although he was impressed with the care and skill of the major, he still felt uneasy about putting total trust in the enemy.

After the initial ordeal was over, they were relaxing for a few moments before retiring. Major Müller turned to David.

"I have suggested to the kommandant that it would be best for you to stay in the infirmary. In this way you can be closer to the prisoners who are not doing so well. I had quarters created for you out of a storage room off the office. We can continue to use German medical assistants as we did in the past, but I suggest that you find two men with medical experience from your ranks and have them work with us. The sick will probably get better treatment from your men than mine."

While David did not want it to appear that he was receiving special treatment, he knew that it only made good sense for him to be close to the wounded. It also meant access to running water and toilet facilities and he was glad for that.

As soon as the wounded were stabilized, David met with Sergeant Bill Johnson, the senior NCO of the camp.

"Well sergeant, how about giving me a rundown of this place and what your needs are."

"There's not a lot to say or be done about things around here, sir, but perhaps you'll have a little more clout. The barracks were designed to hold about fifty men each, but we have seventy-five. While you may see thirty-six barracks, only twenty-four of them are occupied. The kommandant has told me on numerous occasions that these are being held in reserve for future prisoners. He imitated the kommandant, "*after all, at the rate the Americans are losing the war, they will be fully occupied in the near future.*" To be honest sir, your men are the first group of any size to arrive in a long time. If you don't mind my asking sir, where was your bunch shipped from?"

"Italy."

"I had no idea we were fighting in Italy, they really keep us in the dark. Nobody's smuggled a radio in here in a long time. Maybe we could get a rundown on what's going on later. Anyhow, let me tell you a little more about the camp. The latrines and showers are located on the back corners of the camp. There's no running water in any of our buildings except for the latrines. The barracks are each heated with a coal stove. Unfortunately, we only get about half the coal needed to heat them. After all, "*this is no pleasure resort for lounging around.*" He imitated the kommandant as he spoke. "You'll hear that a lot.

"Next, don't trust the krauts farther than you can throw'em. There's a lot of 'em from the states here, New York especially. When the führer told them to return home, they flocked like geese. They sound American and they would have you believe they're your friends, but they're krauts through and through.

"The worst of the lot is Corporal Rothenberger. He is vicious! You'll know him when you see him. He is small and

17

looks like a rat. The men have nicknamed him Rotten and you'll soon know why. Next, in the mornings we stand in formations. I suppose as senior officer here, you will stand at the head and give the report. If you should be needed at the hospital, I'll be glad to stand in for you, just let me know."

"Thanks, Sergeant. You've been a big help. I expect you to continue your duties as you have been doing in the past. Let me know the problems and I will meet with the kommandant to find a resolution. You're welcome to be in attendance when it seems appropriate. Let's play it by ear and see what happens."

"Thank you, sir. We're glad to have you with us."

With that, he saluted and turned to leave.

"Just a minute, Sergeant, I'll need two men with medical experience to work with me at the infirmary."

"That'll be Henderson and Briggs. Neither of them are medics, but both have experience. Henderson is the most experienced. The medic in his outfit was wounded, so he took over until they could get a replacement. He's pretty good too. We always use his services unless it is absolutely necessary to go to the Krauts."

"Maybe we can change that. Have them report to me this afternoon."

Chapter 5

"Henderson and Briggs reporting as ordered, sir!"

James Henderson was a young clean-cut soldier who enlisted as soon as he turned eighteen. Jack Briggs, on the other hand, was older and tough looking. Since Briggs had no known experience in medics, David had inquired about him around camp. What he found was that Briggs was competent and would do any job he was assigned.

"Okay men, your new assignment is to become medics and look after those in the infirmary. You will screen the men on sick call and bring in only those that are truly sick. If I find you letting one of your buddies slip in, you will be out of here and on permanent latrine duty so fast you won't know what happened. Do we understand one another?"

"Yes sir!" They both answered.

"At different times each of you will be expected to scrub up and stand in on surgeries. I want you to learn all aspects of this work. You will NOT pass out medicine unless you check with me first. However, I do expect you to watch and learn what we use for different illnesses. I have had cots set up behind the office here and this is where you will stay. You are expected to work in shifts. Briggs you are in charge and care for the sick and wounded at night. Any questions?"

"No sir!"

irst major problem David had to deal with was the
ty of medicine. Major Müller may have had the
n artist when it came to the scalpel, but if the
ᴋᴏᴍᴍandant would not provide the drugs they needed to
fight infection, much of the work was wasted.

David walked what would become a familiar path to the
kommandant's office. Taking a deep breath, he stepped in
and asked to see the colonel.

"Colonel Baumgartner, we do not have adequate
supplies of medicine for a camp this size. Add that to the
influx of wounded that came in on the train with me, and it
becomes criminal!"

"Criminal? Don't think you can come in here and tell me
how to run my camp. We are doing all we can to help your
men. Haven't we provided you with a fine doctor? We have
provided you with the finest infirmary of any Stalag in
Germany. Besides that, we need the medicine for our own
wounded and the civilians that your bombs have needlessly
injured. I see no need to waste German medicine on
American weaklings. When the war is over, they will have to
be disposed of anyway. This way we save time."

"Let me remind you Colonel, there is a possibility that
Germany will not win the war. Please understand that there
will be trials for those who committed war crimes. You DO
remember the Geneva Conventions don't you?"

The colonel stood up. "I believe this meeting is over!"

David stood up. "Doesn't the Red Cross have medical
deliveries here the same as to other Stalags?"

"I will see what we can do."

Two days later a delayed shipment of medical supplies
arrived from the Red Cross. This brought a smile to David's
face.

Even though the men were recovering from their
wounds, it seemed that the infirmary remained at near
capacity. At least three times a week, a man would be
brought in with major injuries from one of the daily work
parties. "Briggs, what is going on with these men?"

"They are malingerers, sir, or at least that's what Rotten calls them. Malingering is the excuse Rotten uses for getting his kicks. Each time a work party is formed; Rotten makes sure that he gets someone that's not strong assigned to it. From the beginning, the person selected is obvious. He rides him from the start. He will give him a job he cannot possibly handle and when his target cannot keep up, Rotten calls him a malingerer. With a guard to stand by and protect him, he slaps the malingerer around until the guy collapses, dies, or Rotten just gets tired."

"Thanks for the rundown." David had a thoughtful but concerned look on his face.

A few days later as the prisoners were coming in from a work detail; two had to be carried to the infirmary. David suspected the problem, but asked anyway.

"What happened?"

"It was Rotten again." A nearby corporal replied.

David knew that meant Corporal Rothenberger had struck again. He stepped to the door and asked: "Corporal Rothenberger, may I speak with you?"

"Certainly, captain."

"What happened to these men?"

"They were malingering!"

"And exactly what did they do to malinger? Did they refuse an order?"

"Not that it is any of your business; they chose to work more slowly than their comrades and caused the other men to have to stop their assigned jobs and help."

"That was not cause to treat these men this way."

"Listen Strauss, we will treat American prisoners any way we wish!"

"Captain Strauss to you corporal and you will address me as sir!"

21

The corporal pulled his pistol from its holster and placed it under David's chin. Then pulling the hammer back replied: "These are my prisoners and I am in charge. You will NOT tell me what to do! Just remember who YOU are. You are also my prisoner and certainly NOT my superior!"

Rothenberger was shaking with fury by then. David's blood ran cold. Thoughts flooded his mind as he wondered what he had gotten himself into. *I should have left well enough alone. Well, I have started it now and I have to follow through. Whatever I do, I can't lose eye contact. If I back down now, a lot of people will die including me.*

David turned to face Rothenberger squarely. In the coldest, calmest voice he could muster, he said, "I may be a prisoner of war, but I am a superior officer and you will give me the respect of the rank. Do you understand? You will also treat my men in accordance with the Geneva Conventions. This war will be over one day, and you will be held accountable for your actions."

"When this war is over, I will be honored as a hero!" replied Rothenberger.

"Brutalizing innocent and helpless prisoners doesn't make you a hero. Only the weak attack the helpless and everyone knows that," said David through clenched teeth.

Rothenberger's beady eyes shifted slightly. David realized that he had hit a cord. Major Müller, having overheard the conversation, stepped into the office and surveyed the scene.

"Corporal, stand down! What is your problem?"

Rothenberger remained with his weapon under David's chin. Looking at Major Müller he said, "This American prisoner has not been showing me proper respect."

Major Müller was stunned. *Corporal Rothenberger was high strung, but was he a cold-blooded killer?*

"Captain Strauss is an officer and will be treated with the respect due an officer. Do you understand me?"

The corporal, still shaking glared at Major Müller. Slowly he lowered his gun and holstered it. *"JaWohl, Herr Major..."*

He saluted and left the infirmary.

They left the waiting room and went into the office. Major Müller looked at David and said, "That was close! Now, don't think you have seen the last of Corporal Rothenberger. All you have done is draw a line. He never forgets, so watch your back."

David sat down a little shakily. "Thanks for what you did back there. I wasn't sure how far he would go."

"Neither was I. I would not have been surprised if we were cleaning your brains off the ceiling right now. When he gets that way, he is capable of almost anything."

David closed his eyes. *Oh great! I guess I'm in for it now. I hope Catherine is happy. I wonder if I am a real man yet. Well I've drawn the line and the corporal and I both know where it is. I hope the major stays in my corner. He has guts, that's for sure. I can't believe he took that kind of a chance for me.*

While David was contemplating the possibility of a new ally in the major, Major Müller was deciding the same about David. He liked this U.S. army Captain. It took nerve to stand up to a crazy man with a gun and not lose his composure. This guy's nerves must be made of steel.

Rothenberger grew even more vicious after that. His authority had been challenged and he was not going to let this lowly American captain think that he had won. He was beginning to wonder about the major as well. Was the major an American sympathizer? Well, he would show them both!

Chapter 6

The weather grew bad for several weeks and everyone was cold and miserable. Things at the infirmary had been quiet since Rothenberger didn't enjoy being out in the weather any more than anyone else. They had their usual bouts with colds, and infections but nothing significant.

The weather finally cleared up and then became unseasonably warm. A scuffle erupted near barracks twenty-three. There was a lot of pushing and shoving with a large dose of profanity from both sides. David knew that it would have to be stopped quickly and dealt with or it would be an open invitation for more trouble. Stepping down from the porch of the infirmary, he began walking toward the scuffle. Bill Johnson, the senior NCO, stepped out of the barracks and pulled the men apart.

"What's this all about?" he asked.

"He said Joe DiMaggio was a better ball player than Lou Gehrig," shouted a burly private.

His antagonist said, "You stupid gorilla! I'll bet your knuckles are rough from dragging the ground!"

"That'll be enough," said the sergeant with an irritated look on his face.

He turned to David and saluted. "Nothing to worry about sir, it's taken care of."

"Maybe these men have too much time on their hands," said David. "See if you can find something for them to do."

"You heard the man, grab some mops and buckets," said the Sergeant. "I believe the latrines can use some cleaning."

Suddenly a voice from behind made them all turn. "Do you gentlemen realize that you are helping your enemies?" It was Major Müller and he had a hint of a smile on his face. "They laugh each time they see you fighting. You are doing their job for them. If you kill each other, that's a few more Yanks they don't have to worry about. On the other hand, as long as you are here and alive, they have to supply men and equipment to guard you."

The men were silent as the major turned and walked away. David followed. Major Müller slowed and let him catch up.

"You're an interesting man," said David as they walked to the infirmary.

"How so?" asked the major.

"Your attitude toward the men," said David.

Walking into the infirmary office, the Major said, "What kind of attitude do you think I have?"

They settled into their chairs.

Swinging his chair around to face the Major, he said, "You talked to those men like a friend, yet we're enemies."

Major Müller said, "Doesn't the Good Book say, 'Love your enemies?'"

"Yes, but we're at war," said David.

"War is our circumstance. If our countries weren't fighting, I could be a friend with these men. We could go fishing together."

"Yes, but most men don't act like that during war."

The Major replied, "I would like to believe that I am the same man with or without war. If you are a soldier, you must kill. That is your job, to stop the enemy. These men have been stopped. There is no reason to treat them any differently than any other men as long as they don't pose a threat."

David said, "I have seen brutality, immorality, and just about everything else from men who would have been considered 'good' men at home, yet, you don't seem to have been affected by these 'circumstances' as you call them. Listen to the language these men are using. Do you think they would talk that way in front of their wives or mothers?"

The major replied, "While I do not consider myself a religious man, I believe in God, and I believe in right and wrong. Wrong is still wrong even if you are at war. My parents had a strong value system and I guess that it has become a part of me. It may sound strange, but growing up, I always had strong moral values because I did not want to disrespect my family name.

"I remember swearing one time in front of my father. It was not a big thing, but I thought I was a man. My father told me that it was the sign of an uneducated man who did not have command of the language. I decided that day that I never wanted to be considered an uneducated man, most especially by my father."

David laughed as he said, "I wish that I had known you growing up. We would have been great friends."

"Perhaps it is not too late to build that friendship," said the major. "War creates strange bedfellows."

"You know Major; you don't seem to fit the mold of the typical Nazi."

"I'm going to take that as a compliment. The answer is, I am not a Nazi, typical or otherwise."

David swung his arm around with a sweeping motion covering the compound. "Look at the guards around us. Many of them lived in the States before the war. I hear New Jersey, New York, and even California accents. They lived with us as neighbors - butchers, bakers, and just about any occupation you can think of. Yet here they are and you can't trust them any farther than you can throw this building."

Heinrich countered. "I think you need to look at their backgrounds. After the last war, men were out of work, their homes were destroyed, and they had very little hope. They went to America because they couldn't stay home. Hitler comes along and sells his fantasy about building a better life and they take it hook, line, and sinker. I, on the other hand, am in the army for a totally different reason. I joined to keep my family out of prison. My father was a well-respected doctor and businessman in Stadthagen. We lived in a large house and had plenty of money. The führer decided that we were not showing the proper respect for the Reich. It was necessary for my brother and me to enlist to show that my father supported the government. I did not need the respect a uniform would bring, I already had respect from all those I cared about. I am here to protect my family to put it plainly and simply."

David smiled and put his hand out as a show of respect and friendship. "Well Major, I have already been warned not to be taken in by your kind ways, but I think you are real. I don't see that it matters much, because I am not privy to any war plans or troop movements. I am just a doctor and go where I am sent. The grunts out there know more than I. The way you have taken care of our men is proof enough to me to think you can be trusted."

"What is this about?" Heinrich slowly took David's outstretched hand.

"Nothing especially, it's just when men work as closely as we do, I believe we should both know where the cards lie. I am a doctor first and an American second. I will do nothing to harm your men and expect the same from you. I am telling you that if the occasion comes when I would need to work on a German soldier that I will do for him as I would do for my own men."

"I would hope that you already know you can expect the same from me."

"Of course I do." Deciding to take détente a little further he said, "I thought I would let you know that I speak fluent German. I would appreciate it if you didn't make it public knowledge to the kommandant."

"I already know that you speak German."

"Oh? How do you know that? I thought I was concealing it pretty well."

"You never seem surprised when you receive an order. I even saw you begin to respond before an order was translated."

"Really?"

"Yes, and I will not pass this information on unless I am asked a direct question by the kommandant. I will not lie for you."

"That sounds reasonable enough."

"Now, as part of our new friendship, let me re-introduce myself, please call me Heinrich."

"And I am David."

With that they shook hands again as though they had just met.

David smiled again and said, "Now, with that behind us, I am dying to know how you speak English like an American. Even these guys from New York still have a pronounced German accent."

"That is simple enough. I seem to have a gift for languages. My father was a surgeon, and we traveled extensively during my youth. Italian, French, Spanish, and English have each become as my native language. At Capri, I sounded like a blonde haired blue-eyed Italian. The girls loved it." He paused and looked thoughtful. "Those days are gone now... the war has changed everything. As for English, I learned most of my English in medical school. I attended medical school at 'Havad'," he said, saying Harvard like a Bostonian. "The other students were constantly harassing me about my accent. 'Sour Kraut Heinie' is what they called me. I determined then that when I left medical school, I would speak better English than any of them. I used to sit alone in my room listening to the radio. I would repeat what the announcer would say until I got it perfect. Not only did I learn to speak perfect English, but I can also imitate most of the accents." He smiled and looked thoughtful as though he was in another time and place. "Eventually my accent disappeared and the other students forgot that I was German. When new students would come in, they didn't think to ask. Of course, when the war started, I kept my knowledge of languages a secret. I did not want the SS to assign me spy duties. I have studied long and hard to develop my talents for saving lives. To be assigned to duties that would aid in destroying lives would destroy my soul. The SS's propensity for destruction is becoming legendary."

"I understand your feelings."

"Okay, you've heard my story, now it is your turn. How is it that you speak German with such a native accent?"

"My story is not nearly as interesting as yours. My parents immigrated to the United States in 1910. They already spoke English, but preferred to speak German at home when we did not have company. I spoke German before I learned English. I had a nanny that spoke English, add that to playing with the neighborhood children and here I am."

"What does your father do for a living?"

"He is a watchmaker who also creates fine jewelry. His shop is considered the most elegant in town. Everyone who is anyone in the area buys from Strauss & Son. It's kind of a status symbol."

"You didn't want to go into watch making?"

"That's a long story. Maybe another time."

"That's fine. Before I leave, I feel I should give you another warning about our Corporal Rothenberger. Don't believe that because you were able to walk away from our corporal with your life that the feud is over. It is not! He is relentless and will not stop until he feels it is in his best interest to do so. I have felt that I should tell you about him ever since your encounter with him and his gun."

"Oh, I think I can handle the corporal."

"Don't believe that for a minute. Let me tell you a little about him. When you consider that he resembles a rat, and combine that with his small size, you will find someone who

29

was tormented by his Arian friends. Instead of learning compassion by this experience, he learned to attack the weak and helpless. He longs to be accepted by those that plagued him in his youth. His greatest pride is his uncle who is a major in the SS. He brags and uses this to great advantage. There is great fear among the German soldiers that his uncle will bring reprisals if they ever disagree with him. He on the other hand, interprets this as respect for his courage and strength. He has been so violent with the prisoners that they truly hate him. I fear that given the chance this will cause one of them to kill him.

"I also believe that the kommandant himself is not above having a certain fear of our little corporal. In the past he has not offered significant support to me when Rothenberger would make surprise visits to the hospital to gather up those whom he considers to be malingering. Rothenberger says to me, 'Why are we wasting good German medicine on the weak? When we are victorious, their bodies will be used to fertilize our crops!'

"I have not cowered to Rothenberger. As long as there is a war on, I know my services are valuable and I will be left alone. Nevertheless, I have lost several patients who were too weak to leave to hospital to some insane work party dreamed up by our little corporal. If ever the day comes when our scrawny little corporal gets ill or injured, I am not sure that I am up to maintaining my oath to help 'all' the ill. Unfortunately, for such a weak little man, he never gets injured and never gets sick."

It was a cold wet morning and Rothenberger appeared at the infirmary to take a prisoner for interrogation. He did this when he was bored just to remind the prisoners "who was boss." Most of the prisoners thought that he felt if he found out some great secret, the SS would realize they had made a mistake by not allowing him to be a member. David was walking in from a meeting with Sergeant Johnson. He could see the corporal beating Private Jackson, a man who had been in the hospital for the last two weeks. Upon seeing what was happening in the yard, David went to the kommandant to file a complaint.

The kommandant responded with a look of indifference.

"Captain, there are rumors of a planned escape and I did ask Corporal Rothenberger to check into this. We are running a Stalag here and we must address any attempt to escape with proper recourse."

"Sir, with all proper respect, how could Private Jackson be involved in an escape plan when he has been ill for the last two weeks. Rothenberger is using this as an excuse to harass the prisoners. If you look out the window, you will see that he has knocked Jackson down into the ice and mud and is brutalizing him in front of the other prisoners. This is in direct violation of the Geneva Conventions!"

"Capitan, don't quote the Geneva Conventions to me. This discussion is over! Good day Captain!"

Colonel Baumgartner waited for David to be out of the building. *What am I going to do with Rothenberger?*

"Sergeant, send for Corporal Rothenberger."

"*JaWohl*, Herr Kommandant"

About five minutes later there was a knock at the door.

"Enter."

"Heil Hitler!" was his salute. "You sent for me Herr Kommandant."

"Yes, corporal, I am concerned about the treatment of the prisoners. Do you really think that it was necessary to pull a prisoner from the infirmary?"

"Well sir, I feel that the prisoners need more discipline!"

"Corporal, haven't you heard of the Geneva Conventions? Your treatment of the prisoners is inexcusable! When this war is over you may have created problems for all of us."

"But sir, when this war is over, the Third Reich will own Geneva and the rest of the world!"

"Has it ever occurred to you, Corporal, that the Third Reich may not win this war?"

"Impossible!"

"Look at the condition of our wounded that are brought in from the Russian front. Why, if they had not been wounded, they would have starved to death. I'm fearful dear Corporal that things may not be as good as we are lead to believe.

"I'm not asking you to allow the prisoners go free, but I am telling you not to punish the prisoners unnecessarily! When you do find occasion for discipline, remember that you may be their prisoner some day.

"You may go." With that the kommandant turned to some papers.

Corporal Rothenberger saluted with a stiff "Heil Hitler!" and left the room.

Back at infirmary, David and Heinrich had just completed rounds together. David had wanted Heinrich to observe and grade him on his technical skills. Despite the fact that Heinrich wore a German uniform, he and David became the best of friends. David continually had to remind himself that they were on opposite sides in the war since their views were the same on so many subjects. They sat down in the worn chairs of what had become their office and lounge. Heinrich reached in his desk drawer and pulled out a worn and tattered photograph.

"Look, my wife and daughter. They were the light of my life. They brought me such joy and wonder."

"Were?" inquired David.

"Yes, they were killed during an Allied bombing raid on Hanover. We lived in Stadthagen, a small town near Hanover. As the planes were leaving, one of the bombers was hit. It crashed into my home, killing my parents, my wife, and my beautiful Gretchen."

David didn't know what to say. He turned to Heinrich and said, "I'm sorry."

"It's not your fault," Heinrich replied. "It's war; people die." He pulled out another tattered photo. "Here, see my home."

"It looks like a castle."

"It is; it has been in my family for over two hundred years. When I was a boy, I would run across the roof and pretend that I was a swordsman fighting off the enemy and saving the beautiful princess. My father would get so upset. He would say, 'How do you hope to become a surgeon if you break your neck saving your imaginary Fräulein in distress.'"

For a moment David had the same distant look. "That's interesting Heinrich, I did something similar, only my castle was a mound of dirt at the end of the street. Our neighbor was building a garage and never seemed to finish. Mr. Rosenberg would get angry and tell us he was going to pin our ears back if we did not keep off his dirt."

Looking over at Heinrich, his attention back to the present, he asked, "How do you cope?"

"It is not easy. My Ursula and our Gretchen were everything to me. When they were killed I did not think that I could go on, but I did. As time passed, I found that I am not the only one who has lost family. By helping others, I have also helped myself. Time heals many things besides broken bones; it also heals broken hearts. In medicine, when you can repair, you repair. When you can't, you continue on with hope that someday it will be better. Were it not so, I could not continue."

"Heinrich, you seem to be a peace loving man. I am sure there are many more like you. What do you think has given Hitler so much support in this war?"

"Good people did nothing. We all believed that it would go away. By the time we decided to act, he was too powerful. He made promises of a better life. So many people were out of work that they were easy targets. Then of course, there were the Jews. By making them the common enemy, he was able to unite the people against an enemy they could see. They now had someone they could blame for their troubles. By acting against the Jews, they felt they were solving the problem. The educated people knew better and tried too late to help. In my town of Stadthagen, many Germans were killed by the SS for trying to come to the aid of Jewish families. The members of the Hitler youth movement have been known to turn in their own parents."

"That must be difficult."

"Yes, it is. But we get by. For a while it looked like we would win this war, but now with the end coming soon, what we have done is destroy our own villages and cities, lost our wives and children and made widows and orphans out of many more."

David shook his head. "War is hell. We have been lucky in America. Other than what the Japs did in Hawaii, our country has escaped direct damage."

"Yes, you are fortunate. What does your family think about you being here fighting your ancestors?"

"They hate war; however, my father was one who wanted the Americans to get involved sooner than we did. One of my grandparents was concerned about Hitler's ideas and corresponded to us. Father did what he could to make arrangements for them to immigrate to America before Hitler cut that all off."

"Was he successful?" asked Heinrich.

"Only my grandparents. None of his siblings were able to leave," said David.

"My father held a high profile in our city and had to be most careful," said Heinrich, "It was felt that with my brother and me in the military he would be spared duty, as he ran a major hospital. He died in our home along with my mother, my wife and my Gretchen."

"When did this happen?" asked David.

"Last Spring," answered Heinrich, "I was able to go home on emergency leave for a week to tend to their burial. It was difficult. I am still in shock. Working has helped me to maintain my sanity, but when this is all over it is going to be difficult to go back and start over."

"I can imagine so," said David, "I also have a fear for my wife and son. Not with life and death like you have had to deal with, but with their lives if something happens to me. I know that my parents will take them in, but that is also my

34

fear. Catherine has a good family, but my father is a concern."

"How so?" said Heinrich.

"Please understand that I love my parents very much, but my father is a very strong willed man. We were taught unquestioning obedience. My opinion did not count if it differed from Papa's. Even as I grew into an adult, I could not break away. I don't want that for my son. I want him to be free to choose his own way, right or wrong. If he and Catherine go to live with Papa, I'm afraid that history will be repeated."

Just then there was a brief knock and a soldier stepped through the open door.

"Beg your pardon sir, Corporal Fryeburg's birthday party is about to start, and you said you wanted to attend if you weren't tied up."

"Well, I am not tied up and I appreciate the invitation," said David.

With that he grabbed his jacket and left.

The next day after rounds and sick call David and Heinrich met in their office and began to visit as was growing to be their custom. Most days in prison camp were routine, interspersed with bits and pieces of drama. They had a lot of time to talk and trade stories of their lives and ambitions.

As they settled back in their chairs, Heinrich began to tell stories of his exploits with his cousin Erik. "We were as close as brothers." He laughed as he told of their excursions hunting and fishing. We both loved to ski. Did you ever do much skiing?"

"Not a lot," David said. "I did love to ice skate though. I miss those days when we were young and war was so far from our minds."

He was quiet for a moment then said, "I wish Catherine and I had had the closeness you and Ursula had."

"You weren't happy?"

"To tell the truth, I put so much time and energy into my education and training that Catherine and I almost became strangers."

"That can happen. Did she become lonely or angry?" asked Heinrich.

"Not really," said David, "She worked nights as a waitress to help support us while I worked days in medical school. We just seemed to drift apart. She was disappointed when I went to medical school. I know that sounds strange, but I really wanted to be a musician. That's all we talked about when I was in high school. My father put a lot of pressure on me to become a doctor. A lot of our problems came because she was disappointed that I was not man enough to stand against Papa. I loved music, but my father wouldn't have it. He told me, 'David, music is a hobby. You need to be a professional man to be respected in America. You become a doctor and play the piano for your own enjoyment.'" David looked off into the distance as he remembered how it had felt to knuckle under to his father's demands. Yes, David had done as his father had wanted, and he still nursed deep resentment for it. Catherine of course had made it abundantly clear that he should have stood up to his father.

"Our last three months together were pretty uncomfortable," said David. "Catherine had just found out she was pregnant, and we knew I would be going over-seas. She was upset because she felt that I was abandoning her. I don't know, maybe we were in love because we had the same dreams. Catherine loved music and she thought I could make it. When I gave it up, I destroyed her dreams as well as mine.

"In retrospect," David remarked thoughtfully, "I could never win."

"Why do you say that?" asked Heinrich.

"Well," said David laughingly, "Catherine once said she loved me because of the kind of person I am. I love and respect my family. I would never do anything to bring shame to the family name. I was always obedient to my father. I am a Boy Scout, trustworthy, loyal, kind, reverent, and obedient. These are the same characteristics that caused the trouble between us when my father wanted me to be a doctor instead of a musician. I just couldn't say no to my father. It's just not in me. She beat me to death about it. On the other hand, had I not been that kind of person, she would not have fallen in love with me. That's why I can't win. Damned if you do; damned if you don't."

"I see what you mean," said Heinrich. "What are you going to do about it?"

David replied, "I can sit here with you and think I would do this or that if I could do it again, and yet I know that if I was faced with the same situation, I would probably give in just like I did before."

David had a distant look and a slight frown on his face.

Heinrich asked, "Is it all that bad?"

"Pretty much. The last thing Catherine told me as I left was if I can't learn to be a 'real man' not to bother to come back at all."

It sounds like she has a bad temper. Don't worry though, from what I have seen you do, you qualify as a 'real man' in my book"

"Thanks, but Catherine has much higher standards than you do," said David with a slight smile. "I'll tell you the real killer. If I get out of this alive I will probably be a hero and Papa will force me into politics. He has always wanted to be in politics but felt that he had to stay in the background because he is a 'foreigner.' Here I am, American born and bred, and a genuine hero. He will never pass that up. I didn't want to be a doctor, but I am, and a good one. That's what I want to be now. When I get home it will start all over again and this time I will lose Catherine. You see, I will probably cave in again and that will kill what little respect she might have left for me. A 'real man' would say no, and do not what he wants, but what his wife wants." There was anger in his voice. "Sometimes life is a bitch."

Chapter 7

There was a knock on the door and the kommandant said, "Enter." Heinrich stepped in.

"It is good to see you Major, are things going well at the hospital?"

Heinrich saluted. "Heil Hitler!"

The kommandant looked slightly bemused as he returned the salute, knowing full well Heinrich's lukewarm feelings about the Third Reich.

"Have a seat. What is this about Major Müller?"

"As you know Herr Kommandant the numbers of wounded coming in from the eastern front has increased to enormous amounts. I am spending more time at the hospital in Barth than I spend in camp."

"Yes, now what is your point?"

"I would like permission to have the American doctor accompany me and help with the surgery."

Major Baumgartner stood up so quickly that his chair rocked precariously and was in danger of tipping over. "Are you out of your mind?" He slowly regained his composure and returned to the chair he had retrieved from its position against the wall. "Let me see if I understand you correctly. You want me to allow an enemy prisoner to leave the security of the camp and then perform medical procedures on our men who are his avowed enemies?"

"I think you have outlined it properly. It is not as bad as it sounds though. As I have observed him, he is a doctor first and an American second. He is of German extraction and does not look at us as 'the enemy.' I have seen him come into the infirmary and see to the needs of our men when I was tied up with another patient.

"My point is this sir, Captain Strauss could be a major asset to us when we have more wounded coming in than we can handle. Many times we have every hall in the hospital lined up with wounded and they suffer and sometimes die because we simply do not have the skilled manpower to take care of them."

Major Baumgartner sat quietly for a few minutes. "I see what you mean Major. I will do this on a trial basis. If anyone reports strange behavior coming out of Capitan Strauss, he will be shot. If he escapes, you will be shot! What do you think of that?"

"I think that sounds reasonable. I believe that if he gives me his word that he will not try to escape, he will keep it."

The kommandant smiled. "You are staking your life on it. I will have Frau Schmidt draw up the proper papers. Is that all?"

"Yes sir!" Heinrich gave a salute with "Heil Hitler!" then turned and left.

Heinrich returned to the infirmary and sat down in his chair on the front porch next to David.

"I know how boring it is to be here day after day, so I have a proposition for you that you may find interesting. I believe it will also help develop your skills as a surgeon and of course that will help you as you attend to the needs of your men."

David looked over at Heinrich with a slight smile. "I feel like I am being set up. What do you have on your mind?"

"I just had a talk with the kommandant and he has given me permission to take you with me to the hospital in

Barth to care for our wounded coming out of the eastern front."

"How did you manage that? I cannot believe that he would stick his neck out like that."

"His neck is not stuck out near as far as yours."

"Mine?"

"Yes, he said that if you even tried to escape or do anything that would endanger our men, you will be shot. Oh yes, and I will be shot as well."

"Why would you do this?"

"It's simple. When a trainload of wounded comes in from the eastern front, we lose a large number of them because we cannot get to them in time. I see this week after week. You could save a lot of lives. If your conscience bothers you, these men are fighting Russians, not Americans."

"You already know that wouldn't bother me. My job is to save lives. As for trying to escape, if I left this beautiful resort, I would not be able to care for my own men and that would defeat my purpose for being here. Then, of course there's Corporal Rothenberger. Someone needs to be here to clean up his messes. Having said all that, I will not try to escape."

"Good! Let me tell you a little about Barth. Our facilities there will be as good as you will find in this part of Germany. Combine that with the number and diversity of injuries that will come in and you will find your skill level increasing at a rapid pace.

The German soldiers at the hospital in Barth did not know an American was caring for them since David would speak to them in German and was now wearing German scrubs that Heinrich had rounded up. David's had turned to rags long ago and it was imperative that his clothes be in good repair and clean for surgery.

He was impressed with some of the new techniques he saw Heinrich using during their surgery. In the infirmary at the camp, the facility and equipment available were primitive compared to the Barth hospital.

"You're going to teach me some of these new procedures you are doing, aren't you?"

Heinrich smiled. "You bet. I believe that is part of our agreement. If the war lasts long enough, you will be a new doctor when you leave here."

During the next weeks, David was amazed at the new skills he developed. Since their relationship was based on friendship, unlike that of a typical teacher and student, his progress was far more rapid than it would have been in a medical school environment.

David thought that it was strange to be learning new techniques working on enemy soldiers; but when the uniforms were off, and they were on the operating table, they were just boys - scared boys, lonely boys, boys who should have been flying kites, or ice skating with a pretty girl. It wasn't right. These boys didn't care about the Russians, the French, or the Americans. They were just trying to stay alive, hoping against hope that they would see their families again

There is something unique that occurs when people face adversity together. They develop a trust and a bond that is welded by the fire of the moment. When the moments extend into months and years, a relationship stronger than that of brothers develops. Over the next eighteen months, David and Heinrich became as close as two men could ever be. Each man looked out for and protected the other. Heinrich knew that if he protected the prisoners, he would be making David's life better. Many times Heinrich quoted the Geneva Conventions to the kommandant and Rothenberger, knowing that if Germany won the war, these things would come back to make life very unpleasant.

"What about you, Heinrich?" David asked one afternoon. "Have you always wanted to be in medicine?"

"*Ja,* all my life. My father was a doctor, and his father before him. From a boy, I knew that I would be a doctor." He sighed deeply. "Always I have loved helping others. Now that I am without my family, this is all I have.

41

"When this war is over, I would like to start my life over, I believe. I am so tired of hatred and destruction. I just want to be left alone to practice medicine. I think that I can save so many lives, I have so many ideas that I believe will advance medicine. Enough complaining. There are too many people with real trouble."

David said, "I disagree, Heinrich. If you don't have dreams, you can never make a difference. If we should both survive this mess, I believe that I can help you get to America. You would love it. The hospitals are modern and they are looking for skilled doctors. My father has some good connections in the government and could probably pull some strings to get you in. I would certainly vouch for your conduct in helping our soldiers in camp. You have stuck your neck out many times to see that my men received good treatment. At least as good as has been available. You will even find that you can make a good living there. I think it will be a while before the economy here will be good enough to earn the money that you will need"

The door to the infirmary opened and Corporal Rothenberger entered. After saluting he said to David, "Capitan Strauss, I would like for you to go on our work party today."

David wondered what ulterior motive the corporal had. "And why would I do that?"

"You have expressed concerns about the working conditions of your men. I would like to demonstrate to you that I am a fair man. Your men continue to demonstrate to me how lazy they are and I would like for you to see that I only wish for a fair day's work. Do you really care about your men or is it only lip service?"

"I will be ready."

After Rothenberger left, Heinrich turned to David. "Are you out of your mind? You know Rothenberger can't be trusted! You had better stay on your toes, or you may come back dead!

Later, as the work party left, David wondered what Rothenberger had up his sleeve. The one thing he knew was that Rothenberger did not care about his concerns. Perhaps if he witnessed Rothenberger in action, he would be able to find a way to help his men.

The project today was to clear out rubble left from recent bombings in the nearby town. Rothenberger was careful to remind them that they were not working on military buildings, but the homes of innocent civilians that had been "ruthlessly" destroyed by allied bombers. "They take no thought but to destroy and maim anyone or anything in their path."

The buildings were constructed, for the most part, of cut stone about eight inches on four sides and twelve inches in length. A man in good physical condition would tire in a few hours of moving these. These men however, were not in good physical condition and were typically about two-thirds of their ideal body weight. If it had not been for the inhumane way they were treated, the exercise would have been good for them.

Suddenly, as bricks were removed from the base, a short wall toppled. The men scrambled to get out of the way. Private Jim Huntsman, a small man, slipped as he was scrambling and his left leg was pinned beneath the rubble. David ran over and helped the men clear the debris from off Huntsman's leg.

"Quick, move him to this clear area. You two support his leg."

David examined Huntsman's leg and found severe bruising, but no broken bones.

Looking at one of the men standing nearby, David said, "Find a board two or three feet long and put it under his leg. Put one of these stones under the end to keep his leg elevated."

Rothenberger fumed. He began to rant and rave that this kind of malingering would not be tolerated. "I see that he brought his own physician so that he can take the day off after a little scratch."

Grabbing Huntsman by the arm, Rothenberger tried to pull him up and only managed to cause him to tumble. As Huntsman fell over, he knocked Rothenberger to the ground. With that sight, the men began to laugh. Rothenberger went into a mindless rage. He stood up and began to kick Huntsman while shouting, "Malingerer!"

When David saw what was happening, he ran over to stop it from escalating. "Stop," he shouted. As he tried to pull Rothenberger away, he felt a sharp pain on the side of his head and the world faded to black. Regaining consciousness, he could feel Rothenberger kicking with blows to the head, chest, and legs. The only defense he could muster was to pull himself into a ball and take whatever punishment was meted out.

One of the guards shouted to Rothenberger in German, "Stop, you will kill him. The kommandant will be angry." At that, the beating slowed until it stopped.

The men begged Rothenberger to take David back to the hospital but he refused to leave until the job was done. He kept walking back and forth mumbling something about "high and mighty Americans" and "malingering." The men worked extra hard that day clearing the rubble in an effort to save the life of 'Doc.' Even Huntsman worked while his leg turned a dark purple.

As darkness approached, the ragtag group came in from the work party. Heinrich looked for David and knew that his worst fears had been realized when two men were carried from the truck. By this time David was unconscious. The entire left side of his face was swollen. He had a cut over his left eye and the area around it was blue.

Heinrich sprung into action. "Place Huntsman on that bed and elevate his leg. Move Captain Strauss to this examination table."

He took scissors and began cutting David's clothes off. Upon a quick examination, he called Henderson over. "Move the Captain to the operating room and scrub up for surgery."

While Henderson prepared David for surgery, Heinrich gave Huntsman a more through examination. "Briggs, clean this man's leg and sterilize the cuts. Cover it with cool damp cloths and change them every half hour. Keep it elevated and let's see if we can get the swelling down."

When Heinrich cleaned and cared for David's injuries, he was relieved to find that while he had broken ribs, none had punctured a lung. He put a number of stitches into David's eyebrow, but found that through a miracle, the eye itself was not damaged. The big concern now was the extent of David's concussion. He knew that it would be a number of weeks before they knew the extent of damage that may have been done to David's brain. If severe enough it could end his career of being a surgeon, or even a doctor for that matter.

David regained consciousness that night. As Heinrich examined him, David said, "You think I'm bad, you should see the other fellow."

"I did, you got blood all over his boots. I am surprised that you are still alive. All Rothenberger wants is an excuse. He is unbalanced, stay out of his way. Defer to me if he ever makes another attempt to put you in danger."

David remained bedridden for the next month. His mind was okay except for a few headaches, but the cracked ribs and bruised legs would not allow him to stand for more than a few minutes at a time. He did not have any apparent damage to his nervous system His hand to eye coordination was as good as it had ever been.

Two weeks into David's recovery a troop train arrived from the eastern front bringing wounded soldiers to the hospital in Barth. Heinrich worked through the day and into the night. Yet, with all his efforts a number of soldiers still died because working alone he could not get to them fast enough to save them.

The next morning Heinrich was fuming when he went to the kommandant and made his report. At the conclusion he said, "I think you should know that Corporal Rothenberger is responsible for the death of twelve of our soldiers."

The kommandant was shocked. "What do you mean?"

"It's his temper, sir. If he would just do his job without deciding that God had elected him to punish all Americans, we would not have lost those men. When he attacked and disabled Captain Strauss, he signed the death certificates of our soldiers."

"But the captain attacked him!"

"We both know better sir. Corporal Rothenberger is unstable and his temper cost us one of our valuable resources. Captain Strauss may be the enemy, but having him in surgery to save our men when a troop train comes in is much more important than punishing some 'malingerers.'"

"Thank you Major, I will take that under consideration."

David later decided that the beating he received was worth it because someone else was assigned to monitor the work parties and none of his men was ever carried in due to a beating. Small steps.

One evening when things were quiet, David and Heinrich listened quietly to the BBC on Heinrich's radio. It was apparent that the Allies were about to make their final push.

Once again David said, "Heinrich, when all this is over, it's going to take a long time for Germany to recover. Why don't you come to the States? You would be well received as a surgeon, especially since you speak English as well or perhaps better than I do. You are the best surgeon that I have ever seen. Your work in vascular surgery could be a ticket to the top in any surgical hospital in the States."

"You know, I almost immigrated to America once, back in '37." Heinrich looked thoughtful. "But there were my parents to consider, and then I was conscripted into the Army. Since my family was lost in the bombing, I have not thought that much past the war. Do you really believe a German would have a chance in America when our countries have been enemies for so long?"

"Americans are a very forgiving people. They beat each other up one day and are drinking buddies the next. Besides, we have a shortage of surgeons, and in your field you could teach and prepare others. I don't believe you would have any trouble. I'll be happy to sponsor you. Once you get established, you could make it to the top in no time."

"It is a thought, my friend." Heinrich's jaw tightened. "My fear is that the Russians are going to get here before the Americans or the British do. The Russians are doing murderous things on the eastern front. We have done our part in this, but Hitler's main emphasis has been the annihilation of the Jews. He is crazy, but the Russians, they are for me a worse choice. I believe Stalin is just a Russian version of Hitler."

"If the Russians get here first it could be a problem for us, too. They are not exactly in love with America. The communists are against free enterprise and democracy."

Heinrich looked to the north when they heard a distant rumbling. "I fear that the Russians will be here within a week or so. The more troubling thing is that we are getting a new commander for the camp today. Colonel Baumgartner is to report to Berlin by Monday. As you know, he has been a hard man, but he is to be replaced by an SS major who unfortunately is an uncle to our infamous Corporal Rothenberger. It is likely that he will be less friendly to the Red Cross and the prisoners.

"I tell you this because I fear for you. I will do what I can for you and your men, but I am not sure what to expect from Major Rothenberger."

"Thanks, Heinrich. Just remember what I said about getting to America. I'll do everything I can to help. You've saved the lives of many American soldiers, and that will be your ticket to America if I have anything to say about it."

David stood and turned to leave the infirmary. He embraced Heinrich and said, "You're a good man, Heinrich. I think of you as *mien bruder.*"

Heinrich returned the embrace. Then, slapping David on the back, he said, "You have been a good listener and I will keep your thoughts about America in my mind."

"Good. I'll be going to make my rounds of the barracks now. By the way, if I don't make it home for some reason, you contact my father. He is a good man and will help in any way he can." David left the building then and hurried back to the barracks, where he shared with his men the bad news of the imminent arrival of another Rothenberger.

Chapter 8

Major Rothenberger, SS, was bidding goodbye to Colonel Baumgartner, who was to be accompanied by his sergeant to Berlin. "Colonel, the trip to Berlin will be long. I hope you are successful in your new position. Things are tenuous there now."

"Do you think, Major, that they are less so here?"

"No. I am aware of the Russians' proximity. I have my orders and will do my best to see they are carried out. You have kept a clean camp, Colonel. It speaks well of your service here."

"We've done our best *Herr Major*. Our staff is well trained and of course your nephew, the corporal, is a stern disciplinarian."

"Travel safely, Colonel. *Heil Hitler.*" The major saluted and clicked his heels.

"Heil Hitler." The departing colonel climbed into the back seat of the command car. His sergeant joined the driver up front and they drove away.

Major Rothenberger turned to his nephew, Corporal Rothenberger. He had contempt for this young man. He was not strong like his father had been. On the other hand, he was a loyal Nazi. The major was confident they would be able to accomplish their assignment. "Corporal, I want you to have the prisoners fall into formation. I wish to address them. Do you have any prisoners who speak German?"

"Yes, Uncle, I mean Major. There is an American doctor among the prisoners who understands some German. He has been working with Major Müller, the camp doctor. I have heard them communicate in German at times.

"Good. Bring him to my office and have the guards assemble the rest of the prisoners in the courtyard. I want to speak to them."

"JaWohl, Heil Hitler." The corporal clicked his heels, did an about-face, and headed for the prisoner barracks, taking a guard with him.

Speaking in German the corporal said, "Captain Strauss, you will accompany me to the kommandant's office after you have translated my orders to the men. The rest of the prisoners are to assemble in formation in front of the kommandant's office for instructions from the new camp commander. Things will not be as easy around here now that my uncle has arrived. Translate this order now. Then we will leave."

David did as he was told, but added words of encouragement. "The new man is SS, so be on your toes and as military as you can be. This is almost over. Let's not be making any mistakes now."

Corporal Rothenberger and Captain Strauss marched to the kommandant's' office in silence, as the men fell into formation. There was a strained silence among the men as they wondered why they were getting a new kommandant, and worst of all, SS. They were careful not to give Corporal Rothenberger any excuse for discipline this close to the end of their ordeal. Especially since no one knew what another Rothenberger would be like.

"Major, this is Captain Strauss," Corporal Rothenberger announced as he saluted.

"So, you are of German heritage, Doctor?" The new commandant spoke in German.

"Yes sir. My parents came from Germany before I was born."

"Your German is quite good for a man brought up in America."

50

"My parents did not speak English at home, sir."

"My English is poor. I understand some English, but I do not speak it well. I am going to be discussing matters of importance with the prisoners. I will need you to translate what I have to say with accuracy."

"I will do my best, Major."

"Very well, corporal, call the formation. I wish all personnel to be there."

"It has been done, sir. *Heil Hitler.*" Corporal Rothenberger was obviously proud of the arrival of his SS uncle. He turned and strutted out of the office.

"Captain Strauss, I hope your stay here has not been too unpleasant."

"We have had very reasonable treatment until now, Major. In fact some of the prisoners would be dead if it were not for the medical skills of Major Müller. He has been most professional."

"And my nephew?"

David decided to be frank. "He has been one of our less pleasant experiences here."

"I can imagine." Major Rothenberger had a wry grin on his face. It was as if he had wanted to hear the truth. "Frankly, he has been unpleasant since he was a boy. But soon you will not have either of us to contend with. I am quite certain that the Russians will be here by morning. Come, let us join the rest of the camp. You will translate my remarks as accurately as possible."

"Yes, Major. I will do my best."

They left the office and joined the prisoners and staff, who were all assembled in the yard. Heinrich glanced at David in surprise as he saw him ascend the stairs with the new Major.

As Major Rothenberger began speaking, David translated.

51

"The Russians are advancing rapidly. It is expected that by morning they will be here. In other camps, enlisted prisoners have been treated fairly, but the staff and officers have not. The Russians either do not believe the Geneva Conventions applies to them, or choose to ignore them." He paused to allow David to turn his words into English for the men. "The best way for you to live to see your homes once again will be to remain quietly in your barracks until told to do otherwise. You may hear gunfire, but your war will soon be over and you will return to your families, while those of us in German uniform will probably join ours in the afterlife. War is never good. This war has been long, and it is painful to admit that we have lost. I for one hope it is the last war I ever have to participate in."

The prisoners' faces were a mixed sea of both disbelief and relief.

"Corporal, you may dismiss the prisoners." Turning to David, the major said, "Thank you, Captain Strauss, for translating." David saluted him and he returned it, without the "*Heil Hitler*". The kommandant then turned to Heinrich and said: "Major Müller, I would like to meet with you in my quarters, if you please."

Corporal Rothenberger was stunned. He could not believe that his uncle would quit. He still did not believe that the Third Reich could lose the war. His uncle must be getting old. He turned, saluted, and dismissed the prisoners, perhaps for the last time in his military career. The men walked to the barracks with a new spring in their step. Once inside, their shouts of jubilation were easy to hear across the yard. They were finally going home!

Major Rothenberger headed into his office; Heinrich turned to follow. His eyes caught David's. Giving him a slight nod, he followed after the Major.

David stood in a slight daze. While he had known that freedom was imminent, his mind had not processed it as an actual event. Thoughts of Catherine, Davy, and Papa flooded his mind as he walked back to the infirmary he had called home for the past eighteen months. A certain dread came over him as the realization of the upcoming battle with Catherine and Papa took form. *Why is it that I would rather face the Germans in battle than deal with the hell that I know is coming up when Catherine and Papa start in on me?*

The two majors were sitting in the kommandant's office. Rothenberger spoke first.

"Major, you have had an excellent record here at camp. It is a shame that the Russians are coming before the Americans. It would seem that the Russians want to build up their scientific and medical fields with the skills and services of the German people, so I expect that you will soon be leaving for Russia. Do you have family?"

"No. All were killed in bombings early last year. I have a brother whom I have not heard from in months, so I do not know if he is alive or not. He was in Italy the last I knew."

"I understand. I wish I could give you better news. Colonel Baumgartner may live to fight for a while by leaving here today. As for me, I am here on a suicide mission. I lost favor with the Third Reich. I have been put here with the expectation that I will be killed by the Russians."

"I am sorry to hear that, sir."

"Don't be, Major. Like you, I have no family to live for and I am tired of fighting wars and losing. Our führer is quite mad, you know. This war would have ended a year ago if it were not so. I can say that today, for tomorrow I expect to be dead."

"I am not sure what to say to that, Major."

"There is nothing to say. I have asked you to come in, Major, to give you some advice. It would be in your best interests to reach the western front rather than to be captured by the Russians. If you were to leave under cover of darkness tonight you might reach the Americans, and I will not stand in your way."

"How close are the Americans?"

"Actually they are only 10 kilometers away. It seems they have made an agreement that the Russians will be given Poland and most of Eastern Germany so they are holding off. Frankly they could have been in here a week ago, according to our intelligence."

"I am not sure how I would be able to get to the Americans without having them shoot me. I may have to take my chances with the Russians. I appreciate the offer sir."

Major Rothenberger stood and said extending his hand, "I understand. Think about it, I will not stand in your way."

Heinrich stood and shook his hand. "I will see you in the morning, then, unless something happens sooner. *Auf Wiedersehen*, Major."

He saluted with no "*Heil Hitler*", turned and left. As he walked to the infirmary, he thought about David's offer. If he went to America, he would have to leave his home, his history, and what little was left of his family. He was not sure he could do that. He would just have to find a way to stay out of Russian hands.

David and Heinrich were sitting around their battered wooden desk in their small office off the main infirmary area. They were having what would probably be their last visit before everything changed.

"I have been saving this cognac for some time. I purchased it after attending the funeral of my family. I had in mind using it to celebrate the end of the war. I suppose for you and me it is near the end."

"It sounds like it."

"This SS major is a strange man. He says he was sent here on a suicide mission. "

"I wonder what he did to make someone do this to him. SS officers are not loved by the Russians. It won't be pleasant if they take him alive."

"You are right. Well … he offered to let me leave tonight to try to reach the western front. That certainly caught me off guard, but I am just as likely to get shot by the Americans in the dark as by the Russians in the day."

"I wonder how you could do it. I can give you a note that would introduce you, that is, if you don't get shot first."

"No, I am going to take my chances here, David my friend. Let's finish this bottle off and get some rest in preparation for the big day we have ahead of us. I appreciate the friend you have been to me and the service you have rendered to our wounded. We have had some strange but interesting times. They continued to talk of old times until the morning sky began to glow.

"*Skoal*" Heinrich tapped his glass to David's and they drained the last of the cognac.

David gave him a weak smile. "Well, it won't be long, the fighting is getting closer. I expect they will be here in less than an hour.

"You know, that gunfire sounds as if it is in the compound. Maybe we should check."

Suddenly the door to the infirmary flew open and a GI burst in.

"Captain, Captain, he's killing everyone. Rotten's gone berserk!"

David jumped up and said, "Just a minute, Jackson, what's going on?"

Jackson was breathing heavily. "Rotten had Barracks One fall into formation and then he and Schultz started shooting everyone!"

Heinrich started for the door, "I'm the only one he'll listen to. I'll take care of it."

Just then explosions began to rock the compound. The walls of the infirmary shook and the roof caved in, as they took a direct hit. Heinrich was down, with blood running into his eyes. When he tried to move he couldn't. He pushed rubble from off his body then tried to stand. There was something wrong with his leg, it wouldn't work. *David, where is David? Over there, he's under that rubble. Got to get him out.*

55

He wiped the blood from his eyes with the back of his hand as he pulled himself to his friend. He rose up on one arm and began to pull boards off David. As soon as he got him clear, he checked his pulse.

No! Not you! Dear God, why? Why must everyone I care about die? I had nothing to live for; he had everything!

Heinrich sat there not knowing if he could go on. The building rocked again as the room next door collapsed. For some strange reason, he wanted to live. Summoning all the strength he could muster, he managed to get to a half-standing position and started for the door. As he did, an idea formed in his mind. He went back to his friend and lifted his dog tags from around his neck. Replacing them with his own he said, "Thanks for this last favor, dear friend, maybe the Russians won't get me after all."

If I can get to the Americans, I will tell them what I have done after we are safely away from the Russians. I'll take American punishment over Russian justice anytime.

Heinrich worked his way back to the door, but as he stepped out, another shell hit the building and it collapsed. He tried to crawl, but his legs wouldn't work. *Maybe I can pull myself,* he thought. His arms wouldn't work either. *Strange, maybe I'm dead. I can't feel a thing.* Then ... everything faded to black.

Chapter 9

"The American is still alive, but he's in bad shape. He's lost a lot of blood and his face is a mess..." The medic was talking. "There is a German here with severe head damage. He's barely alive. He should be moved to the hospital in Barth immediately. I don't think he will make it, but let's let him die in a German hospital, not ours. We can take care of the captain at our field hospital but we've got to get him there in a hurry."

The American medics had been brought in to examine the results of the shelling of the camp. The Russians were embarrassed at what had happened with their artillery so they blamed it on the Germans. Not wanting to deal with all the wounded they asked the Red Cross to assist the American personnel in the cleanup. Most of the prisoners and two tower guards appeared to be the only survivors besides these two men they had found in the infirmary. They also found the bodies of many prisoners in the courtyard in what appeared to have been a firing squad. Those prisoners were out in the open as the bombardment from the Russians hit the camp. It was a horrible sight, bodies and body parts everywhere.

Two hours later at the American field hospital, Major Heinrich Müller, based on his dog tags, was logged in as Captain David Strauss, MD.

At the same time, David was admitted into the American hospital for Germans as Major Heinrich Müller, MD. He would not have been there except for the glowing reports of his heroism on the behalf of the American prisoners. From his head injuries alone, it was a miracle he was alive. If you add in the broken ribs, arms, and legs the doctors felt that his guardian angel had been working overtime. He was still unconscious when the war officially ended. Since he still had family in Germany, they were notified and they moved him to a hospital in Switzerland as soon as his condition stabilized. It seemed that he and his father were folk heroes in the medical community in Germany and Switzerland and everyone wanted to help. The Americans were glad to see him go since he would likely be a vegetable for the rest of his life.

David finally regained consciousness in the Swiss hospital. "Major Müller, do you know where you are?"

David just stared without comprehension.

The doctor rephrased the question. "Do you know who you are? If you cannot talk, just shake your head."

David hoarsely said, "No I don't and what am I doing here?"

Everyone in the room smiled. The same spokesman said, "You are Major Heinrich Müller. You are in Switzerland recovering from your injuries."

Looking bewildered David just stared at them. Injuries?" He tried to raise his hands to touch his face, but they were in casts and were useless for all intents.

Looking down at his arms and legs and seeing that he was almost entirely covered in casts and bandages, he asked, "What happened to me?"

Again the spokesman began, "When Stalag 21 was being liberated by the Russians, they shelled the camp. You were seriously injured; we weren't sure if we would ever talk to you again."

"I'm afraid that I don't remember any of it. What was I doing in a prison camp?"

Chapter 10

Pain... *Well, I guess I'm not dead. You're not supposed to hurt this much if you're dead.* Heinrich Müller tried to open his eyes, but to no avail. Next, he tried his fingers. No luck there either. Upon trying to move his arms, he found they were in some kind of bandages. *I must be a real mess. I'm too tired to worry about it anyway.* He drifted off to sleep again.

Some time later he felt himself come back to the surface. He could hear part of a conversation taking place nearby.

"Did ya see what those krauts did? Took the prisoners and just shot 'em. What kind of a sick animal would do that?"

Another voice said, "I'd like to get my hands on one of those guys. By the time I got through with him, he'd wish he'd never been born!"

Well, Heinrich thought, *so much for the friendly Americans. I better come up with another plan.* Before he could think any more about it, he drifted back to sleep. It was not a restful sleep though; he kept seeing stacks of bodies. None of them had faces. He was looking everywhere for David but couldn't find him. Sometimes he felt as if he were climbing out of a deep hole, but couldn't make it. Voices and pain became his life. He knew they were talking about him and wanted to answer. What would he say? He didn't know what the question was; there was something he needed to say; some dark secret he must reveal; what was it?

"Captain, Captain Strauss, you need to wake up."

The voice seemed to be in a tunnel far away. Heinrich tried to wake up, but couldn't. It was just too hard. *Let me go back.*

"Captain, you need to wake up."

"Wo bin ich?"

"He's talking. How about that? I'm afraid you were in Germany too long Captain. We only speak English here," came a voice with a decidedly English accent.

"Where am I?" came his reply in a pronounced Oxford accent.

"Welcome back." The nurse was talking excitedly. "I'll get Dr. Crookshanks."

Heinrich lay there, trying to come back to the surface. The voice he had heard was familiar and there was a smell that he knew. What was it? Antiseptic, of course! He was in a hospital.

A few minutes later the door opened and a tall lanky man in a white lab coat and a stethoscope came in.

"Captain Strauss, I'm Doctor Crookshanks, the nurse tells me you're talking again."

Heinrich's eyes popped open. "Strauss?" he said questioningly. "There must be some mistake, he's dead."

The doctor took his wrist and looked at his watch to check his pulse. "You're suffering from disorientation. You've been in and out of consciousness for some time." The doctor checked Heinrich's eyes as he continued his examination. "This is the first time you have spoken since you've been here. You know, a lot of people have been worried about you."

"They have?" he said, switching to American English.

"Yes, everyone from Eisenhower down has called at one time or another. You must have some connections in the states."

"In the states? Where am I?" Heinrich didn't understand. It seemed as if he and David had been talking just a few minutes ago. *How did I wind up in a hospital and an American hospital at that?*

"First things first." The doctor continued his exam. "Do you know your name?"

"Not exactly," said Heinrich. "You called me Captain Strauss."

"Do you know where your home is?" questioned Dr. Crookshanks.

"Germany?" answered Heinrich haltingly.

"No," said the Doctor. "You were there for a number of years though. Do you have any idea what has happened to you?"

"No, I've just had this long nightmare and now I'm awake," answered Heinrich.

"I guess that's to be expected. Just relax, we'll talk later," said Dr. Crookshanks as he hung his clipboard on the foot of the bed.

"No doctor, I don't want to talk later." Heinrich was getting upset. "I need some answers. I don't know my name, I don't know where I am, and I don't know what's happened to me."

The doctor stopped as he was leaving and turned back to Heinrich. "Okay, I guess you have a point. I'll give you the Reader's Digest version and we can fill in the blanks later. You're Captain David Strauss. You were found barely alive in the rubble of what used to be the infirmary at Stalag 21. This was courtesy of the Russian army. While fighting the camp commander, Major Rothenberger, outside the camp, they managed to send an artillery barrage that completely missed the Germans and destroyed the camp. Seeing that it was full of Americans, they called our boys in and let us bring out the wounded. They really weren't interested in dealing with prisoners or wounded so they turned the whole thing over to us.

"Well, to make a long story short, you were found under what was left of the front porch of the hospital. Your face was crushed by debris, your nose was spread from one ear to the other, your face, hands, and arms were burned, and your right leg and several ribs were broken. There were internal injuries and a knot on the back of your head that probably knocked you well into the next week. If you don't know who you are, I'm not surprised. I do believe your memory will return shortly. There may be missing patches, however. They may or may not return.

"You have been in and out of a coma for about six weeks. We weren't sure if you would ever come back. On the off chance that you would, we have put you back together as best we could. Due to the fact that someone thinks you will be president someday, we were told to make you look pretty. We couldn't do that, so we made you look like you used to. Your family sent photos and of course we had those on file in your service records. All in all, I think we did a pretty good job. You're lucky this happened at the end of the war instead of at the first. Over the past four years, we have put a lot of GI's back together and have developed some good techniques. I dare say that this facility is the most advanced in the world for plastic surgery. Oh yes, and you're in London."

"Six weeks?" Heinrich's head was spinning.

"Don't get in too much of a hurry; we still have a lot of touch-up work to do. The basic foundation work is in place, but there's still quite a lot left. We'll have you in rehab starting tomorrow. I suspect you'll have to learn to walk all over again. We'll be putting you through some mind gymnastics to see if we can get that cranked up as well. Now, are you satisfied?" The doctor smiled as he turned to leave.

"It's a good start," Heinrich replied.

"Good," said the Doctor. "We'll let that soak in and start in earnest tomorrow. Don't worry about your wife and family, a wire is being sent as we speak, letting them know you're talking. They've really been worried, you know."

"Wife?" said Heinrich, his mind reeling.

"Now, I'm serious, you relax and let this soak in. We've a long way to go so get some rest. We're going to run your butt off before this is over and you will pray for relief." Then he grinned and said, "Welcome back, soldier!"

Heinrich thought he would never go to sleep, with so many thoughts racing through his mind, but he did. In fact, he slept better than he had in years. Sometime in the early morning hours when he was not awake and not asleep, he thought, *they've got something mixed up; I'm Heinrich Müller, not David Strauss.* As he drifted back to sleep, he suddenly jerked awake and thought, *Oh no!*

Chapter 11

The next morning Heinrich was awakened before dawn. It was the nurse that had been at his bedside the day before. "I'm Lila Turnbull," she said with a brisk British accent. "I will be your nurse, therapist, friend, and taskmaster for the next few months. I have been caring for you for the last six weeks, you just haven't been aware of it. You have been up and around for a while, but yesterday was the first time you weren't in a fog."

"Let me give you our routine." She was talking as she tidied up the room "The first thing in the morning you get a bath."

"Sounds interesting." Heinrich was grinning under his mask.

"Not that interesting." She was smiling. "We'll give you a good English breakfast and then work it off. You've got a lot of catching up to do and I'm just the girl to help you do it. After lunch, we'll exercise your mind while we give your body a rest. After two hours of mind gymnastics, we'll round up the day with a little more physical training. After dinner, you will have the evening off till 9 o'clock. You get Sunday's off to rest and attend church if you desire. This is your life in a nutshell, at least for the next three months."

"I guess it's time to get started," he said as he attempted to grin. "How about that bath?"

Nurse Turnbull smiled, "I'm glad you are so enthusiastic, let's take care of it right away." She was talking as she stepped into the hall. In a few minutes she returned with two male nurses. "Captain Strauss, this is Corporal Jones and Private Yardley, they will be helping with your bath."

Jones was a large black man who looked like he could have been a guard on a football team. Yardley was a large, fair-haired boy who looked like he had just come in off the farm. As soon as he opened his mouth, it was obvious that the farm must have been in Georgia or somewhere in the Deep South.

"Suh," Yardley said. "Let's see if we can get you cleaned up without breaking anything new, or adding insult to your injuries."

With that they stepped on either side and picked him up in his sitting position and carried him to the bathroom as though he weighed no more than a feather pillow. As he undressed, Heinrich realized that he probably wasn't that heavy. His body had shriveled up until he was not much more than a skeleton with skin stretched over it. He guessed he had not overeaten while he was in a coma. As he tried to stand, he realized he couldn't. There just wasn't any strength left in his body.

Jones said, "Don't worry about it sir, that's what we are here for. Most of the guys are shocked to find out they're almost helpless when they start. I promise you though; Miss Turnbull will make a man out of you before this is over."

As they helped him through his bath, Heinrich realized he had never met two men as kind and gentle as these. Over the next weeks, he grew to love and appreciate these two gentle giants.

His first attempt at physical training was a shock. They started him rolling and crawling like a baby.

He was a little embarrassed, having never been a patient. He wasn't sure he liked it either. Of course, there wasn't much else he could do. "What are we doing this for, I feel really stupid."

Lila Turnbull stepped into the room. "We start you the same way babies learn. Rolling over and crawling will develop the muscles and coordination you need to walk. Besides, you will be surprised when you find that you haven't the strength for much else."

Heinrich was shocked to discover how much energy it took to roll over. Jones started him at one end of the exercise mat and had him roll to the other. By the time he had rolled the first lap, he was covered with sweat.

"I'll never look at babies the same way again," he said panting. "Who'd have thought it takes that much strength and energy to roll over." With that, he started rolling back the other direction.

After lunch, he started his mind exercise. Lila had him doing his multiplication tables. His printing was not much better than a first grader's. After a while of that, she had him doing division and estimating in his head without pencil and paper. He was stunned. He couldn't do it. He had always thought of himself as a bit of a math whiz. Now, the simplest tasks were beyond him.

"You will marvel at how these simple exercises will help you regain your memory," she said with her crisp British accent. "Don't worry about it, I promise you that it *will* come back."

He was embarrassed, here he was a doctor and he couldn't impress this beautiful nurse with his superior intelligence and wit. Nitwit was more like it.

After about two hours of torture Jones and Yardley came into the room. "You ready for a little relief sir?" asked Jones.

"You bet," said Heinrich putting down his pencil. "My brain is exhausted. I thought I would never have to do that again when I left high school. I don't know if I can handle three months of this."

"It'll get easier as time goes on suh," said Yardley with his slow Georgia drawl. "After a week, you'll be qualified to help your kids with their homework. You got any kids suh?"

"Yes, a son," replied Heinrich. "It's hard to believe since I've never seen him."

"It looks like your memory *is* coming back. There are a lot of guys like you around suh. A lot of them will never see their kids. You're one of the lucky ones," said Yardley. "Our job is to see that you can walk over and pick him up. That's what makes this job worthwhile. You may hate us before this is over, but when you walk out of here, you'll be glad we did what we did."

"I'm sure I will," said Heinrich. "I guess if I'm going to hate you, we better get started."

When Heinrich had rolled about halfway across the mat, he wondered why he had been in such a hurry to start again.

After dinner, he knew he wouldn't have trouble sleeping. He was completely exhausted. He had done just about everything in a hospital at one time or another, but he had no training as a patient. He didn't have much training in physical therapy either. He had never understood the patience and determination that it required of both the patient and the therapist.

One day after about a week of rolling over, Jones informed him that today he would graduate to crawling. "What a relief," Heinrich said, "I was beginning to respond to rolling on command, like Rover."

Beginner's crawling was easier than rolling over. He had been doing isometric exercises on his own while lying in bed at night. Knowing that he would need to develop them sooner or later, he would press his hands together for a few seconds, then his knees. The exercise had stimulated his appetite as well and he was starting to gain weight. He wondered if he would ever be normal again.

Sometimes Lila Turnbull would take the late shift and roll him on the grounds in a wheelchair. One night Heinrich said, "You put in a lot of hours here, that doesn't give you much time for a life. How about your husband and children, don't they object?"

"No," she replied. "I have no children and my fiancé was in the RAF. He was shot down at Dunkirk. This is my life now."

"I'm so sorry," said Heinrich. "It must be hard on you, patching us up and sending us home to our wives."

"Yes, it is hard. But if I can save some soldier's wife or mother from going through what I suffered, it is well worth it," she replied with a catch in her throat. "I didn't think I could live without James. Life was only existence, putting one foot in front of the other. Then a friend told me about this hospital and how much they needed qualified therapists. Well, I tried it and found that I could breathe again. Life began to have meaning and I looked forward to the next day. It's not the same, but there *is* satisfaction in helping others."

Heinrich thought about his situation with Ursula and how the hospital had given new meaning to his life. He wanted to tell her that he had suffered the same pain but couldn't. Wasn't he the enemy? Wasn't it the Germans that killed her fiancé? Their lives had paralleled in so many ways. Questions plagued his mind. *What is going on with you? Are you falling for her? What kind of idiot are you? You are an imposter, surrounded by people who would kill you if they knew. Now you're falling in love with someone who would put a knife in your heart if she had even a hint of who you are. I want to swear and I don't swear, am I uneducated or maybe there are not the right words in the English language to describe what I am feeling? Maybe I am just going nuts having this conversation with myself!*

Crawling was a new experience indeed for Heinrich. He had not realized that crawling could be so complicated. Trust it to the military. They could make anything complicated. Once he could actually crawl comfortably from one end of the mat to the other, they threw him a curve.

"Now I want you to move your left arm and your left leg at the same time, then your right arm and right leg," said Lila.

Strangely enough, that was complicated. He found that he had to shift all his weight on his right side and move his left arm and leg, then rock to his left side to move his right arm and leg. He was amazed that he had to focus to do this in the right sequence.

Chapter 12

Bombs were bursting all around, he could hear machine gun fire nearby, "Heinrich, help us!" He quickly turned around. There were Ursula and Gretchen standing in the ruins of his home. "I must reach them, help them," he ran, but he just couldn't reach them. He looked down, there was David covered in blood, a bloody hand holding his leg. "Don't leave me here, please don't leave me." "You're dead," cried Heinrich, "You're dead!" "David, David," cried Ursula. "David, David, wake up." Heinrich jerked awake to see Lila standing above him with her hand on his shoulder. "You're having a dream, it's just a dream," she said.

Heinrich looked about; he was in his wheel chair in the garden on the west side of the hospital.

"You must have fallen asleep," she said. "Look at you; you're covered in sweat and such a cool afternoon."

"No, I wasn't having a dream, it was a nightmare. The same one over and over again," he said. "It was a visit from those I have failed."

"Would you like to talk about it?" she queried.

"It wouldn't change anything," he said. "We could talk all day and they would still be dead."

"You might be surprised," she said, "You're not the first man through here to have dreams. Now tell me, who comes to visit?"

"Okay, I had a friend at the camp hospital, Heinrich Müller. He was also a doctor and he became the closest friend I have ever had. We worked side by side, teaching one another new skills. He was one of the finest doctors I have ever known. During the quiet times we talked of boyhood, growing up in different worlds, but the same. He became my brother. The day we were freed from the camp, he was killed and I let him die."

"What could you have done?" she asked.

"Nothing," he said. "It's not fair though, why am I alive and he is dead? In my heart, I feel that it should have been me."

"But it wasn't you," she answered. "Now what are you going to do about it?"

"There is nothing I can do about it," he said. "I just feel so ashamed."

"Why are you ashamed?" she asked. "Do you think God made a mistake or that your friend got in the way and messed up God's master plan? I don't think so. God doesn't make mistakes. You are alive because he intended for you to be alive. Now, as I see it, you have got to decide what you are going to do with the time He has given you. You can go around and feel sorry for yourself because you're alive or you can decide to make a difference with the time He has given you. What'll it be?"

"You know," he said. "I think you beat around the bush too much. Why don't you just come out and say what is on your mind!"

Lila had a shocked look on her face, and then they both burst into laughter.

After he calmed down, Heinrich said, "Thanks, I needed that. It's just that occasionally life gets a little confusing."

"Oh, I am so sorry," she apologized. "I'm far too outspoken and I had no right to say those things."

"Yes you did," he said. "Life has not been so kind to you either, and you have every right to call me on it. Besides you are right on every count. I think it is getting a little chilly out here. Maybe it's time to go in. What do you think?"

"You sound like a doctor to me, Captain," she said. "Let's follow the doctor's orders and do go in."

Heinrich was getting good at crawling right arm, right leg and was feeling ready to move on from this stage. One day Lila came in at the end of his exercise period and said, "Okay, I think you have graduated from this."

Heinrich sighed with relief. "Good, this will wear a guy out. Besides that, my knees are getting callused.

Lila smiled, "Don't get your hopes up too much, now I want you to move your left arm and right leg, then your right arm and left leg."

He wanted to bang his head on the floor.

This turned out to be one of his hardest exercises, and he fell over many times. "I don't think babies are required to do this. You're just trying to humiliate me. I think you should pick on someone your own size."

"You'll be my size before long if you gain any more weight. You're getting heavier than your legs can hold. I think that while you are doing this, we will start you on the parallel bars."

With Yardley on one side and Jones on the other, he began the task of trying to walk. No surprise to him; his legs would not even hold him upright. Jones reassured him, "You didn't actually think you would walk yet, did you?"

"No, but I had hoped I could."

"Here's what we are going to do. We will do this in stages. Your first goal is to stand. Yardley and I are going to see that you don't fall, but I want you to hold on and just push up with your legs."

Day after day, Heinrich pushed. He even got one of the nurses to place a box at the end of his bed so he could do isometrics at night while he waited to sleep. Then one day it happened. Yardley and Jones were like two parents that saw their child stand for the first time. You could hear them across the room and down the hall.

Lila came in and watched and smiled. "Get the Kodak in my office. This deserves a photo for my scrapbook."

Chapter 13

"Time for your afternoon stroll in the park," Lila said as she rolled Heinrich away from the lunchroom after evening tea. She had taken to having him eat in the staff lunchroom in an effort to stop him from being so reclusive.

"Excuse me sir, I have a letter for you," said the nurse at the front desk as they passed by on their way out.

The late afternoon sun was breaking through the clouds as they emerged from the main hospital doors. There was a light chill in the air. Raindrops were dripping from the rooftops and trees as one of the frequent London showers had just ended. Lila tucked a blanket around Heinrich's legs to keep out the chill. He still felt a little humiliated at being so dependent on Lila's help, but he rather enjoyed it too. *If you're going to be taken care of, it may as well be by a beautiful nurse.*

He was brought back to reality as Lila said, pointing to the letter, "I see you've received another letter from your wife. Why don't you ever write her back? Every week it's the same thing."

"What would I write? I was never much for pen pals, I don't know her and I wouldn't know what to say," said Heinrich

"Why not just respond to her questions or comments? Sooner or later you'll have to get to know her, it might as well be now," said Lila. "Don't you think she deserves it? I'm sure this hasn't been easy on her, raising a small child and not knowing if she would ever see her husband again."

"I know that I should, but I just don't know her. I don't want to get her hopes up that I am going to come home and be this wonderful husband. I may never remember her, maybe she won't love the new me, maybe the new me won't love the old her. Seriously though, I feel like a man forced into an arranged marriage. I'm supposed to walk in and live with and love someone I've never seen," said Heinrich. "What are *my* rights?"

"Now you know what the women in China and the middle east feel like," laughed Lila.

Suddenly there was a scream as a woman carrying a small boy in her arms came running up the curved sidewalk from the street. As everyone turned to look she cried, "Help, I need a doctor!"

"Bring him here!" shouted Heinrich from his wheelchair.

As the woman placed the child on Heinrich's lap, he could see that the boy was turning blue. He immediately began to examine the boy's mouth and throat.

"What is the problem?" he said as he reached in his pocket for the small knife that he always carried.

"He's choked on something. I tried, but I couldn't get it out," she tearfully cried. "Please help him!"

Heinrich turned to Lila. "Tear a sheet of paper from the middle of your notepad and roll it into a straw with a pointed end," He turned the boy over and rapped smartly on his back between the shoulder blades. When nothing came out, he turned the boy back over so that he was face up on his lap. He then opened his knife and made a small incision in the boy's throat.

"Ayyyy!" cried the woman. "What are you doing?"

"Move her away," Heinrich told an orderly in the gathering crowd.

He placed the homemade straw in the incision of the boy's throat and turned it so that it spread at the bottom. Placing his mouth over the end of the straw he gently began to blow air into the boy's lungs. His right hand was on the boy's chest and when he felt it inflate, he gently pressed to expel the air. The boy's color began to return. He continued this routine until the boy was breathing on his on.

By this time there were orderlies with a gurney nearby.

"Take him in and get a doctor!" he commanded with authority.

The orderlies gently took the boy from Heinrich's lap and placed him on the gurney keeping the homemade straw in place.

"It looks to me as if he has already found a doctor," Lila said as the orderlies pushed the boy away.

"Welcome back Dr. Strauss!" she said with tears in her eyes. "It looks as though there are a few things you do remember. Where did you learn that straw thing?"

"In combat, you use what's available. I remember doing that once, I don't know where," he lied, "but I can still see his face."

"I think any doubts you have about your skills and abilities should be gone," she said.

Then she did something that caught him off guard. She leaned over and gave him a kiss on the cheek. His only wish was that the bandages were not in the way.

"It was marvelous to see you in action," she said as she turned his wheelchair toward the building. "I think we've seen enough excitement for one day, don't you?"

Heinrich didn't answer; his heart was beating so fast he was afraid she would hear if he opened his mouth.

By the time they came through the door, the word of his actions had passed through the hospital. There was a large crowd gathered in the foyer when they rolled in. Applause amid cheers rippled through the hospital as everyone crowded around and congratulated him. "Here you're supposed to be the patient and you saved the boy's life," said a nurse with a Cockney accent. "Thanks, love."

It took a while to get to his room, as everyone in the halls wanted a chance to congratulate the hero. Small victories were appreciated in these times of gloom when people were trying to put their lives together again.

Lila smiled and said, "I guess you can do no wrong here, Doctor. You are a true hero. Now get to bed."

If only they knew, he thought as he undressed and slipped into bed. *If only they knew.*

The next morning as he rolled himself into physical therapy, Yardley said, "Well, suh, I guess it's time for you say goodbye to your beloved wheelchair. Miss Turnbull left instructions that you have graduated to the next level. It's now crutches for you. By the way, congratulations on saving that little boy yesterday. The whole hospital is talking about it. They say you are a genuine hero."

"I don't know about the hero stuff," said Heinrich. "I do know this, I could never have done that or much of anything else without the work you and Jones have done. I will be eternally grateful to you. You can know this, anything I am able to do with the remainder of my life will be in part due to your work."

"Thanks, suh I appreciate that," said Yardley. "Now let me introduce you to Tit and Tat. You might as well make friends, 'cause you will be together for a while." Yardley brought out a set of well-worn crutches. "One of the nurses made these special cushions for the top. She filled them with goose down. She was proud to be able to do something for you."

With that, they began the slow task of learning to walk upright. His exercises on the parallel bars helped immensely. What he did find, though, was the technique was totally different. Now he began to understand why Lila had him doing so many different styles when he was crawling. He found the easiest method of using the crutches was to use them like a pole vault and swing his legs together. While that was easiest, it did not improve his ability to walk. It was just a method of transportation.

The methods that Jones and Yardley encouraged were left crutch, right leg, and then right crutch left leg. Then, of course, there was left crutch, left leg, then right crutch, right leg. He laughed when he realized that these were the same movements he had learned for crawling. It was slow, but he knew that this would help him develop the coordination for walking again.

A few days later, there was some unusual activity at the hospital. That's not to say it wasn't always busy, but this was different. As Heinrich was taking his morning and afternoon walks, he saw painters everywhere. He wondered if this was therapy to keep the GI's busy or if something was up. Items that had been in disrepair for months were suddenly getting fixed. He began to feel uneasy as if something bad was about to happen. One of his worries was that in a few days the bandages would be coming off his face permanently and it would be confession time. He really liked these people and felt bad at deceiving them, but he just didn't know any other way. What if they stopped part way through his facial surgery and he was left looking like a creation of Baron Frankenstein.

His day of reckoning finally arrived. After months of waiting, his bandages were coming off permanently. They had been reluctant to let him see the results of the interim surgeries. The doctors said that the artist never allows anyone to see his painting until it is complete. Every one of his doctors was there for the unveiling along with his ever-present Lila. The bandages were removed and they just stood and stared.

Finally Heinrich said, "Well, do I look like Frankenstein or what? Say something! Better yet, give me a mirror and I'll look for myself."

As they handed him the mirror, they suddenly began to laugh and pat each other on the back. It was almost as if they had forgotten he was there.

"Beautiful work."

"Look at those ears."

"I got the dimple in the left cheek just like it used to be."

"I cannot believe it came out so good!"

"Captain, you look beautiful," Lila said.

Heinrich put the mirror in front of his face and was stunned. His emotions ran from one extreme to the other. What he saw was a familiar stranger. He could see that it was he and yet it wasn't. He wondered why someone didn't call the police and have him arrested. As he studied it however, he could see David in the mirror as well. He didn't think it looked like David, and yet it did. It was like looking at one of your children. One person would say, "He looks just like his father." While the other would say, "No, he is the spitting image of his mother!" Still, something was wrong. It was the eyes, yes, the eyes. You can never change the eyes. What he was looking at was Heinrich wearing a David mask. He knew he should tell them his secret and get it over with, but they were so happy that he didn't want to break the spell.

When he was alone reality settled in and remorse came over him. For better of worse, he would never look like Heinrich Müller again. He began to understand more fully what many soldiers felt when they had been disfigured by injuries. He felt shame at having hidden behind David's name, and now his face. Well, it would all be over soon enough. Tomorrow he would talk to Dr. Crookshanks privately. That would be the best way. They would bring the MP's in and quietly take him away. No one would ever have to know, especially Lila. He had grown to love her these past months and he did not want to see the disappointment in her eyes when she realized he was a "Kraut" and had stolen her time and friendship just as they had stolen her fiancé.

Chapter 14

The next morning after breakfast Heinrich stopped the orderly and asked, "May I see Dr. Crookshanks? I have something very important to discuss with him."

"Sorry sir, he is not available. Perhaps after the meeting you can see him."

"What meeting is that?"

"Didn't you know sir? Everyone is to assemble in the mess hall at 0900."

"I guess I do now, thank you Corporal."

Now that he had decided to do it, Heinrich just wanted it to be over with. He guessed one more morning wouldn't make that much difference. Just then Lila came in and said, "Get dressed; you and I have a date. You'll find a dress uniform in the closet. I'll be back for you in 15 minutes."

What was going on? Just when he thought he had these Yanks figured out, they suddenly got secretive. What if they've figured out his secret? Maybe they were going to arrest him publicly to make an example for any others. Heinrich felt his palms getting cold and clammy. He knew he would have to face the music sooner or later, but not like this. Not in front of Lila. These people had treated him so nicely and now everyone would know.

Heinrich reluctantly changed into his dress uniform. It felt so strange. This was the first time he had worn an American dress uniform. It was much different than his. Not so much adornment. Lighter, too.

There was a knock on the door and Lila stepped in.

"Ooh, you look dashing. I hope you don't mind, but the meeting is ready to start and it wouldn't do for you to be late."

"I guess you're right," he said. "Let's don't keep them waiting."

They entered the mess hall from a side door. The tables had all been folded and stacked to the side. Chairs had been placed in rows with three aisles separating them into four sections. There was a portable podium with a microphone in front of the room. People crowded every available spot. It looked as if everyone who could move or be moved was in attendance. The far side was filled with patients in wheel chairs. Along the wall beside them were reporters and photographers from the news service. Knots were forming in his stomach. He felt his face flush and he could feel all eyes boring through him.

"You are to take that seat on the front row," said Lila. "I'll be over here."

Heinrich could feel his head pounding. *Something is wrong. Something else is going on. They didn't go to this much trouble just to arrest me. No point in making a run for it. I'm too crippled to get far anyway. Oh well, I guess I've been through worse. I should just take it like a man. Whatever it is, it'll be over in a few minutes and I won't have to worry any more.*

He had just got to his seat when a voice shouted, "Attention!" and a group of highly decorated officers walked into the room. He could hear the pop of flash bulbs as the photographers were shooting pictures as fast as they could.

He recognized the hospital's commanding officer as he stepped up to the podium.

"At ease, men," he said. "It is a pleasure for me to be here and help take care of some business that is long overdue. So, with no further adieu, I will turn the time over to the Commanding General of the Army, Dwight D. Eisenhower."

79

The man who stood up and came to the podium was everything Heinrich had heard. He was a tall man with poise and a presence that commanded attention. What caught Heinrich off guard were the genuine smile and a kindness in his eyes he had never seen in a high-ranking officer. Most high-ranking officers in Germany had a stern, aloof look. *This man really cares about these soldiers.*

"It is a pleasure for me to be here to personally thank each of you for the sacrifice you have made for your country. It saddens me when I think of all those who didn't make it. Theirs was the ultimate sacrifice and nothing can repay them for it. Among those who are here today, however, there are some that we would like to single out for special recognition."

A voice called out. "Corporal John Taylor, front and center."

A young Corporal stood up, and marched to the podium standing at attention.

"Corporal John Taylor, on the 3rd of December your squad was pinned down by enemy fire..."

The General went on and on talking about the bravery of different individuals and handing out medals. For some he went over to their beds and handed them their medals and always ended with a handshake and a "Thank you, son." Then he would salute and go to the next one. Heinrich began to think of some of the brave men he had known on both sides and was saddened that they were gone. He was thinking of his friend David, and how much he wanted to survive the war when he heard "Captain David Strauss."

Lila bumped his arm and said, "Get up! He's asking for you."

Heinrich jumped up and almost fell. He was glad he had his crutch to lean on, because he was shaking all over as he walked to front and center. *What's going on?*

General Eisenhower began talking. "I have been given an unusual honor. As many or you know, with the recent death of President Roosevelt, things in Washington have been in turmoil. President Truman personally sent me this request to honor Captain Strauss. With the war in the

Pacific going as it is, the President did not want us to wait for convenience to present this award to Captain Strauss."

He looked at Heinrich and began speaking, "On December 2, 1943, at the aid station near Isernia, Italy, word was received that the camp was about to be overrun by the Germans. Most of the vehicles had been damaged by a mortar attack earlier in the day. The unit was ordered to retreat, but there was not transportation for 52 of the injured. Knowing they could be killed or taken captive and many would die without proper medical attention, Captain Strauss, with complete disregard of his personal safety, went above and beyond the call of duty and volunteered to stay with the wounded. He knew there was a significant risk and he might lose his life in this endeavor, but stayed and tended to the injured. Over the next 18 months, he put his life at risk on a daily basis by protecting the soldiers from inhumane treatment. On numerous occasions he stepped into the line of fire to protect the lives of those who could not protect themselves. His actions under the most difficult conditions reflect highest credit on himself and the armed forces of the United States of America.

"By order of the President of the United States and the Congress, I hereby present you the Medal of Honor, our country's highest award."

The general then took the medal out of a large satin-lined case and, stepping up to Heinrich, placed it around his neck. He took Heinrich's hand and shook it with a "Thank you son." With a salute, Heinrich stepped back and tried to march the best three-legged march he could come up with.

What have I gotten myself into? The hole just keeps getting deeper and deeper.

The rest of the meeting was a blur as he sat with his head reeling. A German officer had just been given America's highest award for bravery. What was he going to do? It just kept getting worse and worse.

As Lila helped him back to his room, he felt like it was some kind of a dream. His emotions were swinging like a pendulum from one extreme to the other. On one hand, he was elated that he was not in handcuffs or in a jail; on the other, he was ashamed that he had just received a hero's medal that wasn't his. He knew that he should have turned himself in, and now he wondered if it was too late. When the photos appeared in the Ohio newspapers, he would be caught for sure. There is no way that David's family would not immediately know that this was not their son.

When Lila turned him to help him to his chair, she brushed very close to him. He could smell the scent of soap and a light fragrance of spring flowers. Heinrich could not resist. He suddenly pulled her to him. Lila melted into his arms. As their lips met, she stiffened and pulled away.

"No!" she said. "I can't do this."

"I'm sorry. I don't know what came over me. These last few months I've grown to love you... your look, your smell, your touch. The sweet and kind way you care for me. I can't go further without letting you know."

"No, David. You are a married man."

"But I don't remember her. She is a stranger to me. I have fallen in love with you."

"I've grown fond of you these last few months too, David, but I just cannot do this to your wife. I lost my fiancé in this war. There is heartache all around us. There are women in America who have lost their men. As much as I care for you, I will not bring pain to Catherine by causing her to lose her husband a second time. Goodbye, David."

Lila turned and left the room.

Chapter 15

Heinrich was in a daze; he knew he loved this girl and he could not, no… would not let her go. When he lost Ursula he thought his life was over, and he would never love again. Now he had a second chance. He didn't care if he wound up in prison, he would not lose her. Tomorrow he would confess the truth and hope she wouldn't have him arrested. After all, he was the enemy. It was his people that killed her fiancé. Why shouldn't she hate him?

He got up and began to pace. His leg hurt. His head hurt. He felt as if he was carrying the weight of the world. Well, tomorrow would tell the tale. He would confess as soon as she came in, and then let the cards fall where they may. If he was not David, then he wouldn't be married. At least that barrier would be out of the way.

There was a brief knock at the door. He stood thinking that Lila had returned. He was surprised when the door swung open and a full colonel stepped in. His heart froze when he realized the game was over. They knew. He didn't know how they found out so quickly, but from the look on the colonel's face, he knew something was up.

"Hello, I'm Colonel Tom Bartlett," he said.

Colonel Tom Bartlett was 5' 8" with the tan of someone who spent time out of doors. His hair was dark brown with gray quietly slipping in at the sides. His medium frame supported muscle. Broad shoulders, narrow waist and no fat indicated to Heinrich that this officer did not spend a lot of time behind a desk. His eyes were blue and had the look of a man who had seen more than his share of pain.

Heinrich remembered seeing him with the entourage that accompanied General Eisenhower.

"What can I do for you Colonel?" he said.

"I have some business that I would like to conduct with you personally. I know that nothing I can say could mean more than the medal you just received, but I wanted to give you my personal thanks for staying with those men."

Relieved Heinrich said, "Colonel, I just did what anyone under similar circumstances would have done."

"No Captain, no one else volunteered but you. Besides that you don't understand who those men were. Those were my men that you stayed with. I gave the order to retreat and I gave the order to leave those men behind. I died a little inside knowing that I almost certainly sentenced those men to death. When it was reported to me that you volunteered to be captured with them, it gave me hope. For 18 months I clung to the belief that they might still be alive.

"I'm a little different than most battalion commanders. I make it a point to know each and every man under my command. This helps me maintain a sense of responsibility when I decide to send men on a mission. I know that I had better make darn sure I have covered my bases because I know the men I am sending out.

"When I sent those three companies out, I knew that there was a chance that we would get flanked, but I just didn't think it would happen. When it did, I felt I should have done a better job. We all know that in war, you can't always be right, but it doesn't make it any easier.

"Anyway, Captain, you saved my bacon. You did more than that though. Besides being a doctor, you also became a chaplain, protector, and a battalion commander. Not officially, of course, but you took charge and responsibility for that entire camp. Every man in my battalion who was in that camp has either written me or come to me personally to tell me about the doc. I brought a letter for you to read; it is typical of the reports that were given about you."

He passed the letter to Heinrich.

Dear Colonel Bartlett,

I am writing this letter to tell you about Capitan David Strauss. He was with us in the German prison camp at Stalag 21. To begin with, he did not have to go; he volunteered to be captured with those of us who couldn't walk when our position was overrun by the Germans. We were in a forward medical unit after being injured. He was our doctor. When they found out that the Germans had snuck around and had flanked us, we had to leave in a hurry. Captain Strauss loaded those who were in the worst shape in the trucks. He got some of the other GI's to help the ones that could walk. There were 52 of us left who couldn't move fast enough to go with the unit. The CO told us we would have to stay behind and be captured or the whole bunch of us would wind up either dead or captured. I'll tell you I was scared. I wasn't in very good shape and figured the Krauts would either shoot me, or just let me die. Captain Strauss just stepped up and said he would stay behind and take care of us as best he could. Colonel, he saved our lives. We told him he didn't have to do it, but he said he was a soldier, and he would not leave his men. Colonel, he walked through the gates of hell for us. We was on the train boxed up like cattle for 10 days. Some of our guys and some of the guys from the other outfits died too. Well the Captain became a preacher and had a funeral for every one of them guys. He said that their moms and dads would want to know that they had a decent funeral. We figured those Krauts wouldn't do nothin' for them, and we was right too. When we got to that prison camp, I was scared, but that Captain, he said, "Don't let 'em know you're scared, you just look them in the eye and be proud you're Americans." Well, we did just that, I don't know what it did for everyone else, but I felt better. Anyway, even though he was a non-combatant, he put his life on the line for us everyday. We had this guard, Corporal Rothenberger; he had a mean streak a mile wide. He beat some of us up every day. I seen the Captain step between Rotten, as we called the corporal, and one of our guys who was hurt. Rotten put a gun to the Captain's head and was gonna blow his head off, but the Captain wouldn't move an inch. If it wasn't for that Kraut Doctor, I guess Rotten would've done it too. Anyway, he did stuff like that for us nearly every day. I can't believe he didn't get hisself killed. Another time he took a beating for Huntsman while we was on a work party. He spent almost a month in the hospital getting over that one. I know that he's hurt real bad from the shellin' we got. Don't let the doctors in that hospital give up on him. He's a lot tougher than any man I know. I wrote and told my folks about him, and they told me that I should tell you and ask if you could give him some kind of hero medal or something like that. There's probably about a thousand or more of us that would all say the same thing.

Yours truly,

Pvt. Hardy Grissett

P.S. The Kraut Doctor, Major Müller helped out a lot too, but I guess we don't give medals to Krauts.

"I guess that letter says it all. It's such a pleasure to know a man of your caliber."

With that he reached into his pocket and pulled out a small box. He opened to reveal two gold oak leaf pins, the symbols of the rank of Major. "It's with great pride that I advance you to the rank of Major, an advancement that you surely deserve."

"I don't believe I understand, Colonel. You know I will probably be mustered out of the army when I hit the states," he said.

"You're right," replied the Colonel, "but if for some reason you must apply for disability, a major's pay is better than a captain's. If you need more medical attention when you get to the states, you'll find that a major gets a little higher priority. It's not much, but it's something that I could do to personally say 'thanks.' All of the letters I received were copied for your file and sent on to the commanding general. I have also written a letter of commendation and sent it with a copy of this letter to your family back home. I think they should know what kind of son they raised."

With that the colonel said, "I must go now. It's been a pleasure to personally meet you." He then snapped Heinrich a smart salute and turned to leave.

Heinrich returned the salute and wondered to himself, *is this ever going to end?*

Early the next day he got up, showered, shaved, and put on his best uniform. He wanted everything to be perfect. When Lila came to work with him on his rehabilitation, he would let her know that it was okay to love again.

There was a knock on the door and a nurse he did not recognize came in.

"Hello, I'm Gretchen Smyth, your new PT assistant. You are Major Strauss?"

Heinrich was stunned. "Where is Lila?" he asked.

"You mean Nurse Turnbull? She has been transferred to the hospital at Southampton. Her mother has been taken ill and she wanted to be near. It will be good for her. They have been short of staff and have been asking for assistance for months."

Heinrich felt as if he had been struck in the stomach. Could he be loosing Ursula all over again? Why had he waited so long? Would he ever see her again? If he confessed now, he would be put into prison and she might never know.

"Is there anything wrong sir? You really don't look so good."

"No, everything's fine. I'm just sorry I didn't get to say goodbye. We had become such good friends. Would you perhaps have her address?"

"Oh no, sir, they never give us that information. Since the war, everything's so hush-hush. Loose lips sink ships you know."

"Thanks just the same," he said.

He felt like things were getting out of control. He desperately wanted to share his life with Lila, but she had left without a word. If he tried to find her, he would be arrested. What a mess. Prison, he almost laughed. He was in a prison without bars. His life was falling apart and all he could do is just watch. When Ursula and the baby died, he thought his life was over. Now, he had a second chance and just when life seemed as though it would start again, God snatched her away. *What have I done to deserve this? All I had ever wanted to do was be a doctor and help people. Now my life is just one big lie. Maybe God is telling me that happiness cannot be based upon lies. I did not want to be here, it was thrust upon me. I guess I should have stopped it before it got out of control. Of course if I had stopped it, I would not have met Lila. Is this one of life's paradoxes we hear about? All I know at this point is that I want to be in control of my life once again. But how? I need a plan.*

What are my needs? First, I need to get through rehabilitation so I will be mobile. Next, I need to stay out of jail. I'm glad I didn't confess to anything. I guess that this will be my greatest obstacle. Sooner or later David's family will find the truth and call the police. At the present time no one in the military seemed to have a clue that things were not as they should be. If General Eisenhower accepted me, I guess no one else is going to contradict him.

Okay, let things ride as they are. As long as I am here, I might as well get all the rehabilitation I can. When I get to the States, I will make my escape. Surely in a place as large as that, I can lose myself. I wonder if I will be able to practice medicine. I hope so. As soon as the army turns me loose, I will simply disappear instead of going to David's home. If I get caught, I'll pretend I don't remember where I live. Maybe I can use this amnesia to my advantage. At least I know a little bit about life in America with my medical school experience. If I can hide for a few months in the states, maybe I can return and find Lila. If she doesn't hate me when she finds out who I really am, we could return to Germany and put my life back together. There are a lot of ifs, thinks, and maybes, but at least it's a plan.

Time seemed to stand still after that. The therapy seemed more aggravating than before. Heinrich felt as if he was ungrateful to Yardley and Jones for the long hard hours they put in. He knew that it wasn't their fault, but things were different.

"You really do miss her," said Jones one afternoon.

"Miss who?" said Heinrich.

"Miss Turnbull."

"Does it show that bad?"

"It started showing about a week after you came to. The only ones that didn't know it were you and Miss Turnbull."

"Well, I screwed that one up pretty bad."

"Don't kid yourself, sir. She had it bad for you too."

"Really?"

"Oh yes, she would light up every time it was time for your therapy or your evening strolls together. I can't imagine why she took off that way."

"Well, when I get out of here, maybe I can fix that."

"I hope so, sir. She was a fine person and deserves happiness. I guess the quicker we get you in shape, the quicker you will be on your way."

Holding his hand out, Jones said, "Shall we begin?"

Things seemed a little better after that. Heinrich did not feel so alone.

Chapter 16

Southampton, England

"Well if a good man fell in love with me, you wouldn't see me running, even if he was married," said Jillian.

Lila looked at her sister with shock on her face. "That's terrible! You know you could never do that!"

"I know, but with the shortage of men around here, I'm going a little crazy. They're either married, missing important pieces, or just plain bonkers! I need a break and a little romance in my life. All I have done for six years is patch them up for their wives or sweethearts, or send them back to the front to die."

"It does get hard. What you need is to go on holiday! You've been working hard in that hospital for six years and taking care of Mum on top of that. Why don't you take a fortnight off and just relax?"

"I don't know. I couldn't do that with you just getting home and all. It just wouldn't be right."

"What is right in this crazy mixed-up world? We need to take happiness while we can. Who knows when you'll get another chance? It's my time to take care of Mum anyway. Besides, while you're gone, I can rearrange our room more to my liking."

"Now the truth is out you rascal!" said Jillian.

Jillian looked out the window. "I just don't know... Before the war started, I was saving for a trip to the south of France" Turning to Lila she said, "Do you think the French coast is still there?"

"That's the spirit! Maybe you'll meet some wealthy Frenchman."

"Now really!"

"You never know... If you do, see if he has a brother for me."

Marseilles, France a few weeks later

A seagull shrieked overhead and brought Jillian out of deep thought. Startled, she looked around to see if anyone had noticed her jump. She began to watch families frolic in the foaming surf. *It is hard to believe that a short time ago people were dying on these beautiful beaches as the Allied troops rushed ashore in the assault to retake France. How could they have forgotten so quickly? I guess that maybe, I am the one who should forget... What am I thinking? I guess I* **have** *been working too hard and too long just like Lila said. I simply need to relax. Besides, I have no reason to complain! If I do, I am no different than the rest of them. I am not going to ruin my deserved holiday feeling guilty because I am alive. I have come to the south of France to relax and have an enjoyable time whatever that may entail.* She stood up from the wooden bench facing the ocean and began to walk. What should she do now?

As she was walking along she noticed a rather dashing gentleman sitting alone on a bench facing the seashore. He looked a little uncomfortable as the sun was shining in his eyes. Wondering why he didn't just move, she saw a wheelchair farther down the bench. *Just like a turtle on its back.*

Jillian stepped around his bench and said, "Me pardonne, peux-je vous aider?"

He answered, "Oui, merci."

He then smiled and said, "By any chance are you English?"

"Yes, is my French that bad?"

"No, mine is. You just have that 'English look.'"

"I didn't know there was an 'English look'."

"There is, but it is a good thing. I didn't mean to sound offensive. But to answer your question, yes I do need help. I seem to have lost my assistant."

"Maybe I can help. Would you like to return to your chair?"

"Well... yes. It's not too hard if you don't mind. Just move it over next to me."

She pulled the chair over. "Not to worry, I work in a British Hospital. I've done this a million times. Just put your arms around my neck."

As he did so, she hesitated, he smelled so clean and fresh. The light scent of cologne tempted her. She almost kissed him. So different from the odors of death that she had been dealing with. She smiled. Placing her arms around him, she said, "Hold tight," then expertly swung him around and deposited him in the wheelchair.

"You're supposed to let go now."

Smiling, he leaned up and gave her a light peck on the cheek. "Thank you."

With a slight blush, she said, "Anytime you need to be moved, I'm your girl.

Well, where can I take you?"

"I hate to be a bother, but I am staying at the Mercure Beauvau across the boulevard. You don't know how much I appreciate this."

"Not to worry, I have nothing better to do than to pick up strangers and take them to a hotel."

She put her hand to her mouth and began to blush. "I don't know what has gotten into me. Normally, I am not so forward. I had a little wine earlier and it must have gone straight to my head."

He began to laugh. "It's refreshing to meet someone who is not so dour and serious."

He quickly stuck out his hand. "My name is Heinrich Müller."

"Müller?" A frown crossed her face as she looked away.

"Yes, I'm German. Please accept my apologies. I am sure that I will be paying the rest of my life for the actions of others."

Jillian turned back and forced a smile. "No, it is I who should apologize. It's just that you sounded so much like an American... I, I made some incorrect assumptions.

With that she began to push him across the wide boulevard that separated the hotels from the beach.

"I hope you don't change your mind and leave me stranded in the middle of the street." He said laughingly. "For the record, I was a good Kraut."

She began to laugh. "That remains to be seen."

A car came dangerously close and blew long and hard on his horn.

Jillian screamed and began to laugh as she ran pushing the wheelchair in a snakelike pattern.

She realized as she was running that she was enjoying herself even if it was with the enemy. Wait, she didn't know that he was the enemy; he might really be a "good Kraut."

As they entered the plush hotel a man in a dark suit met them. Looking flustered, he began speaking rapidly. The man she knew as Heinrich smiled a gentle smile and quietly spoke to the man. Turning to Jillian, he said, "This is Erik, my cousin. He is my able assistant and good friend. We traveled late last night and he went to sleep while reading the newspaper. That's why you had to rescue me. I would like to repay you for your kindness. Would you have dinner with me this evening?"

"Yes! I mean no, it's not necessary to repay me. I was just trying to be helpful." She began to blush again.

"Please do. I am a stranger in town and have no friends. Besides I am sure I would recover from my injuries much more quickly in the company of a beautiful woman."

"Oh really," she said smiling, "Does that line actually work?"

"You tell me. Are we having dinner together?"

Jillian smiled. "You win. I would hate to be responsible for your relapse."

"Okay, let's say seven then. Shall I have Erik pick you up?"

"That won't be necessary. I'm not staying far from here."

As she turned to leave she looked back and said, smiling, "Oh yes, my name is Jillian, Jillian Turnbull."

David waved back and thought *what a beautiful name.*

That night as Jillian was dressing, she thought how different her room must be than that of Heinrich. She was just two short blocks away and her room cost about one tenth of what his surely did. She did not know why she was fantasying about a man she had only met. He was obviously wealthy. He was the enemy. Well, maybe not. He was in a wheelchair and had some major health issues. She likely wouldn't have to worry about her virtue. At least she might not have to spend her holiday alone. She smiled to herself. At home men were scarce as hen's teeth and she had a date on the first night of her holiday. Not bad!

The meal was amazingly delicious although the menu was thin. The wine was very good though ordinary by French standards. Fortunes of war. *Two years ago, I would have been happy for a full meal and now I am complaining about the lack of variety on the menu. I am as bad as the rest.*

"You look as if you were a million miles away."

Jillian flushed. "I guess I was. I was thinking about how enjoyable this meal was, yet, a short time ago people were dying on these beaches and we were all scrambling for food. I'm sorry, I hate to be a sourpuss but I can't turn my feelings off and on. I guess I've been working too long. Some holiday, eh."

"You have a right to feel as you do. This war has changed all of our lives. Here I roll in out of the blue and you are wondering what am I doing sitting here having dinner with the enemy."

"I thought you were a good Kraut?"

"I am. At least I think so."

"Now you are qualifying it. Are you going to change your story now? Tell me; just what makes you a good Kraut?"

"This is going to sound strange, but I can only go by what I am told. I'll tell you what, why don't we go sit on the patio and I'll dazzle you with my life as I know it."

"Okay, this sounds intriguing."

David smiled, "Better yet, my room has a terrace with a view of the seashore. How about taking in the view?"

"That was fast. Without so much as a breath, you move me to the patio and on to your room."

David was embarrassed. "I'm sorry I guess that was a bit fast. You really don't know me."

Jillian laughed. "Not to worry, it doesn't matter if I know you or not. If things get desperate, I do believe that I can outrun you in a race. Let's go."

When the lift door opened, there was the foyer and only one door - his. The foyer was almost as large as her entire sleeping quarters. It was ecru with ornate gold trim everywhere - from the crown molding to the gold-framed pictures on the walls. The lift operator stepped out and unlocked the door. Room was not an adequate description of his sleeping accommodations. Two streets over and nine pounds *did* make a difference. As Jillian rolled David in, she saw white marble floors with ornate rugs everywhere. There were two spacious bedrooms off a large living area the size of her flat in Cornwall. At the far side of the living area was a marble topped dining table with six chairs. To the side of the table were double doors leading to - yes - a large terrace. At that moment she was so grateful that this building had not been destroyed during the war. It would have been a disgrace to lose such a thing of beauty. In a way, these rooms were like art.

"If you will roll me across we can sit on the terrace as I promised and I will tell you my short, boring story. I apologize for the rooms, but my uncle made the reservation and I had no idea I would be staying in a palace.

After they had settled on the terrace, a waiter rolled in a cart with coffee. He poured the coffee and left.

David began. "Anyway, my life, as I know it, started just over a year ago when I woke up in a Swiss hospital covered in bandages. I have no memory of my life before that time. This is how I know that I was a "good Kraut." If I had been a "bad Kraut", the Americans that rescued me would have sent me to a German hospital. Who knows what would have happened to me there? As I understand, I was a doctor in a German Stalag, caring for the American wounded and ill. When the camp was liberated we were shelled by Russian artillery. I was wounded and a number of Americans were killed. I was taken with the American wounded to the American hospital and many of the liberated prisoners told the authorities that I had done glorious things in their defense.

"You know, this is embarrassing. I don't know if I can continue."

"Go on, I'm all ears. I do want to know why you are a 'good Kraut.'"

"Okay, anyway the Americans kept me longer than was necessary, treating me for a few weeks after I was out of immediate danger until the war was officially over. By that time Uncle Hans had been notified and he moved me to a Swiss hospital where I have been ever since. We were fortunate that my father had moved most of our money and valuables out of Germany and into Switzerland when he knew that war was inevitable. Quite a number of his friends did the same. Otherwise there would have been no Swiss hospital and I would be hopping around like the hunchback of Notre Dame. That is, if I could walk."

96

"How extensive were your injuries?"

"I don't think there is anything you can see that is original. My face was smashed and I had some burns. I had many skin grafts, I don't know where they got the skin, but every time I have to go to the bathroom, my left cheek twitches."

Jillian began to laugh. "You rascal! You had me there for a moment. But seriously though, your face is quite pleasant. Did they have to do much work there?"

"Oh yes, a lot. Uncle brought pictures of me before the war and they were able to reconstruct it well. I did have them make a few improvements while they were at it. All in all, I am as suave now as I was before the war."

"How are your legs doing? I hope I am not out of line, but I have dealt with this so much that it is second nature. What is the prognosis?"

"In theory I can walk. I have feeling in my back and legs and the joints are in working order, but for some reason I can't walk. With all the surgeries on my face and arms I spent a lot of time in bed. Add that to being in traction and having my legs in casts and who knows what could be wrong. There are plenty of excuses for not walking, but the doctors think that isn't the problem. They are of the opinion that I have some emotional trauma."

"What do you think?"

"I don't know. The only thing I know is that I tell my legs to walk but I get no response. I wonder if the loose connection in my brain that has given me amnesia is also stopping me from walking. I don't even remember ever walking. Perhaps I have forgotten how."

Jillian moved her chair over until she was directly in front of David. Reaching down she lifted his leg and placed it in her lap. She untied his shoelace and removed his shoe along with his sock.

"I'm not that kind of boy."

Glancing up and smiling she slapped his leg and said, "Pay attention!"

Running her forefinger under his toes, she saw them wiggle in response. "You will walk again. That is, if you are willing to pay the price."

"What do you mean pay the price?"

"Regaining the ability to walk after the extent of the injuries you have received requires a lot of work and dedication. I have seen many men who should have walked leave the hospital in wheelchairs because they weren't willing to make the sacrifice and do what it takes to walk. Are you willing to pay the price?"

"Yes."

"What is it that the doctors think is in your mind that is stopping you from walking?"

"While I was away in the war, my family was killed when an allied bomber crashed into our home. It killed my parents, my wife and daughter. Uncle Hans and his family are the only members of my family to survive. Erik is his son. I went to war and my family died!"

Tears filled his eyes as he looked away.

Jillian reached and gently took his hand.

"I am so sorry for your loss. Life is full of 'What ifs,' and 'If I had nots.' We all have things that we wish we could change. Unfortunately we can't. I certainly have my share. The only thing we can do is understand that for some reason God kept us alive. For that reason it is our duty to use that life as best we can. Honor the memory of those that have passed, by leading a life that will let people know what wonderful parents you must have had. Let them know that you are such a man that your wife must have been special to have been married to you."

Suddenly her face brightened. "Some date, eh? Here you thought you were taking me to dinner and suddenly you are in a therapy session."

"Some wonderful date, yes. I told you that I would recover faster in your presence and here we are. Honestly though, I have not felt this good in a long time. The doctors and nurses at the hospital are wonderful, but you have brought a breath of fresh air into my life. You didn't have to help me this afternoon, but you did. It has been a long time since I have met someone who was kind because it was the right thing to do. Thank you."

Jillian began to feel a little self-conscious.

"Maybe I was trying to pick you up because you were helpless and couldn't get away. Did you think of that? See, without you realizing it I have taken your shoe off and I have your foot in my lap. I now have you under my power, if you don't do my bidding, I will tickle you to death."

With that she started tickling the bottom of his foot. David started laughing and jerked his foot back. Startled, he pointed to his foot.

"Did you see what you did? My foot moved!"

Jillian began laughing excitedly. "It did, didn't it? Maybe you're closer to walking than you realize."

Placing his hands in a begging position, he said, "Please never leave me. You're a miracle worker."

"Speaking of leaving, it's time for me to go."

She began gathering her things.

"Go? You can't leave at a time like this. I didn't think I would ever walk again. You have moved me forward in just a couple of hours and you weren't even trying. Think what we could do if you tried. Can we meet for breakfast?"

Smiling, Jillian said, "Meet you for breakfast? If I remember right, I am on holiday. This is what I left in England. However, since you are so special, I believe my calendar is open for tomorrow."

"You have made me so happy. Is there anything I can do for you?"

Jillian turned back. "Yes there is."

99

With that she walked over and kissed him on the lips. Looking at his stunned face she said, "Thanks, I've wanted to do that since the first time I saw you."

A big grin spread across his face. "Anytime. You don't even have to ask. I am here for you. Shall I see you about nine?"

She turned and began walking out. "Yes, nine will be just fine."

As she walked to her hotel, she thought about the day's events. *What am I doing? My first day here and I have been to the room of a man that I hardly know and have practically thrown myself at him. I can only imagine what he must think of me. Not to worry though, in another week or so, I will never see him again and this will all be just a memory.*

After Jillian left, David just sat grinning. He could not remember ever feeling this good. The fact that he could not remember much anyway didn't count. All he had known since awaking in that Swiss hospital was pain and fear. He had lost a family he couldn't remember and he was a cripple. He had decided that no woman could ever find him appealing. Now this English beauty had given him a kiss. He wondered how long her vacation would last. Could he keep her attention that long? He was not sure he would be able to sleep this night, but it would be worth it if he stayed awake the entire night remembering that kiss.

Chapter 17

Jillian's sleep was restless. All night long she dreamed of helping Heinrich walk again. He would take a couple of steps, throw his arms around her and give her a kiss as they fell to the ground. They would laugh as they rolled over and over across the sand in a long embrace. Needless to say, she was exhausted when she finally got up.

She looked in the mirror at the bags under her eyes. Her hair was a mess and would not cooperate. She must have tangled it into a thousand knots as she rolled over and over in her sleep. Of all the times to look a fright, not this morning, please! He may be a German, he may be a cripple, but he was a dish. She wasn't sure how he looked when he went into that hospital, but they must have done a superb job.

She felt giddy all over as she hurried down the street for breakfast. Just before she knocked on his door, she thought about that kiss last night, *what could she have been thinking? How could she face him? Well, here goes nothing...* and she knocked.

Erik answered the door. He was smiling and looked like a different man than the one she met yesterday.

"Heinrich was hoping you could have breakfast on the terrace, if it would be okay?"

"Oh yes, that would be fine," she answered as he lead her across the room. As she walked through the door,

Jillian could see that the terrace was covered with beautiful flowers.

David was wearing a white shirt with red stripes. It was opened at the collar revealing just a touch of blonde chest hair. A white belt, pants and white shoes completed his outfit. Jillian felt severely underdressed in a blouse tied at the midriff, casual shorts and sandals. She wore a scarf around her hair in a bit of a ponytail. That was all she could think to do with her hair to try to make order out of chaos.

David pushed himself up from his chair slightly in an effort to show respect.

"Please don't get up, it's okay. Perhaps I should say please do get up under the circumstances." She felt her face flush as she stammered.

"May I say you look like a flower in the spring? You are positively radiant."

"Me? No, my hair is a mess. I simply couldn't do anything with it!"

Jillian felt her face flush again.

"I'm sorry; I hope I haven't embarrassed you. I tend to say what is on my mind and all I can think of is that you look absolutely stunning!"

Once again Jillian's face turned red. What was she going to do?

"I guess I better sit down and eat before I embarrass myself again."

She looked imploringly at David. "Can you ever forgive me for last night? I don't know what could have gotten into me. Maybe I had too much wine. I am normally not so forward."

David laughed. "Please do sit down," he said as he gestured to the seat opposite him. "It is so refreshing to finally meet someone genuine and open. I have been in hospitals so long where everyone is quiet and reserved and polite that I didn't think I could stand it one more day. Then a miracle occurs on my first day of holiday. An angel

102

walks up and literally sweeps me off my feet! How could heaven have been so kind as to send you into my life?"

"I think I should eat before I do something stupid. You're only one step from getting kissed again," she said nervously.

David smiled. "Don't be embarrassed, if you want to kiss me again, it is perfectly fine with me."

The meal was something to behold. There was a tray covered with the most delightful of breads. Butter, jams of every variety, and fruit completed the repast. A silver teapot sat to one side with a pitcher of orange juice next to it.

"I believe I have died and gone to heaven," she giggled. "The French have not lost the art of baking. These croissants are fantastic."

The tone of the morning became more relaxed and they talked for a couple of hours. They laughed and told stories of their youth. David could only tell what he had been told by his uncle.

Jillian commented, "It must be hard not to remember your past. Sometimes I wish I could forget parts of mine."

"It is quite frustrating. Uncle and Erik forget and say things to me expecting an answer, but there is none. It is as though I was born last year. I still remember how to be a doctor. I am told that information is stored in a different part of the brain and appears to be completely intact. Occasionally I see a flash of a memory, but I have no knowledge of when it was or where. I have tried not to think on it too much. I am told that it could come back suddenly or a little at a time. Perhaps if I don't focus on it, it will appear and I will be a complete man again.

"Enough of talking about me, tell me a little about you. The only thing I know is that you rescue lost little boys. How long have you been a nurse?"

"Actually, I am not a nurse in the truest sense. I became one by default. My sister Lila and I were PT instructors at a girl's school near London prior to the war. All PT instructors had to teach other classes as well. She taught French and

103

subbed for me in German. I taught German and subbed in French when she needed time off.

"What is a PT instructor?"

"Physical Training. You know gym classes."

"Okay, go on, where did the nursing come in?"

"When the war started, they closed the school and we were out of a job. We got word that physical therapy nurses were needed as a result of the injuries our boys were receiving so we applied. A short class in first aid and we were in business. Lila went to work in a hospital in London and I went to work in a hospital near home. My mother wasn't doing so well with the loss of my father, and I wanted to be near. That's it in a nutshell."

"I believe you are in your true calling. Only a person who truly cares about people would have come up out of the blue to help a perfect stranger. Once again let me tell you that it is not only a pleasure, but a blessing to have met you."

David rubbed his hands together. "What shall we do with our day today? Are you willing to share it with me, or do you have plans?"

"Actually, I have no plans at all. I left home with nothing but a desire for a change of scenery. So, if it would not be an imposition on you, I would be glad to accompany you anywhere you desire to go."

"Imposition? You are joking, of course. When in my wildest dreams would being with a beautiful, intelligent woman be an imposition? I was hoping you would agree to visit with me today. With that in mind, I had Erik secure us a convertible car. He will drive us along the coast and we can see or do as we fancy."

The drive along the French coast was wonderful. The wind was deliciously refreshing as it blew through her hair. Jillian was amazed at Heinrich's knowledge. He could tell about Hannibal, or historical facts about the area. When questioned, David said that he could remember facts; it was personal events for which he had no memory. Some doctors said that his past was so painful that his mind blocked it

104

out. David told her that he wished that someone could convince his brain that not knowing was more painful than the past could ever be.

They continued to see one another every day. Jillian could not believe how much she enjoyed Heinrich's company. To think, only a short time ago she was standing in her mother's kitchen talking with Lila about her lost love. The thought of finding someone for herself had been a tease and yet here she was with one of the most wonderful men she had ever met. What was she going to do? The days were going by too fast. Soon she would have to leave and she could not bear the thought of never seeing Heinrich again.

One morning she arrived a little early and David was not finished getting ready.

"Erik, do you think Heinrich would enjoy going for a swim?"

He replied, "No mum, he is afraid of the water without the use of his legs. Before the war, he loved the sea."

"He did?"

"Oh yes, we would go sailing on a lake near our home. Most of his family vacations were by the seashore. His family would go to Capri, sometimes here at this very hotel, and of course Mallorca. That was perhaps his favorite"

"The reason I ask is that I think it may help his legs to be in the water. Water exercises stimulate the muscles and nerves of the legs. Why don't you suggest we go and play in the water?"

Erik shook his head. "He wouldn't do it for me, but if you suggested it I believe that he would do most anything. He thinks highly of you, I believe."

"I guess I will then. You two seem more like brothers than cousins. I have never seen a cousin or even a brother that would do what you do."

"What do you mean?"

"Well, you have left your wife and children to help Heinrich for all these months. I don't see that kind of devotion very often."

Erik smiled as they sat on the patio. "Our friendship is stronger than you would ever believe. I owe Heinrich my life."

"You do?"

"Yes, it happened when we were teenagers. We went hiking and camping in the mountains near our home. As it happened, I fell into a ravine and broke my leg. Instead of going back to town for help, Heinrich climbed down and helped me. When I protested, he said that if he went for help, it would be long into the night before he could return. With the cold and the wild animals I could easily be dead. Well, he set my leg and then splinted it. Using ropes and trees at the top, he pulled me up to the top. That was no easy task. He made a drag sled and then dragged me all the way to town. It is amazing that we both didn't die. I have never been so cold or miserable in my life. It was near freezing and there was no snow on the ground, so he just kept pulling me across the rough terrain. He was near death when we reached town."

"That's quite a story and he probably doesn't remember any of it."

"No he doesn't, but I do and I can never repay the debt."

"How did he know how to set your leg?"

"Oh, he learned it from his father. His father was a fine doctor. Heinrich worked in his father's office as much as he would let him. I guess a doctor is all he ever wanted to be."

"Hey you two. What are you plotting out there?" David rolled his wheelchair across the room toward the patio.

Jillian laughed. "I was trying to get Erik to ask you to take me sunbathing. We have been driving all over the south of France and haven't been back to the seashore since the day I found you there."

"You have, have you? Well, I guess I could be persuaded, but just for you. You just have to promise me that you

106

won't laugh when you see me in swimwear. I look pretty scrawny and white as a sheet."

"I am not sure that I can promise that, but I'll do my best."

"That's settled. Erik, will you drive Jillian to her hotel to get her swimwear?"

Jillian smiled and released two ties on her dress revealing a swimsuit beneath. "I don't think that will be necessary."

David had a shocked look. "You are sure of yourself aren't you? What if I had said no?"

Jillian's confidence was almost tangible. "You wouldn't. Now quit messing around and get ready, the sun and the sand are waiting."

They sat and let the waves roll over their legs. Jillian closed her eyes and felt the sun baking through her body. Those dark days working in the hospital were fading away now. She had not believed life would ever be good again, yet here she was. If only it would never end...

She was brought back to the surface of reality when David spoke.

"Isn't it strange that I have been in battle and faced death many times, well, if I could remember it anyway, but the thought of getting into the sea without the use of my legs terrifies me. I feel so helpless."

"Well," said Jillian looking down, "You are not nearly as helpless as you believe, look at your legs."

"They're moving! I think you are a witch. How did you know?"

Jillian smiled. "I have been noticing that when you are not paying attention to them that you have movement in your legs. I am beginning to think you are a fraud. You just want someone to push you around and baby you." With that she splashed him with water and started laughing.

David rolled toward her and splashed back. "You are only picking at me because I am alone and helpless," he laughed.

"Naa, naa, naa, naa naa," she said as she moved just out of his reach. "Bet you can't get me." Then she splashed him.

David splashed back and began to crawl with his hands and kick in the water as he struggled to reach her. Each time he almost reached her she would slide just out of his reach.

"If I ever catch you, you're going to get it!"

"Get what? You'll never catch me!"

Just at that time he quickly reached out and grasped her arm and began to pull her to him. She lightly struggled at first and then gently slid herself into his arms. He pulled her to him and kissed her. This was not like any kiss she had ever received. Heat spread down through her body. Her feet began to tingle and her body shuddered. He released her, caught his breath and said, "There, that was payback for our first night."

Her eyes fluttered and she caught her breath. "I don't think so, my kiss was much better than that!"

He pulled her back and kissed her again. "Was that better?"

"A little better, but you still have a way to go."

"I guess I will have to practice."

With that they kissed again and again. They were brought back to their senses when they heard children giggling. Looking up they saw a small group of children standing a few feet away giggling and chattering in French. When Jillian and David looked their way, the children scattered, laughing as they ran.

Jillian had an embarrassed smile. "I think you have had enough lessons for today. Maybe we should go in."

She turned and waved to Erik sitting on a bench on the promenade. He put down his paper and walked through the sand as Jillian put her hands under David's arms and began to pull him out of the water. Her legs were weak and she stumbled and fell. She hoped that no one would notice that her legs were shaking as she pulled on David.

"I feel like a child being helped by his mother," he protested.

"Well, if you would learn to walk, we wouldn't have to do this. Look at your legs. Your feet are pushing against the sand. I know that you will walk again. You just need some practice."

"I wanted to ask you about that," he said, "let's talk when we get out of this mess."

By this time, Erik had arrived. He put a towel over David's shoulders then scooped him up and began to carry him up to the cabaña that had been set up for them on the beach.

"This is what I am talking about!" he said over his shoulder as Erik put him down.

Erik straightened a light blanket and put it over him. "Thanks Erik." With that Erik walked back to his spot on the promenade, picked up his paper and began reading again.

David looked at his cousin sitting patiently on the bench. "Erik is such a good friend. I can't have him relegate his life to being my babysitter. Did you know that he has a degree in engineering? Yet here he is, patiently taking care of me like I am a child.

"That leads to my dilemma. Erik is married and has children. He needs to be with them. His wife is so understanding, but Erik has been with me constantly since I left the American hospital."

"And...?"

"That's where you come in."

Jillian raised her eyebrows in shock. "What do you mean?"

"I would like to hire you as my personal nurse and physical therapist."

Jillian began to shake her head from side to side. "After that little exercise in the water a few minutes ago, I don't think I could be *that* personal a nurse."

David leaned forward anxiously, "No, this would be strictly business. No hanky panky."

Once again Jillian began to shake her head no. "I'm sorry Heinrich. I already have a job and I have responsibilities at home. A fortnight romance is one thing, but this is different. No... I don't think so."

"You don't know how much this means to me. I'm willing to put romance on hold temporarily until this is over, only temporarily though. It will be strictly business until you have me walking."

"No, I don't think so. It just wouldn't be right."

"How much do you make being a nurse?"

Jillian's face reddened as she began to protest, "I don't see that that is any of your business."

"I will pay you one hundred pounds a week with a minimum of three months!"

"One hundred pounds a week?" Jillian gasped. "That would be twelve hundred pounds. That's more that I make in two years."

"I'll pay you more if you like. It means that much to me."

"What about my mum? She needs me. What would she think?"

"Bring her here. I will rent a chateau and we can stay near the seashore. She can chaperone and I know she will love the weather."

Jillian smiled, "Anything would be better than the weather in England."

David was excited. "So you'll do it?"

"She has never been to the south of France..."

Chapter 18

London, early morning

The morning was cool and overcast as Heinrich boarded the old military bus that would take him to the London docks. From there he would board the hospital ship for his trip to the States. The wind blew the fine mist that the Londoners called rain into his face. He was glad to have the topcoat as he turned up the collar. He thought that the gray day fit his mood as the bus rumbled down the cobblestone street. Once again he was leaving familiar surroundings to go into the unknown. He didn't want to leave, but it was a necessary step if he was to ever reach Lila again. This was a long way to go to reach someone who was no more than one hundred kilometers away. It would be a miracle if he pulled it off.

Damaged homes and shops flashed by the window as the bus traveled down the bumpy road. He was amazed at the resilience of the British. Hell had just passed them by and there they were cleaning up and rebuilding. Heinrich felt a deep sense of shame that his people had done this. How could they have let that madman Hitler do this? What did they have to show for it but destruction? Their beautiful Berlin was destroyed, London destroyed, and so many dead and injured on both sides. His beautiful Ursula and his darling Gretchen were dead. His family estate was half in ruins; his heart ached at all the reminders of what had happened. Was God going to punish him for his part? It was true that he had not participated in the killing, but he and his family had allowed it to start. Well, if he got through this, he would devote his life to helping others

I must not let these dark moods control my life and I will take each day as it comes. I will try to be positive, scared probably, but positive, he promised himself.

They soon arrived at the docks and pulled up next to a large warehouse constructed from sheet-metal. A gust of cold wind struck his face as he stepped off the bus. He felt like one of the lucky ones, as he was able to hurry from the curb through the front door. The thought struck him that he could have stayed behind and helped the others. If he was going to have this new sense of morality and save the world, he might as well start now. He started around to go back when those behind bumped him. An official sounding voice said, "Keep it moving people. We don't have all day." Inside were rows and rows of battered wooden tables with official looking people lined behind. It was still early in the morning but they already looked tired. He was glad he was not in one of the later groups. This was going to take all his nerve as it was.

The room was stuffy after the morning chill. It had the aroma of a room that was being heated by human bodies. Orders were being shouted in all corners of the room. People were everywhere. Long lines were formed leading to the rows of processing tables where official looking people were asking questions and stamping papers. At the other end of the warehouse, there were large groups of people milling about like cows waiting to be penned. Men and women with red armbands were shouting to go here or go there. Others were streaming out a large metal door at the far end of the building and looked to be heading for the ship. Heinrich wondered why they had to go through this when everyone at the hospital knew who they were and where they were going. He decided that this was primarily a military operation and that was how the military operated, no matter what the country.

Heinrich saw a soldier in a wheel chair in the line. It was quite obvious that the man was having problems. He decided that if he helped by pushing a wheel chair with a patient in it, he could speed things up. This would also take pressure off his legs so he walked over, handed his cane to the soldier and said, "Let me help you. Maybe between the two of us, we can get through this quicker. I'm David Strauss."

"Thanks Major, I was really getting tired. I'm Corporal James Greer. Most folks just call me Jim."

"Good to meet you Jim, when no one is around, just call me David. We are both so close to being civilians; we might as well get into practice."

"Major, follow me and we will get you processed and out of here," an orderly said.

Heinrich turned to follow the orderly still pushing the wheelchair.

"Oh no, sir," she said. "He will have to remain here. The enlisted men are being processed later."

"It's no trouble; I will take him with me. He has his papers in his lap and that will be one less for you to worry about."

The corporal grinned as Heinrich pushed him after the orderly.

"I don't know sir, I may get into trouble."

"Don't worry about it," said Heinrich, "I will take full responsibility." Heinrich wasn't sure why he was doing this, but it felt good. It was as if a large weight had been lifted from his shoulders.

"Sorry sir, but enlisted men are going to be processed later," the sergeant behind the table said.

"This man is a friend of mine," Heinrich said. "How about it?"

"Sir," the sergeant said, then his eyes locked on the Medal of Honor ribbon pinned above Heinrich's pocket. Suddenly the sergeant stood up, saluted and said, "Yes sir, Major, anything you want." He picked up Corporal Greer's papers, looked around and said, "Jameson! Front and center. Take these papers over to table seven and get them processed ASAP!"

"Yes sir, Sergeant," he replied and hurried through the crowd.

"Now sir, if you will let me have your papers, we'll get this taken care of right away." With that he began flipping through papers and stamping with a speed that Heinrich found amazing. Not once did he miss hitting the center of a square. Heinrich idly thought that surely somewhere there must be a job for someone as accurate with a rubber stamp as the sergeant.

"Now sir, if you and the corporal can wait over here in the lounge area, I will send the corporal's papers over as soon as they are back and we can get you two on your way."

"Thanks Sergeant," replied Heinrich, "I appreciate your extra care."

"It was nothing sir," said the sergeant. "Nothing at all."

Within a few minutes Jameson hurried over and handed the papers to Heinrich. "You should go over to the area with the green flags. They will make arrangements for your sleeping quarters and send you on to the ship." With that, Jameson saluted him and left.

Heinrich handed the packet of papers to Greer and said, "You had better hang on to this yourself; I wouldn't want to see you left behind because I tried to help."

As they reached the area designated with green flags, a nurse in a white uniform stepped in beside them. "I believe that I can take the corporal from here Major, thanks for your help."

"I don't mind helping," said Heinrich.

"Thanks anyway," she said, as she took over. "It's no trouble for me; he is going to be in my ward so we might as well get to know one another. My name's Sally and you're Jim," she said as she looked at his papers. "Let's see if we can get you on board right away."

"Don't forget this sir," said Jim as he passed over Heinrich's cane. "You might need it later on."

"Over here, sir," said a navy quartermaster. "Let's see if we still have room for you," he said with a grin. He looked at Heinrich's papers and had a startled look. "I've got just the spot for you, sir." With that he made a note in Heinrich's papers, placed them in a large basket, and handed him a blue tag with 353 in large black numbers on it.

"If you will go over to that door and show your tag to the seaman, he will get you taken care of. Let me say 'Welcome aboard, and welcome home.'"

Heinrich felt a lump in his throat. He didn't know why, but he felt as though he was going home. *'I guess I must be getting into my role as David. What in the world am I doing?'* he thought as he mentally shook his head.

Once again he felt the shock of the cold damp wind in his face as he stepped out of the processing center and began walking toward the hospital ship. He had a surreal feeling as he looked at the ship. There were lights everywhere, a far cry from the blackouts of the recent past. The ship was a blinding white except for the large red crosses on the smoke stacks and the black rings at the top. The lights reflected off the white paint and back again as the fog and light rain obscured the scene. The mist swirled about the lights and gave the feeling of slow motion. It was as if time had slowed and the world had begun to drift. A shrill whistle broke him out of his revelry as a man in a British seaman's uniform said, "Let's move along sirs, we plan on leaving today." Heinrich chuckled to himself in spite of his pain. He was glad to be on the road again.

His joy was short lived as he looked at the line leading to the narrow gangplank. It went across a large staging area for cargo and up the ramp. He wished they had kept him inside until the line was shorter. His legs were aching more as the cold found its way through his uniform. There were large flats of cargo scattered around that blocked some of the rain and wind. He guessed that the Brits were used to this weather and thought nothing of it. Well, they weren't saving time by waiting in line. He wondered how Jim was faring. He considered himself one of the healthier ones. The others must be in real pain. As he looked around, he noticed another line about fifty meters to his left. It was moving faster than his. There was Jim and his nurse getting ready to roll up their gangplank. He guessed they were not total idiots. Those who needed special attention were being loaded on a wider ramp and were being taken care of on an individual basis. Good.

As Heinrich was about to step on the gangplank, he felt the urge to step out of line for a moment. He looked to the east, toward his beloved Germany, and his heart ached. What had they done? His home was destroyed. His beautiful Ursula was gone and with her his flower, Gretchen. He had kept it blocked out of his mind for so long but now it started flooding to the surface. His body shook as tears began to flow. Suddenly he felt an arm across his shoulders. "It's all right," a quiet voice said. "It's over and you're going home. Don't look back. Things will be better from now on."

He looked up to see a chaplain standing beside him. "I know what you're going through Major. We can't change what has happened and we can't bring the dead back. I'm sure that those of your men that have passed away are in a better place and would not want you to mourn for them."

"Thank you sir," he said. "I'll be okay now. Just lost it for a minute."

"It's okay to cry, you know. That is also part of the healing process. We know how to heal broken arms, but we have a lot to learn about broken hearts. Things that are not visible are the hardest to heal because we have no way to measure the damage. Don't be too hard on yourself. Take your time and one day you will look and realize it's over and you're okay. It's hardest when we try to force it, remember, God is on your side."

"Is he? Sometimes I wonder if He can ever forgive me."

The Chaplin gave him a small smile. "There is nothing to forgive. All we can do is give life our best shot. We don't have all the answers and God knows that. We work with the best information we have at the time and leave the rest up

116

to Him. He understands. It's part of the plan. Talk to Him about it and you will find that He has a lot of understanding and a lot of forgiveness if you feel you need it. Now turn and look in one direction - forward."

"Thank you, sir."

Heinrich turned and started up the ramp. Strangely enough he did feel a little better.

There was a real mix of men in his line, Air Corps, Navy, and Army (both American and German he guiltily thought). He wondered if he was the only German sneaking in. As they were stepping on the ship, he noticed the sailors would turn to face the rear of the ship and salute. There was a flag visible hanging from a staff. As he stepped on board, he turned and saluted. The other soldiers had a questioning look but the Navy men smiled. He guessed then that it might not be a bad thing to have the friendship of some of the Navy men working on board.

Once he was on board, a seaman with a blue armband asked for his paperwork. "If you'll follow me, sir, I'll take you to your quarters." The sailor walked briskly across the deck. As he started up the broad staircase, he realized that Heinrich was having trouble keeping up with him. "I'm sorry, sir, I'm not used to being an escort. I was on a cruiser for most of the war. We were sunk just before the war ended. We made it all those years only to lose at the end. What a shame. I'm sorry sir, I shouldn't complain, we did a lot of good before we went down. I didn't even get hurt. Am I walking too fast, sir? Do you need some help?"

"No, I'll be alright. I'm just not as fast as I once was."

The sailor slowed down. "This is a pretty nice ship. In case you can't tell, it was once a luxury liner. They pressed her into service after the war started. You won't find a navy ship with wide ladders like this. Let's see, 353, one more level up and we'll be in business."

As they finally reached the next deck, Heinrich was exhausted. He had been working out every day, but had not dealt with stairs. Well, at least not two flights after a ramp.

117

"Why don't you rest a minute, sir? We have time. It's not far, just down this passageway on the starboard."

"It's okay. I can make it. Let's not make the others wait any longer than necessary."

Heinrich couldn't believe his room. Its appearance was as it must have been when it was a liner. He was also the only occupant. He almost asked the seaman how he wound up with such nice quarters but decided to keep his mouth shut in case it was a mistake.

After the sailor left, he decided to rest a bit. First though, he stowed his gear to get it out of the way. He actually had a closet and a dresser. It reminded him of the cruises he had taken with his parents in his youth. His room had been larger, but it was not a lot different. He guessed that if he had been an enlisted man, he would be in a room with six or eight others. He tried to rest but had too much on his mind. He was a kid again and wanted to see what was going on around him.

Chapter 19

After resting a little while he thought, *I don't have any assignments or any place to be, so why not explore.* He decided to make his way down into the lower reaches of the ship and work his way to the top; at least as far to the top as they would allow him to go.

The engine room was noisy, busy, and hot. Large furnaces were heating boilers to drive the large steam engines. Men were scurrying around checking gauges, and making adjustments on large valves the size of a melon. They were courteous enough as they slipped around him on the catwalks, but he decided that if he wanted to make friends with the crew, the best thing for him to do was keep out of the way - at least until they were well at sea. Out and up again he went. The nicest part of the engine room was that he was no longer cold.

On the vast main level he stopped to rest for a few moments. The stairs were almost more than he could handle. After resting, he decided to explore the main level while he still had the energy. He found that they had converted the grand ballroom to a hospital ward. The room that once housed cocktail parties for the very rich was now filled with beds in orderly rows, home for those needing the greatest care. The large windows that gave a view of the main deck and the ocean beyond now had canvas curtains that could be drawn closed to make the room dark. He noticed that the legs of the beds stood in cups that were attached to the deck. This would allow them to be lifted out

119

and rolled away, but would keep them stable in rolling seas if they hit really bad weather.

Once again, nurses and sailors were scurrying around getting everyone settled before they went underway. The beds were being filled from the center out, with some being brought in wheelchairs while others were on stretchers carried by seamen. He knew he would be in the way, but he wanted to see what was going on in the adjoining rooms while he would not be noticed. He found that operating rooms had been set up in six rooms that had housed private dining areas in another lifetime. Other rooms were set up for routine medical procedures that would be done in any hospital. This ship was as well equipped or better than any hospital that he had worked in before. He knew that the staff was serious about the treatment of their patients and this made him feel good.

He laughed to himself as he walked around the promenade areas of the ship. The deck chairs were lined up just as they must have been when it had carried paying customers. He sat in one and took a few minutes to rest and take the weight off his legs. They had been aching since he had made the journey to the engine room and back. The stairs in the working areas of the ship were steeper and harder to navigate than those in the guest areas.

The sun was up and the fog and clouds had finally burned away. He leaned back and felt the warm sun melt the tension from his aching body. Despite his aches he felt good inside. He could not remember when he had felt this good. He felt confident that everything was going to be okay. Someone bumped his chair and he jerked awake. Men and women were lining the rails of the deck. From the position of the sun, he realized that he must have been asleep for hours.

Like the others, he found a spot at the rail then realized that the ship was already getting underway. The deck vibrated as the large engines came to life. Men were shouting orders as the large lines were lifted from the bollards on the docks and thrown aside. The ship's whistle blared with such force he thought he might be deaf for life. Just then the ramps were lifted and rolled back. Suddenly the ramps were getting smaller as the ship began to pull sideways from the dock. He wondered how they could make such a large ship drift to the side the way it was doing. Excitement was in the air. Everyone was going home and they began cheering. He wasn't sure why, but he found himself cheering as well. His cheers turned to laughter as he clapped others on the back and said, "We're going home."

As the ship began traveling down the Thames, the crowds thinned out and the crew began the earnest work of running a ship out at sea. A whistle sounded over the PA system and a voice announced, "Now hear this, now hear this. Chow will be served on Level 2. Enlisted men will eat in the dining area forward of the fantail. Officers will be served in the dining area at the bow." Heinrich realized that he was hungry. He guessed it was about time to be locating the dining hall.

Sitting in the dining hall, he looked at those at the table around him. Most of them looked as though they were sitting with friends they had known for years. They were laughing and joking despite their physical condition. Heinrich wondered about the reception they would receive at home. Would their wives and sweethearts accept them with the limitations that had been created by their willingness to defend their country in a war they had not created? Or would they be rejected like an automobile that had not met expectations? Would they be willing to forgive themselves for being human or doing what was necessary at a time when the opportunity for analysis was not available? He knew that the hardest battles some of the men fought would not be on the battlefield, but during the quiet times when the words "what if" or "I wish I had done that" would creep into their minds. For some, the healing would be quick; for others, the healing would never come. Their families and friends could easily see a missing arm or leg and make allowances; but it was the hidden wounds that would cause the broken hearts and broken homes and no one would ever know why.

After seeing a young Lieutenant, looking older than his years sitting alone, Heinrich decided to continue his

"Florence Nightingale" routine and go over and visit. He picked up his meal tray and walked over.

"Is this seat taken?"

The Lieutenant startled and started to rise. "No sir!"

"Keep your seat. The war's over and I'm too tired to care."

The kid grinned and said, "You took the words right out of my mouth, sir."

"You have someone waiting back home?"

"Yes sir, my girl, Linda. We were going to get married before the war but..."

And it went on and on. Heinrich grinned inside and felt good. Throughout the trip he found someone to eat with at each meal. At each meal he heard a story. Sometimes the story was the same and sometimes it was different, but the end result was almost always the same. They felt good and he did not have to think of his own story. He noticed that no one ever asked what was waiting for him. Wouldn't their eyes light up if they knew what he had coming?

Mornings and afternoons he would take those in wheelchairs for a stroll on the deck or sit with them in the sun and talk. It was a nice existence. Occasionally he would help the nurses change dressings or move patients. When they protested, he would pretend to beg and tell them he was like a firehouse dog without a truck. They would be a little embarrassed but were glad for the help and the days passed faster and faster.

After what seemed an eternity, actually twelve days, a voice came over the PA system, "Now hear this. Now hear this. Man the rails. Lady Liberty is coming up to the starboard bow and wishes to greet her returning sons and daughters! A cheer went up as crowds rushed to the rails, straining to see a sight they had been dreaming of for years.

Heinrich felt elated and nervous. He knew that this would be by far the greatest test he had encountered to date. Perhaps tomorrow his fears would be realized. What if she was waiting at the dock? Would he recognize her? He had seen the pictures she had mailed to him in the hospital, but it was not the same as the real person. Well, he would know soon enough.

Chapter 20

The ship stopped as the sun faded. Heinrich could hear the anchor chain drop and wondered what was going on. He had planned on leaving the ship in the dark since it would be the best opportunity to disappear. Everyone was excited at the prospect of touching American soil again but their excitement was soon abated. The voice over the PA system informed them that because the ship had arrived two days early, the billets were not ready for their arrival and they would be required to remain onboard for one more day. Only those in need of immediate medical attention would be taken ashore. Heinrich thought to himself that this probably never happened when this was a liner with paying customers. To the military, those aboard were a commodity to be dealt with just as if they were trucks or tanks. The only difference was that if they were trucks or tanks, they would just leave them until they could locate a warehouse.

The next morning at about ten o'clock he felt the ship begin to vibrate. He wandered out to see men begin to line the port rail. About a half hour later he heard noise as the anchor chain began to rattle and the large ship began to drift. Soon tugboats were on either side as they made their way toward the docks. There was no need for him to pack his bag. He had been ready to jump ship last night and had everything with any connection to him packed and cleared out.

The crowd gathered on the dock was huge. They had been alone so long that Heinrich had not imagined that there would be such a large number of people interested in their return. Well, that should make getting lost that much easier.

A military band standing on the dock was playing a selection of patriotic songs as the ship pulled along side the dock. The dock appeared to be a sea of American flags waving from the hand of every child present. As he looked from the rail Heinrich could see a Salvation Army station set up behind the crowd passing out coffee and donuts. He knew that transportation would be waiting to take them to hospitals for relocation or release. He wanted to just walk off the base and into oblivion rather than wait. Thinking about it, he realized he didn't want the military looking for him as a deserter. *Keep your focus Heinrich.* Walking down the offloading ramp he heard "David, David" from the left side. At first he thought he would ignore it, but the caller was persistent. "David, David" came again. Heinrich took a chance and glanced to the side. There was no doubt in his mind who the speaker was. The pictures did not do her justice. Her hair was dark as ebony and a perky little nose adorned a face with eyes so blue they put the ocean to shame. This beautiful face sat on a body that was slender with curves in all the right places. All the parts individually were beautiful, but put together they made a breathtaking sight. Heinrich stumbled and would have rolled the remainder of the distance to the end of the gangplank had the man behind not grabbed his shoulder. "Easy there Major. Beautiful isn't she. Anyone you know?"

"I think she is my wife."

"Well, don't wait here, get on down there and introduce yourself."

Heinrich felt like a fool, as he turned left at the bottom of the gangplank. "Excuse me, are you Catherine?"

Tears were running down her face as Catherine threw her arms around Heinrich and said, "You bet I am!" With that she gave him a big long kiss. "Welcome home soldier!"

Heinrich didn't know whether to smile or run. "Your pictures don't do you justice. I can't believe I am so lucky as to be married to a girl as beautiful as you."

Catherine stepped back with a shocked look on her face. "You don't remember me?"

"If I had half a brain I would fake it but I guess I'm running a little short on that end."

Catherine excitedly stepped back a little. "Well, I remember you. That will have to do for now. You are as handsome as ever, I can't wait for Davy to see you."

They turned and began to follow the drift of the crowd. What a pack! Tears and smiles, babies crying, wives crying, and men crying.

"They told me that you would have to catch the bus over here to go and get processed out or something like that. If you are in good enough shape, you can go on home and finish your recuperation there. You look in pretty good shape to me. Are you feeling alright?"

"I think I am in pretty good shape, but let's see what they have to say at the hospital."

"It says here that you require the use of a cane Major. I don't see it."

Heinrich smiled at the doctor reviewing his records. "Next time you need to give someone therapy for legs that are recovering from surgery, send them on a sea cruise. Nothing on a ship is on one level. After going up and down those stairs for twelve days, I believe my legs are in pretty good shape. They still have a way to go before I would rate them A+ but I think they will pass for transportation."

"Well, that was our main concern. If you would like to do the remainder of your convalescence at home, we will include three months pay to cover lost wages and go ahead and muster you out today. Normally, we wouldn't do this, but as you can imagine we have an extreme shortage of space. We're concerned about your memory loss and would like you to check in at St. John's Hospital in Columbus in sixty days. You will receive a letter from them scheduling an

126

appointment. Is this address of your parents still a good one?"

"Yes, I will be staying there while I get settled in."

"I guess the only thing left is for you to sign here and we are through with you unless there are further problems."

Heinrich smiled and signed the papers in triplicate.

"Done! It was nice visiting but I think it's time to go home."

Waldorf Astoria Hotel, New York City.

As they stepped in the room, Catherine suddenly turned and kissed him. Heinrich was taken by surprise when her dress slipped to the floor. As she kissed him again, she slipped his tie off and began to unbutton his shirt. He began to panic as images of Lila and thoughts of escape raced through his mind. *I can't just sleep with her and then disappear. Besides that, this is David's wife. Where is all the honor and integrity now that I need it? Am I going to dishonor Ursula for a night of passion? Black underwear, oh... she looks good and... her skin is so soft... what am I doing? What if I do this and they find out who I am?*

"Stop!" he said, "I think we're going too fast."

Catherine laughed, "Isn't that supposed to be my line. What was it you used to say, 'I'm sorry, I just couldn't help myself.' What's the problem David?"

"I don't know how to say this, so I'll just lay it out. You are a wonderful, beautiful girl, and a guy would be crazy not to want you. My problem is that I can't remember being married to you. Yes, I've seen your pictures, and I have been told that we are married. I just can't remember it. This wouldn't bother many men, but it bothers me. It's like going to bed with a stranger... please don't look that way."

Catherine looked embarrassed and sat on the bed. "I don't know what you expect of me David."

127

Heinrich turned away for a moment and then turned back to face Catherine squarely.

"When I was in the hospital battling for my life, I promised God that I would be a better man than I am," he lied. "Sleeping with a stranger just doesn't seem like the right thing to do. Maybe we could sort of date and get to know one another."

Catherine suddenly relaxed and said, "Thanks. You don't know what a relief it is to hear you say that. When I saw you come off the ship, I was somewhat taken aback. To everyone else you may look like David Strauss, but to me you look like a stranger who has been made to look like David. Add to that your amnesia and I felt like I was going to bed with a stranger.

"When you joined the army, I was angry. Your father had made arrangements to get you deferred, but you would have no part of it. All I could think is that you would do anything to get away from me. I know that before you left, things were a little strained between us. I guess that I was kind of a bitch. But when you were taken prisoner, I died a little inside. I was so afraid that you would die, and I would never be able to tell you I was sorry. I made myself a promise that I would do better and I would be the wife you deserved. When I saw you this afternoon, I was shocked, but I was not going to add to the pain that you've already had by stepping back from you. You did a very brave and honorable thing and your injuries were not your fault. I just felt I had to go through with it.

"I *will* say this, my intentions were not completely honorable, you were handsome when you left and even though you have had some modifications, you still are.

"Besides that, I can tell that you are David now."

"How?" questioned Heinrich.

"It's simple, what you just did was an honorable thing. It's just what David would have done. My boy scout," she answered.

"Let's order room service and go to bed. To sleep of course," she added. "It's been a long day and I'm tired."

After the meal was finished, they quietly settled into bed. She lay on her side and he on his. Heinrich could feel the heat from her body and a warm feeling began to settle over him. He was beginning to wish that he had not been so honorable when a sharp pain suddenly hit the calves of both of his legs.

"Ow," he shouted. "That was cold."

"I'm sorry," laughed Catherine, "but my feet were cold and you seemed so warm."

"Stick them over here and I'll warm them up," he fussed. He sat up and pulled her legs across his and began to rub them vigorously.

"Your feet are so soft, how do you do it?"

"Long baths and lotion," she replied.

"Lotion?" He lifted one foot to his face.

"Mmm... they smell good too. Not much of that in the army." He began to kiss it as his hand caressed her leg. Warmth began to spread over his body... Her breathing became more rapid and pronounced.

He stood up unceremoniously dumping her legs. "I think I'll sleep on the couch. I don't believe your feet can reach me there."

As he settled in on the couch, Catherine pulled the covers and snuggled. She smiled. She was happy but maybe just a little disappointed.

Chapter 21

The next morning they boarded the train for Roquefort, Ohio. As they rode along, Heinrich noticed that Catherine was looking a little uneasy.

"I haven't known you very long, but I would have to be blind not to notice that you have something on your mind."

Catherine gave him a weak smile. "I guess I should give you a warning. Your father is arranging a parade for you from the train station to the town hall. There will be a band and everything at the train station. When you get to the town hall, the mayor will present you with a key to the city and proclaim 'David Strauss Day.'"

Heinrich sat quietly for a few moments. "I guess I should have expected something like that. Everything I know about Papa tells me this is what he would do. It really bothers me that he doesn't respect my feelings."

"I don't know why you would think he is suddenly going to be different. He loves you David, but he is still Papa. There is something else you are not thinking about David. A number of our boys were killed during the war. You weren't. For all the sons, brothers, or husbands lost, you're here to show their families that our boys, their boys were heroes. They need something tangible to look at. They want to say, 'My son was like David. He was a hero too.' They want to parade you around so that people will know that Roquefort is a good place. It's a place that heroes come from."

"Well, I am certainly no hero. I'll tell you about the real heroes. Al Johansson went on patrol with only a side arm

130

because I had patched up his right shoulder two days before and he couldn't use a rifle. The lieutenant asked him what he was doing leading a patrol in his condition, he answered that he wanted these men to come back. He had been raised there as a child and knew it like the back of his hand. Then there was Dub Plemmons. He was a medic. Every day he ran onto the battlefield under fire and rendered first aid to the injured. After he stopped the bleeding, he would pick them up and run back to a safe area. A news correspondent asked him how he could do that. He answered, 'It's my job. If I don't go get them they will die. One day he brought his man in and dropped him on a cot. As soon as he did, he fell over and died. He had been shot in two places. He did not have a medic to help him so he made sure that he took care of his man before he collapsed. I could continue on for hours. Those guys were the heroes, not me."

A tear ran down the side of Catherine's face. She put her arms around him and began to cry. "All I could think of was that if you made it back I would be a better wife. I know that things weren't right between us when you left, but I promised God that if I could have another chance, I would be a better wife. You are my hero. No parade, no band, no mayor. I love you. I promise right now before God and the angels that I will spend the rest of my life proving it to you."

Heinrich did not say a word. He put his arms around her and pulled her close. His mind was racing. *How can I break her heart by disappearing? Lila was right. What am I going to do?* The day wore on and they sat each deep in his own thoughts. Finally Heinrich said, "Just so I don't appear as a total idiot, why don't you tell me a little about myself. I know this sounds crazy, but my experience to date is that people don't understand amnesia."

"What do you mean, they don't understand?"

"It's simple. You knew that I had amnesia, but you were still shocked when I did not recognize you."

"You're right. I'm sorry; I know that this has to be hard on you. Okay, you went to Roquefort Elementary. Your best friend was Scott Nelson. He is married to my best friend Ann Marie."

Heinrich spent the rest of the day learning about his life from Catherine's viewpoint. He discovered that he knew quite a bit already from those long days talking with David. This came in handy since he would occasionally be able to complete a story. Without realizing it, Catherine was giving him the background to complete the illusion. As the day wore on, Heinrich realized he was having 'feelings' for Catherine. He tried to push them away since it would make disappearing that much harder.

The rhythmic clanking of the wheels on the track and the gentle rocking of the train finally lulled them both to sleep. As before, Heinrich's sleep was troubled with nightmares of David and Ursula. This time it was different. Catherine was there.

Heinrich suddenly awakened. He looked around, where was he? Bam! Bam! Bam! He jumped to the floor in a crouched position. "One hour to Columbus. Are you awake?"

It was the conductor. "Yes sir, thank you." He felt a little silly crouched on the floor ready to run. How long would it be before his reflexes would give the right answers? He stepped over to the sink and began to wash his face to prepare for their arrival home. He knew that by the time he cleaned up and had breakfast, they would almost be home in Roquefort. *Home? Who was he kidding? One look at him and he would be in the nearest jail. There is no way I am going to fool David's parents.*

"What was that?" Catherine had risen up from the bench where she had fallen to sleep.

"That was the conductor calling reveille." Heinrich had already learned that Catherine loved to sleep late. "We'll be getting to Columbus in about an hour. Thirty minutes there and another half hour to Roquefort. I guess I'm a little nervous. I hope I don't scare the children."

"You'll not be scaring children, I can guarantee that. You are much too handsome for that. I'm worried about the women hanging all over you. They did a good job on you.

You look handsome with just enough scars to make you dashing. You're a blonde version of Errol Flynn."

"Who?" That was a mistake. He was supposed to know who Errol Flynn was. "I guess that must be another of my relatives I don't remember."

"Wow! I've got my work cut out for me. Errol Flynn is a famous swashbuckling actor. All the girls think he is dreamy."

"I'm sorry; I guess this must be driving you crazy." Heinrich had reddened a bit.

"Not at all," She laughed. "How many girls get to create their own husbands? I can be like Baron Frankenstein and create my own man. The problem is if you turn out wrong, it's my fault."

How could you not fall in love with a girl like this? He wondered. *If I wind up with this girl, life could be good again.*

All too soon they were pulling into the station at Roquefort. Heinrich was dressed in his uniform with medals adorning him like jewelry. He glanced down at the Medal of Honor hanging around his neck. He thought of how ironic it was when so many of his countrymen had dreamed of having the Knight's Cross hanging there. He had decided to hang back a little and let the rest of the passengers get off first so that he would not get in the way. As the train pulled in, he looked out the window and was shocked at the number of people there. *How many of these people was he supposed to know? There was Scott and Ann Marie standing near to the front. She was Catherine's best friend. Papa and Mutti were standing with two men in tuxedos, probably the mayor and one of his henchmen.* These he knew from the pictures that had been sent to him plus Catherine's wallet. *This town must be larger than David had said and everyone in town must be here.* As the train came to a stop, the Roquefort High School band began to play one of John Phillip Sousa's patriotic songs. The other passengers did not get off as he expected, they looked at him and stepped back smiling - some with tears on their cheeks. Heinrich began to silently pray that he would get out of this unscathed. He wasn't sure if he could live like this, always afraid. He had promised himself that he was not going to live in fear so he threw his shoulders back, smiled, and stepped off the train into a new life.

As he stepped down, Papa and Mutti came up and put their arms around him. David's mother was crying as they parted and allowed the dignitaries to step up. One of the men with a cutaway tux and a top hat reached out his hand. "Welcome home son, we're proud to call you our own." He then stepped back and swung his arm out with his palm open and with a loud deep voice said, "It is my pleasure to introduce Marvin Crenshaw, Mayor of Roquefort."

The other man dressed in a tux stepped forward and grabbed Heinrich's hand. "Welcome home. If you will step this way, we can let the parade begin." With that he escorted Heinrich to a large black Cadillac convertible with the top down. They had Heinrich and Catherine sit on the back of the seat so that they would be visible to everyone as they traveled to the town hall. Men, women and children with small flags waving, lined the streets of the parade route. Heinrich sat there feeling awkward and waved as the car traveled through the city.

On arriving at the town hall, they left the car and walked to a raised platform with red, white, and blue banners everywhere. The mayor stepped up to a microphone and tapped on the top to verify that it was operating. "Humph," he said, clearing his throat. "Fellow citizens of Roquefort, it is with great pleasure that we welcome home our own Major David Strauss, a hero in every sense of the word." With that, he outlined David's high school career, and on and on and on. Heinrich thought it would never be over.

Suddenly, he was handing Heinrich a key to the city and declaring today as "David Strauss Day." He then stepped back to allow Heinrich to speak.

Heinrich was nervous about speaking. "I may have faced Germans and bombs, but that was nothing compared to speaking here today." The crowd laughed. "As I think on the past four years, I realize that I am not a hero. The real heroes are buried in unmarked graves along the way. I was like everyone else there, just hoping against hope that I would come back alive. They didn't and I did. I feel a great responsibility to make sure that their lives weren't wasted and the time that God has given me to remain will be used wisely. Someday I would like to walk in this town square and see a monument with their names listed on it so they will never be forgotten. They were your husbands, fathers, brothers, and sons. My heart aches for each of them and I am ashamed that I am here receiving their honor. I would like you to rename this day 'Fallen Heroes Day', and remember them and not me. Thank you."

With that he stepped back and stood at attention. He turned toward the flag that was prominently displayed in the town square and saluted. The crowd was quiet, as though they did not know what to do. The mayor stepped up to the mic and said, "There is a real hero for you!" He started clapping and the crowd went wild with applause. The band began to play as everyone stepped down from the podium. People that David knew crowded around and began to shake hands and welcome him home

Heinrich was speechless and felt a little ashamed as he shook hands and thanked people. He was getting invitations to dinner, to play golf, or just to sit around and talk of old times. He was astonished. Was he actually pulling it off? Eventually, he and Catherine were able to work their way to the edge of the crowd as it was thinning out. He was afraid that Papa and Mutti would be tired from the crowd and all the noise. As he met them at the car, instead of tired, Papa was elated. It seemed that this was exactly what he wanted.

Papa could not stop talking about Heinrich's speech. Perfect! He would say. "Turning and saluting the flag was the perfect ending to a wonderful morning. You are a shoe-in for the nomination for governor. By the time the reporters get through writing that up, we'll have a million dollars worth of publicity."

Heinrich knew that while he had played into Papa's hand perfectly, he might have created a monster that would pull him down. Publicity was exactly what he did not want.

He knew that he would have to stop this train before it rolled over him. He also knew that it would not happen without someone being hurt. David's voice was ringing in his head, "what Papa wants, Papa gets."

As they arrived home, He was surprised at the size of the house they lived in. The jewelry business must have done well. The house was a large three-story brown-stone home with a wrap-around driveway in front and a drive down the side that fed a four-car garage. It was situated on a half acre of well-manicured lawn dotted with trees. There were a variety of shrubs in the flowerbeds that went across the front and down the sides. It looked more like Germany than any place he had seen since he left home.

Papa had talked non-stop since they got in the car. How Papa wished he had brought little Davy so the reporters could have snapped pictures of David as a family man. As they stepped into the house, a young child ran across the floor to him and stopped a few feet away. Heinrich knew that this must be Davy. He was the spitting image of his father.

He felt sick inside for his friend; he knew David would never see his son. He knew that he would have to go through this if possible for the sake of his friend. He just could not abandon David's family. For all their faults, they were wonderful people who should not lose their son and husband a second time.

"I must call some of the men from the Democratic Party and have them over tonight. It is never too early to get started," Papa was saying.

"Wait! This is going too fast." Everyone stopped in their tracks as Heinrich spoke. Shock was on Mutti's face. People just didn't speak that way to Papa. Heinrich walked over to David's father and said, "Papa, I love you and appreciate all you have done, but I will not be running for governor, mayor, or dog catcher."

"But, I thought we agreed before you left that you would run for governor if things went well," Papa said.

"No Papa, you agreed, not me. I love you and respect you, but I must lead my own life. Please understand when I was in that camp, I had a lot of time to think what I want in life. I laid my life on the line every day I was there. My comrades did the same. Many of them died with me at their side and many died alone. If I learned anything from the experience, it is that life is precious. We only get one chance. If I live this life for you, there will not be a life left for me. Every day I was there I thought of Catherine and Davy and what I would lose if I did not make it. I am here now and I do not want to lose the second chance that God has given me at life."

"But..." Papa interrupted.

"Please, Papa, let me say what I must say. You encouraged me to be a physician. You said that it is an honorable profession. You were right. Not only is it an honorable profession, but I am a very good physician. I have found that I can do things no other physician around can do. As a result of this, I can save lives that would be lost without my services. I have saved limbs on men that would have been crippled for life. I feel good about myself and what I can do. Maybe someday I will want to run for office, but not now. I certainly do not want to get elected based on the fact that I lived when my friends did not. Do you understand?"

Karl Strauss looked defeated. "No, I do not, son. I do not. I think of the millions you could help if you were governor or even president and I do not understand. I will honor your wishes, but I will never understand."

Catherine's eyes were misty. Whatever horrible things her husband had endured, he came back as the man she had wanted all these years. Well, he had done his part; she would have to do hers.

"Thank you Papa. I will try and be the best doctor in the state. I will earn the respect that you have wanted for our family. Now if you don't mind, the morning's activities have tired me and I would like to get out of this uniform."

"Can you wait a few minutes longer? I have a photographer coming and would like to get pictures of you and your medals for the foyer wall. Whether you run for office or not, I am very proud of you and your accomplishments. I love you, my son, and would like everyone who walks through that door to know that my son is my hero. Oh yes, and there is a reception this evening in your honor. The mayor insisted and I couldn't say no. It is a little late to change that now don't you think?"

"You're right, and I appreciate the honor."

"You will wear your uniform right?"

"Yes Papa. I will. Now perhaps Catherine can show me to our room and I can at least unpack and rest for a few minutes."

"You will be staying in your old room. Surely you haven't forgotten your own room."

Heinrich followed Catherine up the stairs. "He doesn't realize how much you have forgotten, so be understanding. Okay?"

"You don't think I was too hard on him, do you? I just felt that I had to get things into the open before they had gone too far."

"No, I think you did well. In fact, I can't think of one thing that you have done wrong the whole day. I am very proud of you. I know it was hard, but you did what had to be done.

That night at the reception Heinrich spent a lot of time dodging questions and offers to run for office. He felt that it was a good opportunity to meet the 'movers and shakers' of business in Roquefort. That afternoon Catherine had made a list of people she thought would be there. They had gone over it several times so that when Heinrich met them in the evening he knew who he was meeting. An especially good opportunity came when he met Dr. Rogers, Chief of Staff at the hospital.

"We are looking forward to seeing you at the hospital as soon as you get your feet on the ground," he said. "Do you think you will be available for a walk through on Monday? If you are half as good as the publicity that has preceded you says, we would like to get our bid in first. You do plan on staying in Roquefort, don't you?"

"I would like to remain here. If I can find the right position, it would fit my plans perfectly. If I do take a position with you, I would like to start slow until I get my strength back. I have learned to empathize with my patients when they tell me how much strength they lose through inactivity. I did a little work on the ship coming over, but have a ways to go when it comes to stamina."

"We will work with you in every way we can. See you on Monday."

As far as Heinrich was concerned, he had accomplished all he could that evening. Anything else was just icing on the cake. Papa was in his element. He, the mayor, and a few other men he couldn't identify did a lot of huddling with quiet smiles. He hoped they could be trusted. It really didn't matter though; he was going to stay out of the limelight as much as possible. The last thing he needed was to have his picture flashed around. He had already had all the publicity he wanted.

The only other tense moments of the evening came when the music started. Catherine wanted to dance. Heinrich had not yet come that close to Catherine except for brief moments. As he began to dance with her, it was amazing. He wanted to look and see if her feet were touching the ground because she seemed to glide. His greatest fear was that David would have had such a difference in style that it would be obvious to her that he was an imposter. Fortunately, he was able to blame his leg injuries for his dance style. He had actually been a very good dancer in the days before the war. His problem was that he didn't know about David. He decided to be clumsy for a while. He thought that if he improved as time went by, he could either claim that his legs were better or he was learning through practice. This being an imposter had its down side. He really did enjoy dancing.

The night was finally over. He was not a candidate for governor, but he did have a job opportunity. He was wondering what kind of American he was going to be. According to David, every little boy in the country wanted to grow up to be president. He did not even want to be elected dog catcher. Time would tell. Whatever happened, he hoped that he would be a credit to David's name or his own for that matter.

Chapter 22

Monday morning found Heinrich sitting in Dr. Rogers' office. "We want this hospital to be at the forefront of technology. I know that Roquefort is a small town, but that doesn't mean that people won't travel for miles to get here. We have space to grow, and with the return of our boys from the war, we can build a community that anyone would be proud to live in. As part of that growth, we plan on making Roquefort Hospital one of the leading medical centers in the Midwest. With doctors like you that dream can become a reality. Let me give you a tour. You'll see that we have the best-equipped operating rooms in the country. Our patient rooms are all air conditioned and no more than two patients to a room."

"Compared to operating in the open air, or a tent, it doesn't take much to impress me, sir."

The hospital was everything that Heinrich was looking for. He was careful, however, not to let Dr. Rogers know that, since he would be a staff surgeon and wanted to negotiate the best salary he could. When they began discussing the offer, Heinrich took a chance. "I'll tell you what Dr. Rogers; I will take your offer for one month. After you have seen my work, you can give me your real offer. If you don't think I'm worth more, I'll quietly leave, and we'll still be friends."

Dr. Rogers was taken aback. "That's the first time anyone has made me that kind of offer, and I believe I'll take it. I have a feeling you know your true value and I will be happy to pay it. Tomorrow I'll have you begin work with Dr. Gray, our chief surgeon and you can get in the swing of things."

The phone rang and Catherine answered. The voice on the other end was Ann Marie. "Catherine, how are things? Have you and the man of the hour settled in?"

"I guess. It is like a zoo around here. All of David's old friends dropping in and he doesn't remember any of them. He won't let me out of arm's reach. My job is to look out the front window as they pull up and tell him who they are and give a brief synopsis of their friendship together. He is actually pretty good at it. He can't remember much from the past, but anything I tell him, he soaks up like a sponge. He is even figuring out inter-relationships between himself and the wild bunch he used to hang out with. The only thing I can figure is that his head is so empty, that it has room for anything I say."

"You are terrible! Don't pick on the poor boy that way. Does this mean that you don't have time to come over?"

"Actually I have plenty of time today. He is out interviewing for a job at the hospital. I have shown him how to get there and back so I am free for the morning at least."

"Well come on then and bring Davy, the girls want someone to play with."

An hour later they were sitting in Ann Marie's den drinking ice tea southern style; the way Ann Marie had learned when she visited her aunt last summer.

"Okay, tell me about David. He looks great. He doesn't look exactly like he used to, but maybe a little better if you ask me."

"I think he looks a little better too. It'll take a little getting used to though."

"Nothing wrong with that! I bet it's like having an affair with a new man. Now that I think about it, this could be fun. Now, give me all the details."

"Details of what?"

142

"Don't try to stonewall me. This is Ann Marie you're talking to. Now tell me. You went to bed with a strange man that has been celibate for at least two and a half years, maybe even five. Was he an animal, I hope?"

"Well, it was a little disappointing. In fact it was very disappointing, nothing happened."

"What do you mean nothing happened? You have got to be kidd... Oh no! I am SO sorry. How insensitive of me. It doesn't work anymore does it? Was it the injuries? Can it be fixed? Oh, what are you gonna do?"

"If you will give me time to answer, I will tell you! First of all, it isn't broken. At least I don't think it is. I haven't actually seen it yet, but I almost did."

"Almost did? What is going on?"

"Just relax. It's more of a technical issue. He doesn't remember me. The only thing he knows about me is from the letters I wrote that he never answered. He says he didn't answer them because he didn't remember me or Roquefort or anything else so he didn't know what to talk about."

"What is the technical issue?"

Catherine laughed a short embarrassed laugh. "Since he doesn't remember me, he doesn't remember marrying me and he just doesn't feel right going to bed with a stranger. There, now I have said it."

"Ha! Since when has that ever stopped a man?"

"Well, it stopped him."

"Of course. You know this proves he *is* David even though he looks a little different. Even with amnesia, he is still a boy scout. He is the only man I know that would let something like that bother him. You said almost. How close is almost?"

"Well, I had my dress off and had his shirt half off before he stopped me. I told him I understood and then rubbed my cold feet down the back of his legs as we were lying on our own sides of the bed. I got him warming my feet and he was warming up pretty good when he jumped up, walked to the closet and got a blanket and went to sleep on the couch."

"Maybe I should get him and Scott to hang out together a little. Scott's like a bee, always buzzing around looking for a little honey. Do you think David could calm him down?"

"You're not helping you know."

"You are a beautiful and intelligent woman. Let's go shopping this afternoon. I bet you can find something that will destroy his willpower."

"It won't do any good. He has his own room. He told me that that was the only way he could be sure to preserve my honor."

"This is serious! Did you tell him you didn't want your honor preserved?"

"Yes, no good. Isn't this terrible, two women spending the morning scheming on how to destroy a man's honor? We are horrible!"

"Yes, isn't it great down here in the gutter? I think that is why we are such good friends. Don't give up now. You don't know how low I can sink. Don't worry, I'll find a solution to your problem."

"Don't take too long. I am beginning to suffer a little. I need help."

Stepping into the next room, Catherine said, "Come on Davy, honey. You and mommy need to stop by the lingerie store on the way home."

Looking at Ann Marie she said, "It can't hurt. A girl needs to be prepared, just like our little boy scout!"

Heinrich hit it off with Dr. Gray from the beginning. One thing he had learned from his father was not to show off. "Come in quietly," he would say. "Don't let them know how good you are right away. Let them believe that it was their idea. You will always find friends, and others will not fear that you have come to replace them."

They started off small doing simple surgeries, first with Dr. Gray in the lead, then allowing Heinrich to take over as Dr. Gray felt comfortable.

Finally the day that he had been waiting for came. Dr. Gray said, "We have a young boy in the emergency room that has his leg crushed in an auto accident. This resembles what you may have seen on the front where you were caring for those injured in battle. I would like to see you take the lead in this one. I'll be there to assist you, but this will give me some insight on where you stand on your major surgery skills."

"Okay," said Heinrich. "Let me visit with the patient and then study the x-rays. Why don't we schedule surgery in forty-five minutes?"

"Okay, meet you in the scrub room."

As they prepared for surgery, Dr. Gray asked, "What is your prognosis?"

"I believe that we can rebuild the leg," said Heinrich. "There is a lot of damage to the arterial system, but I believe that we can reconnect and restore the blood flow to the lower part of the leg. Once that is accomplished, we can set about rebuilding the bone structure."

"Are you sure? I think the leg is lost and should be amputated. I did say, however, that this is your lead so I will go along with your prognosis as long as we don't put the boy in danger."

"Hopefully you will be surprised. In the army, our only constraint was time. If we had the manpower, we would always try to save a limb. So, after surgery is over, we will monitor the limb closely for infection or gangrene. We can always remove it if it gets infected and the infection gets out of control. My goal is to try to save a limb first, and then work from there."

That night in the changing area Dr. Gray told Heinrich, "That was the most amazing experience I can remember. I wouldn't have believed it could be done. I really felt that amputation was the only answer. I know that the kid is not out of the woods, but I have no doubt that you saved his leg. A real miracle! I can't get over it. Amazing! Absolutely amazing!"

"In the army we had a lot of opportunity to experiment and develop our skills. The most important thing is to be brave enough to try. I have yet to talk with a soldier that wasn't willing to take a chance in order to save an arm or leg. After a while, the impossible became routine," said Heinrich. "To keep things honest though, I have worked with surgeons better than I. There was one that I worked with in the prison camp that did wonderful, almost artistic things."

"We'll see if we can get him to come here", said Dr. Gray excitedly. "Was he German? I'm sure we can work something out."

"No, we can't", said Heinrich sadly, "He was killed during the liberation of our camp. He was a good friend. Yes, he was German, but he was a doctor first, last, and always. I get angry when I think of the talent lost. He went all through the war, and when it was all but over he was killed by misdirected artillery."

"I'm sorry about that," said Dr. Gray, "but we can't live in the past. This is here and now. You've got talent and you should be teaching others these revolutionary new techniques. As you know, Dr. Rogers asked me to grade your skills to see if your services would be what we're looking for. I am going to call him tonight and tell him to get his checkbook out. You have far surpassed our wildest dreams!" Shifting around on his bench he excitedly looked Heinrich squarely in the face. "Now, I think you should be teaching in conjunction with Ohio State in Columbus. The hospital could get a lot of good publicity out of it."

The one thing Heinrich feared the most was publicity. While he knew intellectually that he looked different, and no one would recognize him, emotionally he felt he could be discovered at any moment. Things were not going as anticipated.

"I don't think I'm ready for that quite yet," He replied, "I just want to stay in my little corner of the world and get to know my family again. I don't want to set the world on fire,

146

and I don't want anything that will pull me away from Catherine and David. I've been away for so long that I feel as if I've been cheated out of all those years. Thanks, but no thanks."

"I guess I was getting a little ahead of myself. Here, we haven't even made you a permanent offer and I'm sending you out on teaching assignments."

The offer he received from the hospital was very generous. Dr. Rogers was beside himself. "I can't believe it. First you're a war hero, and then you turn out to be the best surgeon Dr. Gray has ever seen, and he has seen a lot. If we were making a movie, we couldn't have chosen a better leading man. Dr. Gray told me about your reluctance at teaching classes at Columbus, so I took the liberty of arranging for the classes to be taught here. That's even better. Say you'll take the job and I'll be happier than the day I got married."

"I think I can work with that Dr. Rogers, and I'll be thrilled to work with students. I had some outstanding doctors teach me, and it's only right to pass it on."

With that, Heinrich's new life as David Strauss was established; not quite as planned.

Chapter 23

Marseilles, France

It had not been easy to convince Jillian's mother to come over. She insisted that although the war was over, she was not going to aid the enemy. What would the neighbors say? What did Jillian mean when she said that this Heinrich Müller was "a good Kraut"? It was only when she found that the chateau had a piano that she changed her mind.

Phoebe Turnbull had been an accomplished pianist when she met Jillian's father. She still had hopes for a career in music when they married. Those hopes vanished when she found that she was pregnant. First, there was Lila, then Jillian. She had vowed to put her career on hold until she had raised her children. Times had been hard on the family and they had to sell her piano. It had been so long that she had forgotten those dreams. Then Ronald, her husband, was killed as the Germans were pushing the English into the channel at Dunkirk. So close, and yet so far. She had tried to forgive, but it was not easy. The past was past and hadn't Jillian said that "he was a good Kraut"? Whatever he was, she was not going to stand in the way of Jillian making such an enormous sum of money when everyone around them was struggling to make ends meet. Besides that, there was the piano...

The chateau was not the cottage Phoebe had visualized. It was more like a small palace. There were huge gardens surrounding the estate. While they were still somewhat in

148

poor condition, René, a small Frenchman, worked everyday trimming, planting, and pruning. He seemed a bit more tolerant toward the Germans renting the chateau than Phoebe was. He explained that during the war, he was with the French underground and they worked with many Germans who did not support the Nazis. He could support Heinrich's story with full faith.

The chateau sat on a hill overlooking the rocky seashore on the edge of town. It had three stories with a basement. The rooms were bright and airy. As Phoebe and Jillian toured, they were almost stunned to silence. They were not sure what to do with the space, but knew that if Heinrich was on the first floor and Phoebe and Jillian were on the second, propriety would be served. They chose adjoining rooms with a shared patio that looked over the seashore. The cooling breeze came through the doors and made sleeping a dream. Erik had brought his family with him and occupied the entire basement. His wife May served as cook and maid while Erik continued as David's friend and assistant.

There was a small ballroom, living room, and a drawing room on one side of the first floor. The drawing room was Phoebe's favorite because it housed the grand piano. The other side included a sunroom, dining room and study. The study was converted into David's bedroom while the adjoining sunroom was converted into a PT room. Erik spent all his time locating things like large rubber balls, weights, balance bars, swings, and the list went on and on. These things would not have been hard to locate before the war, but now they were scarce. It helped to have what appeared to be an endless supply of cash. If Erik couldn't find an item, he would have it built. Before long he was friendly with every merchant in town.

As Jillian worked with him, David began to have hopes that she would see him as something other than a cripple. He was determined not to let her see that inside he was weak. Time after time he wanted to quit but he didn't want to let her down. He knew the first time she had spun him in a circle on that boulevard in traffic that this was not an ordinary girl. It did not take him long to fall in love. In fact,

149

when he hired her as a therapist, the main reason was to keep her from leaving. He knew though that he could not tell her his feelings until he could walk. He would not have her love him out of pity.

Jillian had no illusions about the job she had in front of her. That first night she kissed him after dinner she knew she was in love. She was so glad when he offered her the job. She had known she must leave and didn't know how she could deal with it. If she told him she loved him, he might accept her because he thought that a cripple couldn't do any better. No, he had to be standing before she could reveal her feelings. Twelve weeks was not a lot of time to do what they must. She would work him until he dropped, but he would be on his feet at the end of the allotted time. She was not going to lose the man she loved on a technicality. What she also hoped for was that he would not see it was breaking her heart to be this hard on him. She did not want him to quit.

On the second morning as the sun was creeping over the horizon, David was lying in bed in that twilight sleep that occurs just before one comes fully awake. He was dreaming of a beautiful piano and he was playing. The sounds were soft and gentle as though they were coming from heaven. His fingers slid lightly across the keyboard and his body swayed with the music. As his eyes opened, he realized the music was not a dream at all but was coming from the drawing room.

He reached for the trousers on the rack beside the bed. Pulling the wheelchair over, he lifted himself in. Dressed only in his undershirt and trousers, he wheeled himself into the drawing room. As he entered he could see Phoebe playing with her eyes closed. Tears were streaming down her cheeks as her body swayed to the beautiful music. Hearing him come in, she stopped. "I woke you, I am so sorry. After seeing this beautiful piano, I could wait no longer. I just had to play. Thank you so much for bringing me here. I had forgotten the joy that comes from creating beautiful music." With that, she walked over and kissed him on the cheek.

"No, it is I who should be thanking you. As I have seen death and destruction on all sides these past years, I too had forgotten that something as beautiful as a melody can heal the soul. Would you mind if I just sit and listen for a while?"

He could tell she was elated. "I would be thrilled if you would allow me to continue."

She sat down again and her fingers began to waltz over the keys and music filled the air. A while later she looked to see Jillian standing inside the door quietly listening. At the end of the piece Jillian came over and put her arms around her mother, "I love you Mum." Tears also filled her eyes. "I had forgotten how beautifully you play. Your music brings peace to my soul."

Phoebe stood up and wiped her cheeks. "I think a good breakfast is in order. I could play until I starve, but that wouldn't do now would it?"

Jillian said, "I guess we should wash for breakfast. We'll see you in a few minutes Heinrich."

"Right." David sat looking at the piano for a few minutes. There was something intimately familiar about the keyboard. Finally he pushed the bench out of the way and rolled his wheelchair into position. It was a little awkward since the wheelchair and piano didn't match in height.

He reached out and placed his hands on the keyboard and gently pressed down. The chord struck a familiar note. He shifted his hands and struck the keyboard again. Lightly and gently he moved his hands from position to position. He wasn't sure what he was doing, but it felt right. It was a little awkward from the wheelchair, but right nonetheless. He continued on until he looked up and saw Jillian and Phoebe standing inside the doorway.

"Don't stop," Phoebe said. "I didn't realize you played."

"I didn't either, if you call that playing. This morning when I was still in bed, I dreamed that I was playing. It seemed so natural." Looking at Phoebe, he said, "When I saw you, I could anticipate the next movement of your hands. I think I must have played at one time. Would you be willing to help me? We could at least see if I actually know anything about the piano."

"Of course I will. I will be thrilled to help in any way I can."

Jillian was all smiles. "Playing the piano will help redevelop your coordination. This can be a big step in helping you to walk again. Now, back to reality. This does not count as PT. If you plan on having time to eat, you better get it in gear." *I guess that Mum doesn't count him as the enemy if he plays the piano.*

After that, David and Phoebe spent two hours each morning with piano lessons. As it turned out, David was an accomplished pianist. The hardest thing he had to deal with was the stiffness of his hands from inaction during those months of recovery. As they limbered up, his coordination began to improve. One day Phoebe asked David why he was not a musician. "You obviously have a love and a talent for music. There is a professional quality about your music. I imagine the piano is not the only instrument you play."

"I don't have a clue why I am a doctor instead of a musician. I asked Erik when I learned the piano and he suggested it was when I was in medical school in the states. I may be a good musician, but I cannot imagine being anything but a doctor. Even now, while I don't like being a patient, I miss the hospital. I want to spend my life helping people. I have a million ideas on things in surgery that can be improved."

Phoebe looked a little disappointed. "You're right, of course. One doesn't see your talent for quality music that often. There are lots of people who can play the piano, but very few that have the keyboard as an extension of their hands. Playing the piano is as natural to you as walking... Oh! I'm sorry. What could I have been thinking?"

David began to laugh. "Okay, Phoebe, you must forget about hurting my feelings. You notice that Jillian has no sympathy for me. I *will* walk again and soon. It's just a matter of time. Even if I never do, don't cry for me. There are thousands of men and women much worse off than I. If I don't, I'll deal with it and develop a way I can function without legs. Now let's get one more song in before Jillian catches us."

"I heard that." Jillian was walking into the room. "If you were with anyone besides my mum, you would be in serious trouble. How can I get mad at my mum though? Just be thankful that she's here to protect you. Now get through your song and let's get serious about walking!"

The weeks flew past. The trees were changing color and fall was coming. The tourists were gone as they strode down their favorite boulevard next to the seashore. They stopped at the bench he was sitting on that first day they met. As Jillian was helping him out of his chair, she slipped and fell. David's right knee hit the edge of the bench and he instinctively pulled it up and grabbed it with his hands. Jillian immediately noticed what happened. "Did you see what happened?" she shouted. Tears of joy were running down her face.

"Yes, I hurt my knee!" he returned, "Ohh... that hurts."

"No you ninny! You pulled up your leg! Now do it again." She wiped the tears from her cheeks.

"No, that hurt!"

"You better move that leg right now mister or I will give new meaning to the word hurt!"

David released his leg and pulled it back, slowly at first then again and again. They both started laughing, almost hysterically as he continued to move his leg. It was as though his brain had learned to say the word 'move' again. Now over and over David kept his brain doing it so that it wouldn't forget.

"I'm almost afraid to stop. I might not be able to start again."

"Let's wait five minutes and do it again," said Jillian.

After waiting for what seemed to be an eternity David moved his leg.

"I'm sorry, but I just couldn't wait. Do you think we can do the same thing to the other one?"

"Sure, but wait a minute and I will kick you in the leg so it will be the same."

"That won't be necessary. I think I'll try on my own."

David sat there and his right leg moved. "Now that it has started moving, it wants all the glory."

"It's okay. Don't worry about it now, I have some ideas we can use later in the room."

They both sat quietly looking at the surf coming in on the empty beach, each engrossed in his thoughts. They were both thinking on the same thing. They were one step closer to their goal.

Later in the PT room, Jillian began having David move his right leg and she would tickle the bottom of his left foot at the same time. Before long they had the second breakthrough of the day. As she tickled his left foot, he brought up his left leg instead of his right. Once again, they practiced moving it over and over to train his brain on this new command.

Jillian threw her arms around David and told him how proud she was of his accomplishments.

"If I had known I'd get a hug, I would have done it days ago."

Jillian blushed and backed away.

The moment was gone. David promised himself that he wouldn't make that mistake again.

As time went by, David got stronger. He walked the balance bars until he could stand and step without aid. He had not realized how weak his legs had become. Once he learned to stand, he could take only a few steps before he was exhausted. Jillian was a relentless taskmaster. David began to wonder if she took pleasure in seeing him collapse. She would drive him until he could walk no more, then she would put him in the swimming pool and have him paddle his legs like a child.

Once he started walking, pain became a way of life for David. Both his legs and arms hurt more than he believed was possible. Yet, they kept on. Every day Jillian would

154

come up with another way to exercise. David was getting a little discouraged, so on a beautiful sunny morning she suggested that they take the day off and go to the seashore. They could play in the surf the way they had done earlier. David still had fond memories of holding her and practicing his kiss. Erik had his wife pack a picnic basket and before long was driving them to their favorite spot. As David looked at Jillian in the seat beside him, he wondered how he could have been so fortunate. If he had not been confined to his wheelchair, he may never have met this wonderful girl. Yet, at the same time this wheelchair stood between him and happiness. Time was running short and he had not accomplished his goal. He could not; no... he would not fail.

So much for vain plans, David knew he was in trouble when she walked ahead and slipped off her robe. As he trudged through the sand he realized he was not going to have enough wind left to practice kissing or even talking. She laughed and teasingly said, "Come on, last one in is a rotten egg."

Erik attempted to help him but Jillian said, "No help, he has to make it on his own."

David felt like a drunk trying to remain upright while staggering down the beach. Fortunately, it was downhill. He did not know how he would ever make it back to the promenade; perhaps he would spend the night right here.

Doggedly he trudged on, stopping only to shed his robe at the cabana that had been set up about halfway down the beach. The going got easier as he approached the water and got in the packed sand. As he reached Jillian and the water, he half sat, half dropped into the water. As Jillian helped him sit up, he wrapped his arms around her and gave her a kiss. Not much of a kiss, mind you, he didn't have enough breath for that.

Jillian pushed him to his back in the water and said, "Strictly business, eh. What was that all about?"

"Well," David said, "I've been doing all the work, so I decided I should have a reward."

155

"Not likely." Jillian laughed and began tickling him.

"Wait cough, cough, you're drowning me."

"I thought you had all this extra energy to waste."

She got out of the water and walked back up to the cabana. There she spread a blanket in the sun and laid on it. "This sun is wonderful, why don't you come on up?"

David lay in the water and thought, *I think I may just have to stay here. That wasn't fair at all. I wonder if it would count if I crawled back up to the cabana.*

Finally he got up and slowly walked to the cabana. His legs felt as if they weighed a hundred pounds each, but he made it. As he was walking up the beach, it struck him that he had accomplished his goal. He was walking, not very well mind you, but walking nonetheless.

He knew what he must do. He wasn't sure how, but he must do it.

"Jillian, I guess that you are aware that your three months for training me to walk are almost over."

Jillian's heart almost stopped. She had been dreading this subject. "Yes, I am."

"I would like you to continue on if you will."

She felt her heart leap. She must retain her composure.

"You would?"

"Yes, I would. However, one hundred pounds a week is a little expensive. I thought I might save some money if you married me, then I wouldn't have to pay you anything; how about it?"

Jillian was stunned. She wasn't sure what she heard. "Let me get this straight, you would like for me to continue working but for free?"

David took her into his arms. "No silly, I asked you to marry me. Will you be my wife?"

Tears immediately rose to the surface in her eyes. "Of course I will. You don't know how long I have wanted to hear those words!"

With that she threw him on the ground and kissed him long and hard. As she drew back he looked at her and grinned.

"One of these days when I am as strong as you, I am going to throw you down and kiss you just like that. Then we will be even!"

"We will never be even my love..." She kissed him again and again.

Chapter 24

Roquefort, Ohio

Heinrich still had one major hurdle to overcome: Catherine. What was he going to do with her? He had been avoiding his personal duties to her as a husband. She on the other hand was getting bolder each day. He had set them up in separate rooms but wasn't sure how long his amnesia story would hold her off. He was actually worried that one night he would wake up and find her in bed with him. She was quite a tempting little vixen herself and didn't realize how hard it was for him to stay away. What was he going to do? Maybe he should just give in. Not yet. He would come up with something.

One morning Catherine was awakened as the phone rang and rang. She decided that she must be the only one around. She reached from her bed to pick up the phone. As she reached, she made humming sounds to clear her throat so it wouldn't sound as if she had just awakened.

"Good morning."

"Catherine?"

"Yes."

"It's Ann Marie. I've got the solution to your problem! It's brilliant! I can't believe it. I was just sitting here in the den mending, and it popped into my head."

"This is not something that could wait until a decent hour? Now, what problem are you talking about?"

"I know that it been awhile, but surely you haven't forgotten. You know... the David problem?"

Oh yes... the David problem."

"It *is* still a problem... isn't it?

"Ooh... yeah! Now, are you going to give me your solution, or spend the morning prying?"

"Okay, okay! Propose to him!"

"Propose? What do you mean, propose?"

"It's simple! Ask him to marry you. If he can't remember marrying you, do it again. You can tell people that you are renewing your vows to celebrate his return home. You lost David to the war, and now you have him back. Now you have another chance at life together and you are renewing your vows to celebrate its beginning. Renewing of vows is the latest rage among people. That way he will have a wedding he can remember and you will have a wedding night you won't forget! Tell me now, is that brilliant?"

"Ohh yes, Ann Marie, that *is* brilliant! If he accepts, will you be my maid of honor?"

"Ha ha ha! You bet! I don't know why I am so excited. You're the one getting married."

That night after everyone went to bed Catherine dressed in her most beautiful nightgown with her sheerest negligee and knocked on Heinrich's door.

"Yes?"

"It's me, can I come in?"

"Please do."

Catherine stepped into the room. Heinrich was sitting at his desk in his pajamas and making notes in a small notebook. He stood and looked at Catherine with a stare that could only be compared to a kid looking at a birthday cake.

"David, will you marry me?"

"What?"

"I said, 'Will you marry me?' It seems to me that if you can't remember marrying me then maybe we should do it

159

again. That way I'll have mine to remember and you will have yours. We could tell your parents that we are renewing our vows in celebration of our new life together."

Heinrich laughed. "Yes I will. That solves all the problems. Perfect!"

Catherine heart jumped inside and she ran over and threw her arms around him and kissed him. "Now since we are getting married can we start the honeymoon now?"

"Girl, you have got a **one** track mind. We are not officially married until we say 'I do'."

"No... you are not married. I still remember my marriage. This way I am not a slut, you are and I don't mind being married to a slut."

"You really have no idea how hard this is on me. I will tell Papa and Mutti in the morning and we will see how quickly we can get this under way."

"Saturday afternoon at 2:00 PM will be perfect. That way it will match the invitations that Mutti sent out this afternoon."

"I think I may be on call this weekend."

"No, I have already cleared it with Dr. Gray. In fact you have all next week off for your honeymoon. All you have to decide is where to have the honeymoon. As far as I am concerned, the nearest hotel will be fine. You think this has been hard on you, you don't know how hard it has been on me. You'll find out Saturday night though."

Heinrich laughed inside. *I guess I'm in this for the long run. David never told me quite how aggressive this girl is. I like it.*

Saturday was a beautiful day. Early in the morning Heinrich got up before anyone else and went for a walk. He found himself in a little park near the Strauss home. There he sat and watched the day come to life. He thought how appropriate it was to see it on this wonderful day when his life was returning. Over the past months he had discovered what a wonderful person Catherine was. His talks with David about her helped because he knew what it would take to fix their problems. They weren't really all as bad as David had thought; they were the problems of the young,

160

when they realize that everything isn't perfect. Heinrich had seen and felt enough pain and sorrow to last a lifetime. He was not going to let trivial things ruin happiness for him and his new family.

He took a few minutes to talk with Ursula. *You know you own a part of my heart that can never be given to anyone else. I love you as much now as I did the day we were married and the day when you presented me with our beautiful Gretchen. I feel in my heart that somehow I let you down by not being home to protect you. I know that I couldn't; what God has decreed we cannot change. The most beautiful thing about love is you cannot give it all away... I know that you will not begrudge me this chance for happiness and I promise that I will never disgrace what we had together. I love you Ursula... now and forever.*

His thoughts then turned to his friend David. *Well David, here I am about to marry your wife. I am sorry you are not here to lead your own life. I will try my best to see that little David is raised the way you would wish. I will try to make... no, allow Catherine to have happiness in her life. She is the wonderful person you told me about and I am not going to let her lose her husband again.*

Heinrich arose from the bench, looked at the rising sun, and walked back to begin his new life. He gave a half-hearted laugh to himself. *Goodbye Lila.*

The wedding was simple but elegant. It was held in the Strauss home. Heinrich was a little embarrassed about the greater than life-sized portrait that Papa had placed in the foyer. It was hard to miss. When one walked in it was staring at the entryway like a sentinel. Just below the portrait were three documents in picture frames. On the left corner was the letter of commendation by Colonel Bartlett and on the right corner was Private Grissett's letter. In between the two was the letter of commendation he had received with the Medal of Honor.

He decided that if showing his picture would keep Papa at bay, it was well worth the embarrassment.

The wedding was attended by all of Papa's political cronies, as Catherine had named them, a few of David's old friends, and of course Catherine's family and friends. Ann Marie was maid of honor and Scott was best man. At any rate, Heinrich didn't know that many people. David Jr. carried the ring on a small satin pillow and Catherine's nieces were flower girls in pink taffeta dresses. After hearing Catherine's opinion of Julie Anderson, Heinrich was surprised at seeing her in attendance. When he asked Catherine about it later, she gave him that look relegated to those of low mental stature. "Of course, I just HAD to invite her." Heinrich decided that American women were not that different than German women after all.

His shock came when Catherine walked in holding to her father's arm. He could not think of when he had seen anything or anyone as beautiful as the vision before his eyes. Her dress was white silk covered with fine lace. It was tight at the waist and had full-length sleeves. Her black hair worn down was cascading over her shoulders. The lace veil and came over the top of her head and stopped just below her hair. He could not get over the blue of her eyes. She seemed to glow as though under a light that followed her as she walked. *Poor David.* That was his last thought of David.

The reception followed on the patio and the back garden. It would not have dared rain. Papa wouldn't have it! All the usual things took place, the cutting of the cake, toasts, and of course the dance. If this was a renewing of vows, Heinrich wondered what it would have been if they were having the full wedding. It was nice and they were officially wed in Heinrich's mind. It didn't matter that she was marrying a total stranger as long as they were officially married.

At long last the reception was over and they were on the train for their honeymoon destination to, where else, Niagara Falls. Heinrich looked at the tiny bunk bed in their compartment on the train and wondered if it would do. It did!

Chapter 25

Marseilles, France

The wedding was not as large as it would have been before the war. David only invited those he considered as family. His biggest problem was that he couldn't remember his extended family. With that in mind, he chose those with whom he had created his family. Uncle Hans, Aunt Adele, Erik and his family were first on his list. Since he couldn't remember any of his extended family, he selected from those persons that had been so supportive. First on this list was Helga, the housekeeper and her husband Bernard. They had taken over running the home with the death of his wife and parents. According to Uncle Hans, Helga had participated in raising him almost as much as his mother. When his sweet Gretchen was born, Helga was there to continue her role on another generation. Then there was Gustav, or Gus, as he was affectionately called and his wife Marta, the cook. Each of them had fussed and worried about him from the time he had returned home. The women, of course, had to mother him back to health. With Helga's "I'll help you remember," to Marta's "He is so thin." David knew he was loved. He had vowed that since he could not remember his former life, he would make new memories with those who loved him now.

Jillian's list was small as well. It included her mother, her sister Lila, and her mother's two sisters. Knowing that the Turnbull family might not have the finances to cover the wedding, David insisted he would cover all expenses. This included bringing the family to the south of France for the wedding. They had decided to have the wedding in France as a compromise. There were still feelings of anger in Britain against Germans and they didn't want this special day spoiled by someone that didn't know that he was a "good Kraut".

The wedding was held in a small chapel on the outskirts of Marseilles. As they were planning it Jillian said, "You know, Heinrich, there will be so few of us that it is not necessary for you to go to the expense of a wedding. We can just quietly have a ceremony and be done with it."

David took her in his arms and said, "Don't worry about it. You are going to have the wedding you deserve. I am marrying the most wonderful, intelligent, and beautiful girl in the world and I want everyone to know.

Uncle Hans walked down the aisle with Jillian and gave her away. He could not have been happier if he had been walking with his own daughter. Erik was best man and Jillian's sister, Lila, was maid of honor.

Jillian was shocked as she walked down the aisle. The room was filled with people. Besides the family, she saw René the gardener and his wife, the baker and his large family, and shopkeepers and craftsmen and everyone in town that had participated in helping them during these past months. Erik had personally gone around and invited everyone he had dealt with in creating the tools they had used in David's therapy.

The reception at the chateau was really more like a festival. Jillian could not remember being happier. She had gotten to know and respect these people during the past months and could not think of anyone she would rather share this special time with. There was nothing quiet or subdued like it would have been at home.

The sunroom was open to the back gardens and the flowers were beautiful. Over the summer René had taken special care to make this part of the grounds the most beautiful. Children ran down the paths and laughed. Music was playing and people were dancing. Jillian saw her mother sitting at the side with a smile and a tear. She went to her mother and put her arms around her and kissed her on the cheek. "He's here, don't you think? Dad wouldn't miss this for anything."

Phoebe smiled. "I know he is. Ronnie loved his girls. This is what he would want for you. Be happy and have a good life." She patted Jillian's arm. "Now go on and find that man of yours. See if he is good for one dance. Ask Erik to have them play something slow."

They had their dance and Jillian positively glowed. David wondered if all brides had this look or just his. He knew he had been given a second chance at life and his heart was full. *How could it be? A few months ago I was sitting by the seashore and wondering if I would ever have a life and this little breath of spring walks in and changes everything.*

After the dance was over, he excused himself and walked over to the band and whispered something to the leader. As the band began playing "Always," David stepped over to Phoebe and said, "I believe that I have one dance left in these feeble legs if you will trust your feet to them."

Phoebe smiled and said, "If I will trust my daughter to them, I guess I can trust my feet."

"Phoebe, I don't know if I can begin to tell you how happy I am."

"You don't have to. I can see it in your face. You look at Jillian the way my Ronnie used to look at me. I know everything will be fine with the two of you."

"There is something else we need to talk about. Now that Jillian is mine, I was wondering if I could call you 'Mum' instead of Phoebe. I miss having a mother so much."

Tears welled up in Phoebe's eyes. "Of course you can call me 'Mum'. Everyone has been so concerned about our losses that no one has considered the pain you have suffered." With that she stopped and put her arms around David and began to hold him tight. David could feel her tremble as she quietly sobbed. "Ronnie would have approved of you. You are the kind of a man he would have wanted for a son."

David led her from the dance floor. "I guess my legs are not as strong as I hoped. Let's sit down over here and rest for a few minutes if you don't mind."

After they had settled on a small couch out of the flow of traffic, David said, "Now Mum, Catherine and I have a home so large that we could walk around and not meet for days."

"Who's Catherine?"

"Catherine? I don't know a Catherine."

"That's what you said."

"I think you heard me wrong. Anyway, I would like for you and Lila to live with us if you would."

"Thank you, but I couldn't. Besides that, newlyweds don't need a meddling mother-in-law around."

"I know that it is a sacrifice for you to have her so far away and I don't want you to think you have lost her. We will visit often, and I want you and Lila to visit us as well. We have all intentions of having a family and don't want them to be without a grandmother." David put his arms around her and held her for a few moments. "I love you, Mum."

Chapter 26

They had their honeymoon in the town of Cannobio on Lake Maggiore in northern Italy. Everything was perfect. They took a room in a small villa on the lake. It was like a dream for both of them. The war seemed so far away and so long ago. There were very few indications in that part of the country that the war had ever occurred. The town seemed to be in celebration. Everyone was smiling and seemed so happy. There was no significant rebuilding to do and the harvest in the nearby fields was good. Life had returned to the way it had been for the last century. Jillian thought how nice it would have been to be married here where the people were so down to earth. Perhaps the stability here would somehow attach itself to them and they could have a long and uneventful life with babies, singing, and birthdays. That was all she really wanted. She felt she had seen enough pain and suffering for ten lifetimes. *Please God, don't let this ever change.*

Reality set in on the train ride to her new home in Stadthagen. As they passed through Stuttgart, they saw hungry children digging through garbage in search for food. Their train had stopped on the outskirts of the city to wait for a passing train. They both felt helpless as they sat in luxury watching the children through the window. They were both quiet as the train started on its way.

Finally David said, "I think we need to do something for the children displaced by the war. I am not sure what to do, but I can't stand idly by while children go hungry. Their only fault was to be born in the wrong place at the wrong time."

Tears welled up in Jillian's eyes. "Thank you, Heinrich, for being the man you are! I knew I made the right choice when I fell in love." A little smile crossed her face. "You're right; you are a 'good Kraut'. I guess the honeymoon is over, welcome back to the world." She snuggled into David's arms and felt safe.

Jillian was amazed when she saw the 'castle.' David called it 'the schloss'. It was a huge castle-like home set on an estate of at least one hundred acres. There was a small lake on one side toward the back. A brown horse barn that looked to have held at least a dozen horses at some previous time sat between the lake and the house. The emptiness of the barn contrasted with what must have been the splendor of the estate at one time. Just down from the barn was a small cozy cottage for the grounds keeper. On the south side of the house and down toward the lake was a beautiful white gazebo with vines growing through the lattice. Beautiful red and pink flowers surrounded the outside. A guesthouse sat on one side close to the road. It had a drive coming off the main drive and a sidewalk lined with flowers that led to the main house. It was beautiful.

Jillian could not get over what a lovely and romantic place this was, that is until the car rounded the curve and she saw the north side of the house. That wing was in shambles. It looked as though a bomb had struck it. Heinrich had told her this was where his family had been when a damaged allied bomber had crashed after making a run over Hanover. She was struck with the reality of the event as the car pulled into the long drive. The telling of the tale could never match the breathtaking tragedy that lay before her. Her heart went out to Heinrich as she realized what he had been through. Perhaps his amnesia was more understandable if it helped him block out the heartache he must have felt. She put her arm through his and pulled closer.

"Oh Heinrich, I am so sorry. Your wonderful family... I feel the pain of your loss." Tears rolled down her cheeks.

David put his arm around her and kissed her hair. "I love you and with your help maybe we can bring back happiness to the innocent people who have suffered so much. I have no memories of my home and family so I will start new ones. I want the new life and memories we have started together to be memories of service and joy. Thank you for loving me and helping me to have this opportunity at life once again."

He turned her face to his and kissed her. As he pulled away he said, "You know, you started it when you walked up out of the blue and helped me that day by the seashore. I believe God sent you that day. You turned my life around and allowed me to live again... and to love. Now we are together about to continue the work you started when you saved me. This day before God, I pledge my love and devotion for this life and for eternity." He then leaned over and sealed this pledge with a kiss.

Chapter 27

Roquefort, Ohio

Heinrich looked up at the bank as he approached. The cut stone reminded him of buildings in Germany. A feeling of nostalgia passed briefly as he stepped in. This would be a new experience for him, borrowing money. At home his accountant would have called the bank and have them allocate funds into a special account for a new project and it would have been taken care of. He wished he could go to Switzerland and access some of his accounts, but there is no way on earth he would be able to explain that one.

As he walked over to the counter marked LOANS, a woman in her mid twenties looked up from her desk. The placard on the corner or her desk read Amy Hamilton.

"May I help you?"

"Yes, I have an appointment with Mr. Odegard."

"If you will take a seat I will see if Mr. Odegard is available. You are David Strauss aren't you?" It was more of a statement than a question.

"Yes, but I wasn't aware that we have met."

"You have got to be kidding. Everyone knows you. Best doctor in the state, teacher, war hero... there is not a girl in town who doesn't wish you were single. I guess I had better get Mr. Odegard before I start drooling."

Heinrich smiled.

She smiled as she turned and gave the door a brief rap.

The voice behind the door said, "Yes?"

Miss Hamilton opened the door. "Dr. David Strauss is here to see you."

"Oh good, show him in."

As she stepped back to her desk, Mr. Odegard followed behind her. He walked over to Heinrich with his hand outstretched. "Dr. Strauss, it is so good to meet you. I'm Stan Odegard. Just call me Stan. Won't you come in?"

Stan Odegard was a man in his early fifties. What hair he had left had been blonde at one time, but had succumbed to the gray that seems to slip in until it had quietly taken over. "I appreciate you seeing me Mr. Odegard."

"Please, call me Stan. The pleasure is mine Dr. Strauss; your reputation precedes you. Take a seat and tell me what's on your mind." He smiled. Heinrich felt like he was looking at the genuine article, a man who cared.

"Okay Stan, if you will call me David. I wanted to discuss a project that I am undertaking. Of course it always seems that these things require money."

Stan smiled. "That's what we're here for. What kind of project do you have in mind?"

Heinrich began to relax. "I would like to build a small doctors building."

Stan nodded. "That's a little out of your line of work. Do you have a location in mind?"

The excitement began to show on Heinrich's face. "I have taken an option on the vacant space just west of the hospital. Frank Boris has been working on the plans." He reached into his brief case and pulled out a folder. He laid a conceptual drawing of the building. "It is going to have offices for six doctors with exam rooms and a small operating area for minor surgeries. The foundation and structure are going to be set up so that floors can be added in the future and we can expand the building into this area that will serve as a parking lot initially." He had risen up in his chair as he described his project. "It gets even better."

"Better?" Stan laughed. "It looks like you have been planning this for a while."

"That I have." Heinrich leaned back smiling, then leaned forward again. "Now for the best part; I plan to start my own construction company. My first project will be this building."

Stan had a surprised look on his face. "That's a large undertaking. I don't want to see you lose your shirt. First of all, what do you know about construction?" He had his business face on now.

Heinrich had to be careful not to reveal his true past. During his early years, his father had done much the same thing before Herr Schiklgruber had taken over the country. While Heinrich's life had a lot of the advantages of the wealthy, his father had a strong work ethic. Heinrich had spent a lot of his younger years working his way from the bottom up. Papa had said, "To properly run a business, you need to know every aspect of it. I do not expect you to be proficient at each job, but you need to know how to do it. Many a business has been ruined because the owner did not know his workers were doing a substandard job."

"I know a little bit about construction, but I know more about people. I saw the look on your face when I told you Frank Boris was my architect. Frank may have lost a leg during the war, but his mind is in great shape. I have had a lot of talks with him and find him very stable. Let me give you the big picture. We have lots of good men who left their jobs to go and fight our battle. When they came home, the women had taken over. They work in factories, mills and every job that used to be held by men. Everywhere you look there are men out of work. I for one plan on hiring only vets where possible. I think our men deserve better than they are getting. If they are missing an arm we'll find a one-armed job. These are good men who did one hell'uva job under adverse conditions. My foreman will be Ed Rodenburger. He was with the Seabees. He directed construction of airstrips and buildings on half the islands in the south Pacific. Anyway, I'm getting ahead of myself. As

I'm sure you are aware, there is a shortage of housing in the area. After we have completed the office project, my plan is to build low cost housing. Frank is going to design maybe four different layouts for three bedroom homes and four for four bedroom homes. They will have common dimensions so that we can prefabricate certain walls, roof joists, bathrooms, closets, kitchens, and anything else we can think of. We will build homes the same way the Seabees built buildings in the Pacific. We can get the costs down so that those same vets can now afford housing. If these projects work out as I expect they will, I have other ideas that will blow your socks off.

Stan looked thoughtful for a moment. "Why don't you get the money from your father, I'm sure that it wouldn't be a problem for him."

"I could, but I'm not going to go that way. I would rather make it on my own. I understand that this may seem farfetched to you, but I will do it, and I will be successful." Heinrich began to gather up his paperwork. "I appreciate you taking the time to see me."

Stan placed his hand on Heinrich's arm. "Wait, I wasn't saying no. I was just asking the questions that a good banker should. You're going to get the loan. I think it's a great idea and with the right team it will work. As far as I can see, I think that you have picked the right team."

Heinrich was stunned. "Don't you have to present this before a committee or something like that?"

Stan laughed. "You don't know who you are, do you? This loan was in the bag before you ever walked in."

"What?" Heinrich couldn't believe it. "I'm not sure what you are talking about. Who do you think I am?"

"You're Mr. Reichstein's hero, that's who you are."

Heinrich couldn't believe his ears. "Who is Mr. Reichstein?"

Stan was enjoying this. "He is the president and major stockholder in this bank. That's who he is. What you don't know is that his grandson, James Henderson was a private at Stalag 21 when you and your crew arrived. Here is the story as he told it: Before you arrived, life was a living hell in that camp. Men died on a daily basis. If they didn't die from natural causes, they died from the brutality of the camp guards. When you came along, things changed. You stood up for the men. You challenged the kommandant and you challenged the guards. The men started getting the medicine they needed and you were the champion. He even said that the worst offender of all held a gun to your head and you wouldn't back down. When Mr. Reichstein heard you were coming in for a loan, he told me to approve it if it even sounded halfway reasonable. He said that if you could turn a German prison camp around, you could probably do anything."

Heinrich was a little uncomfortable. "I am not nearly the man he thinks I am."

"I don't believe that and I am not going to tell the president of the bank that he is wrong either. I wouldn't worry about it anyway. I think that you have a great idea and a great plan. I would have approved it even if Mr. Reichstein hadn't put pressure on me. We will have to do a little paperwork now, but I would like for you to meet the boss."

Mr. Reichstein was a tall man on the slender side. His hair was gray and thinning on top. He held himself erect as he stood and shook hands with Heinrich. "You don't know how much I have looked forward to meeting you, Major Strauss."

Heinrich flushed. "It's not Major any more Mr. Reichstein. But please, call me David. I remember your grandson, James; he was my right hand at the infirmary. What is he doing now?"

Mr. Reichstein looked proud. "He is going to Harvard. He says he wants to be a doctor. I think that I can give you credit for that. He has a lot of admiration for you." He glanced at his watch. "I have a lunch appointment that I can't be late for, my wife, so I must leave. It was good to finally meet you. Thank you for bringing James home alive. He is my only grandson and I don't know what we would have done if we had lost him. I know that there is no way I

174

can ever repay you. Don't be a stranger. If there is anything we can do to help in your success, feel free to call."

Heinrich never ceased to be amazed at the legacy David had left. The funny thing was that David had no idea how much he had been admired.

The work on the medical building went better than Heinrich had hoped for. The work crews were dedicated and hard working. They were thrilled to have good jobs and equally thrilled to be working for "The Major" as they called him. They worked in teams just as they had in the army and the discipline they had learned paid off. Their workmanship was of the highest quality and everything was completed on time. Other contractors tried to hire the men away, but their loyalty couldn't be breached. Interestingly enough, the returning veterans began to be given preferential treatment by employers in the area because of their work ethic.

The offices were all leased long before the building was completed and Heinrich saw the first phase of his project become a success. It felt good to give some repayment to this country that had taken him in. He guessed he would always feel some responsibility for the many loses that these people had suffered because he and his family had stood by and let a madman take over their country.

As his building was complete, those working on this first project became leaders of the new teams created for the housing developments. Many of the aging farmers who had lost sons in the war were ready for retirement. With no sons to take over, they gladly sold their property and moved into the new planned communities that were being built.

Once the initial projects were initiated and underway, Heinrich was able to step back and let the company run itself. He had leaders that he would have trusted with his life and they didn't let him down. Medicine was his first love and he was now able to focus full time in his new office complex. Shortly before he moved in to the new offices, his personal life took a big leap. Catherine presented him with a new daughter. He called her Gretchen. Life was good.

As the years went by Heinrich often thought of his friend David and the wonderful gift that David had unknowingly given him. Life had ended when his family had been killed. Now through this twist of fate happiness had returned. Never in his life could he have dreamed that love would return. He was happier than he had ever been before. What he didn't understand is why David had to die in order for him to have happiness. Was there a rule that required balance? Someone had to lose in order for another to gain?

Chapter 28

Stadthagen, Germany

David's next years were filled with joy and lots of hard work. Using the vast resources that were at his disposal, he worked with Uncle Hans to get the family construction business running again. He knew that there would be plenty of construction projects in the rebuilding phase of his country. He also knew that this would provide jobs and income to families that needed them. Over the next years, he was so grateful to a father that had the foresight to move almost all of their liquid assets to banks in Switzerland prior to the start of the war. The first project they started was for an orphanage for those children who had lost or become separated from their parents. This is where he discovered some of Jillian's hidden talents. Jillian, it seemed, had an eye for aesthetics. Her nursing training allowed them to develop some very creative projects. Her other talent, one that David had already been introduced to, was her intelligence. With a sparkle in her eye and a captivating personality, and she could sell almost any project to anyone. After the success of their first project, David and Jillian worked with various towns and cities to rebuild or renovate buildings to be used to house the orphans. As he became intimate with the leaders of communities throughout the country, David established a network of lists of families looking for their children and children looking for their families.

The reputation that "Dr. Heinrich Müller" had developed when working with American prisoners during the war opened doors with the U.S. military and thus with the U.S. government. He received cooperation from the U.S. everywhere he went in this quest to help since they were both working for the same goal. The U.S. wanted to help Germany become financially and politically stable as soon as possible and David was personally taking on a major task by helping families reunite. If "Dr. Müller's" name was associated with a project, the "red tape" seemed to disappear.

David's family began to rebuild at the end of their first year as well. Jillian had a beautiful little girl. Jillian called her Gretchen Marlene Müller after Heinrich's Gretchen. "Would it hurt too much if we called her Gretchen," she had asked David.

David smiled and held her close, as he looked at the most beautiful baby he had ever seen. "No, now my little Gretchen will have the chance to live again and grow up. Thank you my dear."

Two years later "Heinrich Erik Müller" was born. David was happy to have a son. He felt that their family was complete. That feeling was short-lived however. One year later, to the day, little Phoebe was born. David had to smile to himself, Phoebe Müller, now **that** was a name. As she grew, she was independent, intelligent, and full of surprises, just like her mother, and David was glad.

Erik had become president of the construction company and ran it as though he was Heinrich. With Erik as the technical leader, and Jillian in marketing, Müller Construction grew beyond their wildest dreams.

In case he had nothing else to do, David began practicing medicine again. While the memories of his family were gone, there was nothing wrong with his job skills. He went on a self-imposed training program, working as assistant to other doctors and surgeons until he felt confident that he was back on track. He worked tirelessly in the hospital trying to repair broken bodies and shattered lives.

As soon as construction on the first orphanage began, his next project was providing public sanitation. With cooperation of the city, he built public bathhouses that operated on public and private funds. He had observed the diseases that come with poverty and lack of opportunity. If he could improve sanitation, he could relieve the epidemics that were popping up all over the country. Eliminating them here could provide the example that would help communities elsewhere.

David's life was filled with happiness. As he sat down in the evenings with his family, he wondered if life could get any better. Yet... sometimes when he was alone, he would try to break through the barrier that hemmed in his life. If he could just remember, he knew his life would be complete. Occasionally, he could feel a memory come near the surface only to fade away. The only clear memory that ever came to the surface was a voice that said "Don't bother to come back." It was in English and very distinct. Once when he was in the train station in Hanover, he saw a small man coming through the gate. The name Rotten stepped to the forefront of his mind. When the man approached him he said, "Rotten?"

The man stopped and looked at David with alarm. Suddenly recognition appeared in the man's eyes. The color drained from his face and he began to run. David chased but he lost himself in the crowd. David was angry. This man knew him and may have been able to help him solve the riddle of his past. What was it that scared him? He began to wonder if he could have been involved in something illegal and the man knew about it and was scared. Why was a man named Rotten? There was apparently something to it or he would not have run. Try as he may, he could not remember anything else. He did make it a practice from that time to scan crowds for clues but to no avail. The only thing this did was frustrate him and keep him aware that his memory was gone.

Chapter 29

Roquefort, Ohio

One day Heinrich came home with a big grin. Catherine couldn't help but smile. She and David had been so happy. It seemed that he was always coming in with a gift or was taking her and the kids out for a treat. Since they had gotten past the first months of his return from the war, they had had a fairy tale romance. Her life was like the one young girls dreamed about when they thought of marriage. The romance never seemed to end. "What are you up to? You look like the cat that ate the canary."

"How would you like to go to New York?" He was grinning from ear to ear.

"New York? Yes! But how?" She was excited too. It had been a long time since she had been to New York. She could go shopping.

Heinrich sat down in his favorite chair. Catherine sat on the floor at his feet and began to take his shoes off. "Come on; tell me what's going on." She placed his feet on the ottoman and began to rub them. This was a routine that they had for years. Some days he stood in surgery for so long that his feet and legs would hurt. It gave her a sense of satisfaction to relieve the pain.

"I've been asked to speak at a medical convention in New York this year. It seems that my research into peripheral artery disease has gotten some attention. Anyway they will pay for our train tickets and hotel bills if I will be a speaker. If things go as I hope, I will teach a class to other doctors from around the country on detection techniques and surgical procedures. We could get a grant to put in a lab at the hospital to do research and development and they would be sending patients to us that are about to lose limbs. If our techniques work out, as I know they will, we could be saving thousands of limbs every year. I'm sorry, I'm rambling."

Catherine smiled. Nothing made her so happy as to see the excitement in David's eyes when he had developed a new technique or saved someone's life. "You just ramble all you want. I am so proud of you. How did this happen?"

Heinrich sat up. "You remember the article that I submitted to the New England Journal of Medicine? Well, it came out last week and when the committee read it they called. They've added it in their program. We'll have to be ready in three weeks, but I'm sure my parents will be happy to take care of the kids. What do you think?

Catherine started laughing. "What do you mean, what do I think? It's New York, isn't it? As far as I see it, a bad trip to New York is better than a good trip to almost anywhere else. You know, the last time we were in New York was when I picked you up from the hospital. That was almost ten years ago." She got up and sat in Heinrich's lap. She put her arms around his neck and gave him a light kiss. As she laid her head on his shoulder she said, "Ten wonderful years. I would never have dreamed they could be so wonderful. You cannot imagine how scared I was. You think I could go shopping?"

Heinrich sat up. "Wait a minute. One minute you're telling me how wonderful our life is, and the next you are talking about shopping. Are you trying to con me?"

Catherine started laughing and got up. "I always heard 'strike while the iron's hot.' I figured that as long as I had you in a good mood, I might as well ask. Seriously though, you need some new clothes and I thought we might as well get them while we are in New York."

181

Heinrich began shaking his head. "Now 'I' need new clothes and you were only thinking of my needs. You are such a wonderful person, thinking of my needs and all. I suppose you would do some shopping for yourself while you're at it?"

"Well, it would be foolish to be there and not pick up a few things for myself. Don't you think?" Not giving him time to answer she went on. "Besides that, I just wanted to look good for your colleagues. Wouldn't want to embarrass you by being out of style." She had a mischievous look in her eyes.

"I don't know if I could live with myself if you were caught dressed out of style. Of course you can go and get me some new clothes, and do pick up a few things for yourself while you're at it."

"Yes!" she squealed as she headed for the kitchen. "Talk to you later, I've got to call Ann Marie."

Life was good.

Chapter 30

Stadthagen, Germany

"We'll only be gone for four weeks," David said. "The conference will last four days and we can take a week or so to tour in America. I was thinking if I visited the university I attended, perhaps it would jog my memory..."

"I know how it bothers you not to have a memory of your past life, but I don't want you to get your hopes up. Remember years ago when you saw the man in the train station. What was his name...? Oh yes, Rotten. It distracted you for months. I don't want to lose you Heinrich. What if you do remember and your love for Ursula is so great you can no longer love me? I want you to have your memory, but I hate to see you in pain, and I don't want to take the chance of losing you."

"Don't be silly," David said. "Could I not love my arm or leg? I know what it is like not to have legs, but I would rather spend my life in a wheelchair than lose you. I made a pledge to you that day in the car and I will always love you. Now, quit changing the subject, the children can do without us for one month. They will be with Erik and May and their children. They will be hiking and swimming and sailing. They will need this before school starts again. If we stayed home, I would be working and would not be here to accompany them, so what is the difference?"

Jillian smiled. "Okay, you win. I don't know what is wrong with me, but I have a sense of dread about this. I know that I have always wanted to visit America, but somehow this bothers me. No reason, just me being a silly female."

"Then it is settled, Erik already has us staterooms on the Queen Elizabeth, sailing out of London in a fortnight. We have rooms at the Waldorf Astoria in New York and our acceptance has been wired to the convention."

Jillian just shook her head. "You are certainly sure of yourself. What if I had refused to go?"

David laughed. "Refused? I knew I had you that first night in Marseilles when you brazenly kissed me."

"You rascal!" Jillian pushed him down on their bed and jumped on him, straddling his waist. "Just remember I can still take you down anytime I wish!" With that she started tickling him.

"No!" David was laughing. "You are picking on me because I am a helpless cripple."

"That's right and don't you forget it!" She leaned over and kissed him long and hard. "Anytime I want, I can own you." She fell on his chest and they rolled over, still kissing...

The trip across the Atlantic took just over four days. Jillian was amazed. America seemed so far away yet four days later they were looking at the Statue of Liberty in New York harbor. She watched Heinrich carefully as they came into the harbor, but he showed no signs of recognition. She guessed that she had been a bit of a "ninny" about the whole mess. Well, not to worry, she was going to enjoy her holiday in America.

New York was so different from London or Hanover or Paris. It was too shiny. That was the only description that Jillian could come up with. Now that she was married to the famous Dr. Heinrich Müller, they received the best of treatment wherever they went. While the Waldorf Astoria was beautiful and nice, it was so new. In Europe, everywhere they went, the hotels had grace and charm. They were old and elegant with an almost reverent feeling

184

about them, a feeling similar to visiting an old cathedral. New York on the other hand was always in a hurry. There was no charm, just new and expensive. As they walked into their suite, she was reminded of the first time she had visited Heinrich at the south of France. Where were the gold-framed paintings or the gold leafed moldings? She remembered thinking that the hotel itself was a work of art. She wondered why she was being so critical. Maybe it stemmed from the feeling of foreboding that threatened to engulf her. She had always wanted to see America and New York especially, and see it she would, even if it killed her.

Since they only had one day before the conference started, she spent it dragging Heinie around shopping. She wanted at least two new outfits to wear at the functions they would be attending. David tried to reason with her that since they were in New York and knew no one, all of her clothes would appear new. This of course was ridiculous because the styles here would be more up to date, everyone knew that.

The first day of the conference David was a keynote speaker. He discussed the changes in medicine and needs Europe faced as a result of the war and the rebuilding process. Being both a doctor and owning one of the larger construction companies in Germany gave him a unique prospective on the problems and solutions they had found. At the end of his session, he was surrounded with people from all over the world, fielding questions from new surgical techniques to hospital design. Had he been on a marketing trip for his construction company, he would have found the trip a total success. Erik would be shocked at the number of proposals for new facilities and designs he had received. This of course was not the reason he was here. He already had all the business he could handle without adding a new division, and he didn't care. Erik on the other hand was going to light up like a Christmas tree when the offers started coming in. What David had not told Jillian or anyone else for that matter was that secretly he hoped to find the key to his past.

He was not sure of the driving force behind this desire. He was happy. He had a beautiful, intelligent wife who loved him. He had three wonderful children. There could be nothing in his past that could make him any happier than he was. Yet here it was, nagging at the back of his mind as always. There was something he needed to take care of. In the past few years he had discussed it, but only casually with Jillian - it made her uneasy. She said that she could not compete with his ghosts from the past and had a fear that they would drive away the happiness that was hers. Again David heard her say, "*What if you wake up some day and suddenly remember Ursula and your love for her is so strong that you have no room for me and the children?*" David didn't know the answer either, he only knew he had to find his past and face it whether it was painful or not.

He did know he had attended medical school at Harvard and hoped someone here might remember him. So far no one had stepped forward and started talking about his past as they had in his dreams. He no longer had a particular interest in the conference. He wanted to visit Harvard and see if he could remember anything. He would complete the conference more for protocol than anything else. Besides that, he had to keep up appearances for Jillian's benefit.

By the end of the second day of the conference, he was beside himself with anxiety. He had not met anyone from Harvard or anywhere else in America that knew him. He knew that it had been sixteen years since he left there, but felt that he must have been a hermit to have not made friends with anyone

"Heinie, aren't you ready yet? The reception starts in half an hour and you haven't even started getting dressed. Now this conference was your idea and I have a brand new evening dress that I bought for this occasion. Please hurry!"

David shook his head. *This is the part that I hate the most, and she blossoms at these gatherings. I feel a little like a displaced wife. Jillian is going to spend the evening talking with doctors about building new hospitals and I am going to stand around trying to figure out what to do.* "I'll be ready in just a minute! We won't be late!"

Chapter 31

Catherine walked aimlessly around the ballroom. David was over somewhere visiting with a group of doctors discussing some new technique or something of the sort. She just hated these events. She loved the dancing part, but David always gravitated to a group of doctors and began some boring discussion that she had no interest in - nor stomach for.

The grand ballroom was large with portable bars set up at each corner. It always amazed Catherine that even though the men in this room were all financially well off, if free liquor was being served, they would drink themselves senseless. Hence, crowds were gathered at each corner of the ballroom. She tried to stay away from those areas because the smoke was most dense there. Cigarettes, large cigars, and intellectual pipes were creating an odor that would take days to get out of her clothes. The large dance floor was almost wasted on the two-dozen couples showing off their skills. How she wished David would just come dance with her! She missed dancing. She turned as the band at the far end began playing *"I'll be seeing you."*

Oh how I love this song; it is so romantic. Tears formed in her eyes as she heard the words *'I'll find you in the morning sun...'* she was transported to those days so long ago when David was in prison camp. She was walking in the park holding little Davy and someone was parked nearby with it playing on the radio. How her heart had ached. As the words *'...I'll be looking at the moon, but I'll seeing you'* wound down, she quickly wiped her eyes hoping that no one saw. *I guess I must be a hopeless romantic but I just can't help myself. I am so glad that David came back from the war. I just don't know what I would have done without him.*

She was so mesmerized by her memories that she did not notice the man who had stopped and was staring at her. When she finally became aware of him, she turned and her breath caught. *What was it?* There was something strongly familiar about him. Was it his eyes? *How do I know this man?*

Suddenly he stepped forward and said, *"Ursula! Sie sagten, Sie waren tot ist."*

"I'm sorry, I don't speak German."

"Ursula! They said you were dead.   How can you be here?"

"I'm sorry, were you speaking to me? You must be confused, my name is Catherine."

Catherine was visibly shaken by this outburst.

"They said you were dead, how can you be here?"

The man reached out and put his arms around her and began to weep.

"They said you were dead, they said you were dead!" he moaned over and over again.

Catherine tried to step back and disentangle herself, but he only held her more tightly.

A beautiful woman stepped in and said in an English accent, "Heinrich, Heinrich, get hold of yourself. What are you doing? Ursula has been dead for years!"

Turning to Catherine she said, "I'm sorry, my husband is ill. This has never happened before. For some reason he thinks you are his wife who was killed during the war."

"I'm sorry, too. I must go," said Catherine. Her heart was pounding as she stepped away. She had never been touched that way by a stranger and it completely unnerved her. Yet, as she hurried away, she knew that there was something vaguely familiar about the handsome German. It was his eyes - yes his eyes.

Jillian led David back to their table. "Heinrich, what happened? What were you doing?"

"I don't know what happened!"

His hands were shaking. One of the doctors that had been talking with Jillian brought a glass of amber liquid over. "Here's some brandy, maybe it will help."

Jillian took the glass and handed it to David. "Thank you, Dr. Keene. That was very thoughtful."

He handed her a business card. "It was nothing, please give me a call. I would like to finish our discussion."

Jillian slipped the card in her purse. "I'll do that."

Turning back to David, she said, "Now tell me what happened."

"I am not sure what happened. I was 'mingling' as you like to put it, and suddenly I saw this woman. I knew her! I stood for a few minutes trying to figure out who she was. When she turned and looked at me, I just knew that this was my wife."

"But Ursula had brown hair and you know she is dead!"

"I know that! I have no idea what just happened. I knew she was my wife, and Ursula is the only wife I have ever had... except you, of course. That's when I fell apart and made an absolute fool of myself. I have got to know more, you know that, don't you?"

"Yes, but not now. We don't need the police hauling you off to jail in a strange country, or worse, the men with butterfly nets taking you away.

"Why don't we relax here a few moments and let everyone calm down."

Catherine found Heinrich standing with a group of doctors discussing some 'amazing' new procedure that they were developing.

"David, I must go."

"Catherine, what is wrong? You're white as a sheet. I'll take you to the room."

"Excuse me gentlemen, but my wife has taken ill."

As they rode up on the elevator, Heinrich put his arms around Catherine and said, "What happened, you're shaking. Did someone try to hurt you?"

"No, just a case of mistaken identity. But it was the strangest experience I've ever had." Just then the elevator stopped and the operator said, "12th floor, watch your step, please."

"I'll tell you the rest when we get to the room."

When they stepped into the room, Catherine immediately went over and sat on the couch. Heinrich closed the door, walked to her and sat down pulling her into his arms. "Now tell me what happened."

"I don't know why I'm so upset," she sobbed. "Maybe it was the hurt and lost look in his eyes. Well, anyway, I was standing by the tables near the edge of the dance floor, when this German man stepped over."

"How do you know he was German?"

"Well," she said, "he first spoke to me in German. He said, 'Ursula' and then something in German. I told him I didn't speak German so he switched to English and said, 'Ursula, they said you were dead.' He just kept saying it over and over. He wrapped his arms around me and started crying. It really scared me. I tried to get away but he wouldn't let go. I am so glad we were in a crowd. I don't know what I would have done if I had been alone, passed out probably. Then his wife stepped over and literally pulled him away from me and said, 'Heinrich, Ursula is dead, she died in the war. What are you doing?' She said that he had been ill and apologized. I felt so sorry for both of them, but I didn't know what to do. I just left. Somehow I feel guilty, like... I should have stayed and helped them figure it out. Like a coward though, I ran. Oh, what should I have done?"

Heinrich felt as if his heart had stopped beating and he felt a chill.

"I don't know if you could have done anything. If you want though, we can try to find them and talk about it. What did you say his name was?"

"I heard her call him Heinrich. David, what's wrong?"

"Did you say Heinrich?"

"Yes, do you know him?"

"No! Where is the list of those in attendance?"

"I believe it is on the desk," Catherine turned. "I'll get it for you."

"No, you stay here, I'll get it."

As Heinrich was walking back from the desk with the list, Catherine said, "The strangest thing is that there was something familiar about him, I don't know what, but I had the feeling we had met before."

Heinrich sat down beside Catherine and hurriedly scanned the list. "Here it is, Heinrich Müller." His hand shook. "Why don't I go down and see if there is anything I can do; or at least see if he is someone we have met before."

As he hurried down the hall to the elevator his mind was spinning. *What is going on? Is someone pretending to be me so he can blackmail me? That's got to be it. Someone has found out about me and is trying to scare me into entering into some scheme. I guess they are going to ask for money and then bleed me to death.*

Just then the elevator arrived. The operator pulled the door open. "What floor please?"

"Mezzanine, thank you."

As he arrived at the mezzanine floor, he began searching the crowd. How was he going to find him? He didn't even know what the man looked like. He was about to ask someone if they knew Dr. Müller when he saw a couple seated at a table in the corner. There was something familiar about the man. They were talking intently and did not notice as he approached. As he drew near, he could hear the man saying, "I don't care if it's not reasonable, I know that woman from somewhere."

As he got a good look at the man, he was startled. *Good God! It's me! Well, at least a poor copy of what I used to look like.* He just couldn't believe his eyes. *What in the world is going on?*

Heinrich moved closer. "Excuse me, sir. Are you Dr. Heinrich Müller?" *What bizarre trick could they be playing? Maybe they were using makeup. This was too far for anyone to go.*

The man, startled, looked up from his conversation. "Yes, I am Dr. Müller. Can I help you?"

Let's take the bull by the horns. "I noticed on the program that you build hospitals in Europe."

Dr. Müller looked at him. "Yes, we do. My wife runs the construction business. Why don't you leave a card and she can contact you? I'm sorry, I don't mean to put you off, but something has happened that we must handle."

Heinrich didn't want to reveal too much. He reluctantly passed a card over and said, "It's okay. I just wanted to chat. Maybe some other time, have a nice evening."

David had a concerned look on his face. "Thank you, sir and you have a nice evening as well."

Heinrich turned and walked away. *What is going on? I gave him his opening and he didn't take it. I believe that my best bet is to get out of here as fast as I can. I'm not sure if it will do any good, he is bound to know where I live. Why in the world did I give them a card! I wish I had never come here. I am too open and vulnerable. I guess I have been David so long that I have begun to think it was so. What could I have been thinking?*

The elevator was still there when he arrived so he stepped on and asked for the twelfth floor. The elevator operator looked at him in a quizzical manner "Are you alright sir? If you're not, I am sure we can find a doctor in this bunch."

192

"I'm fine, just a little tired I guess." He gave her a weak smile. "Thanks for asking though."

"Here you are sir, why don't you take it easy. Things always seem to work themselves out." The elevator jerked a little as she evened it up with the floor. "Watch your step." The door opened with a clank and he stepped off.

Heinrich wondered why all of a sudden he was so visible. He could have ridden this elevator a hundred times and the operator would have never noticed him. Now, everyone seems to be taking an interest in his welfare.

He tried to compose himself before he opened the door to the room. He didn't need to upset Catherine anymore than she was already. What would she do if she found out? She was his whole life.

He stepped into the room to find Catherine more composed. She had changed into her nightgown and was propped up on the bed.

Catherine turned and looked as he stepped into the room. "Did you talk to the man?"

"Yes I did. He wasn't anyone I knew. He didn't know me either. I think he might have had too much to drink and got carried away. I felt sorry for him but there's not much to do." Heinrich took off his coat and loosened his tie. "Why don't we just go to bed and see what tomorrow brings."

"I think that's a good idea sweetheart. You've already given your speech, why don't we relax and not worry about the conference?" She looked at him pleadingly. "Can't we just take a little vacation for the next few days and play hooky? Besides that you already know more than the rest of them put together." She stuck her lower lip out in a fake pout. "I get so tired going to luncheons and having to make pleasant conversation."

Heinrich felt relieved. "That sounds like a good idea to me."

"Okay. Let's start now." She patted the bed next to her.

Chapter 32

The next few days were a whirlwind. They went sight seeing and rode to the top of the Empire State Building. The hotel made a picnic lunch and they went for a picnic in Central Park. The carriage ride driver began to expect their visits and they became friends. He wondered occasionally if they were newlyweds because they snuggled and laughed so much. Catherine couldn't remember when she had been so relaxed. These past years she had been worried either about David's health or having babies, or the chicken pox or something else. Now she didn't have to worry about anything but what their next adventure would be. Finally though, reality caught up with them. David had called his partners and had them take his patients for a few extra days. That too was used up. It wasn't that she didn't love her life, because she did. These last few days were different though. David had been so serious since he had returned from the war. He had been so intent on regaining those years he had lost. Now suddenly, he was relaxed. He seemed to be living every moment they were together as if he didn't want it to stop. He laughed, joked, and acted silly, not the way a distinguished and respected doctor would act. Occasionally she wondered if something was wrong, but she didn't want to break the spell by asking questions.

On the morning they were to leave for home, she lay in his arms and told him how much she loved him. "When I was a young girl I dreamed of having a wonderful husband, beautiful children, and a loving home. I didn't really believe that I could be so lucky as to have them but here I am. If I were to die tomorrow, I could not have wished for a more wonderful life. Thank you my darling, thank you." With that she rolled over and kissed him. As they tenderly made love, a tear quietly slipped from her eye and trailed down her cheek.

David and Jillian decided to wait a few days before pursuing the incident with Catherine any further. Jillian had quietly asked around and found that the woman Heinrich had accosted was Catherine Strauss, wife of Dr. David Strauss. Their thought was that if Heinrich actually knew this woman from the past, pieces of it might appear voluntarily. Jillian talked with her husband about getting too upset the way he had done with the man in the train station. David reluctantly agreed, but in his mind he knew he was not going to let this go away. Jillian had wanted to do some shopping in New York and used this time as an excuse. Even though the war had been over for ten years, Germany was still living a Spartan existence and very stylish clothes were hard to find. She did not like shopping in Paris, because the French had suffered severely at the hands of Germany during the war and tended to be extra rude when they encountered Germans. The Americans, while they had suffered from the war, had not had their cities destroyed and seemed to be more forgiving.

One day they bought hot dogs from a vendor in Central Park and sat on some newspapers under a tree while they ate. It was a wonderful day and as they were talking, Jillian realized that they had not taken any pictures together. Generally Heinrich had taken the pictures of her at different places insisting that the camera would break if she took a picture of him. She and David went over to the man that sold them the hot dogs and David asked if he would take a picture of them together.

"I would be glad to." He took the camera and snapped a couple of pictures with them by his hotdog stand. "So, what brings you to New York from Ohio? On vacation or business?"

David was startled. "Ohio? We're from Germany. Why would you think we were from Ohio?"

Mr. Hot Dog laughed. "Hey, don't kid a kidder. I was raised there and I would know that accent anywhere."

David looked at Jillian and laughed. "Well, I guess you got me there. We were just trying to not look like hicks from out of town. Thanks a lot for taking the pictures, our kids will love them."

As they returned to their room, they both tried to keep the excitement out of their voices as they discussed what the man had told them. Heinrich had an American accent and from Ohio of all places. Jillian had a dark feeling about this. She didn't want to dampen her husband's excitement, but how would he have acquired an Ohio accent? They'd heard that Ohio had a large German population and that opened all kind of possibilities. Suddenly Jillian got a wild idea. "I wonder where Dr. and Mrs. Strauss are from. Where's his card?"

David began to look through all the papers on the coffee table. "Here it is. He's from Roquefort, Ohio. I wonder how close that is to New York. Call down and have the concierge get us a map of the United States."

A little while later they were pouring over their newly acquired map. "Here it is." David was pointing on the map. "Roquefort, Ohio. It's about twenty miles east of Columbus. What do you think it means? What made you think to check where the Strauss' were from?"

"Well." Jillian was smiling proudly. "I was trying to put everything together. For instance, where would you have met his wife? How would you have acquired an Ohio accent? Now, suppose she was a medical student and the two of you met when you were at Harvard. You had an affair and so you remember making love to her. It has been a number of years since you were at medical school. Add that to the surgery you have had due to your injuries during the war and maybe she didn't recognize you. On the other hand, maybe she did recognize you but she didn't want her husband to find out about you so she fled. Of course the worst of all would be that she was married at the time you had your torrid little affair and she is afraid her husband would shoot you if you unknowingly blurted out the whole thing right in front of him. I vote for the last one.

I don't know how any woman could be around you for any period of time and not fall in love."

With that she lovingly gave him a quick kiss. "Let's go to bed and worry about it tomorrow. Tonight I'll see if I can keep my hands off you."

"Don't try so hard," he said, and put his arms around her and gave her a long kiss.

A few days later they had to make a decision. The conference was over and Jillian had so many clothes that they would have to book an extra room on the ship just for baggage. David's memory had not come up with extra clues and he was getting anxious.

"Okay," said Jillian nervously, "we've come this far, let's don't stop now. I know that you want to track this as far as you can. I will support you all the way. I don't want to lose you, but I can't compete with a ghost."

"Don't be silly," said David. "You own me and you own my heart. There is nothing to worry about."

"But what if you find that you were in love with someone else? I don't know what I would do," said Jillian.

The next morning they checked out of the hotel. Before leaving they made a tentative reservation for two weeks in the future. They had the hotel store their extra baggage to be picked up on their return. Jillian thought how nice the people in New York were. They had heard such terrible stories about New Yorkers and she had been afraid that it would be like London at the end of the war. They took a taxi to Grand Central Station and when she walked in, she was overcome with its size. Jillian's mind jumped back to a night long ago in London. She was with her beloved Roger, the man she was to marry. Like today, there was turmoil in the large terminal. People were hurrying with looks of concern, babies were crying and families were being separated. She stood there with tears in her eyes as Roger assured her that he would return. She never saw him again. Less than two weeks later he was killed on the beachhead at Anzio, Italy. Just like that and life as she knew it was over. Tears came to her eyes once again as she thought of Roger standing there so gallant, so proud. A shiver ran down her spine. *Would this bring peace or turmoil?* Heinrich was excited that his life may be coming together; she was worried that hers may be coming apart.

The train station was so noisy. People were everywhere; announcements were coming in on the public address system. Whistles were blowing and travelers were hurrying to reach their trains. There appeared to be multiple societies thrown together in an incongruous mass. Businessmen with fine suits and newspapers tucked under their arms hurried for their commuters, while older people were saying goodbye to their grandchildren. Smiles for those arriving; tears for those leaving. She saw the rich and the poor side by side as though it had always been that way. Once again she was in London at the end of the war. Ruin and devastation were everywhere. Her train to Southampton was more like a cattle car than a passenger vehicle. The shrill whistle of a train brought her back to the present. They were at the ticket window and Heinrich bought two first class tickets to Ohio. They would have their own compartment with a bed above the seats. How different life was. Still, Jillian was uncomfortable. She had had a bad feeling about this trip from the beginning, now she wished they had never come here. It seemed only yesterday that she was so excited to come to this great land, a land that had not been ripped apart by the war that destroyed so much of her life. Now that same war could once again destroy her life, not quickly, surgically, as it had before, but quietly as memory upon memory reappears and a new Heinrich emerges... a Heinrich that loves someone from his past.

Chapter 33

As they arrived at the station at Roquefort, David felt excitement coursing through his body. Could this be the answer to so many questions? What lay in store? He wondered again why he felt this drive to uncover the past. He had such a good life in the present, yet there was still this drive to remember. It was as if he had only half a life, one that started ten years ago in an American hospital. Maybe the people in this town would remember him, and the giant dam would be removed and allow the past to flood in.

The town was so familiar to him that he was beside himself. He was like a kid in a candy shop, not knowing which way to turn and having a delight at every move. They took a taxi to the hotel in the middle of downtown. It was not much when compared to their New York accommodations, but it was nice enough.

After they were settled in, David suggested that they take an afternoon walk to relax. "Maybe we'll find one of those quaint shops people always talk about."

Jillian smiled, trying to react enthusiastically, "Let's do, it will be fun."

As they stepped out of the hotel, they turned right and only walked a short distance when David stopped before a jewelry store. It was called 'Strauss and Son Fine Jewelry.' As he looked inside, he had a mental image of every room.

199

"Let's step inside," he said with a slight tremor in his voice.

The door jingled with a familiar sound as he stepped in. "May I be of service?" said a familiar voice with a German accent.

"Perhaps you can," he answered. "I believe I may have been here before the war. I have been showing my wife a little of America before we return to our home in Germany."

"You are German? You sound so much like an American. Where in Germany do you come from?" said the older gentleman.

"We're from Stadthagen," said David. "Are you familiar with it?"

"Of course," said the older man. "My family emigrated from Hanover when I was a young man. Stadthagen is only a short distance away. I have been there many times. What is your family name?"

"Müller, I am Heinrich Müller," said David.

"Müller, that name is so familiar, it has been such a long time," said the man. "Was your father a doctor?"

"Yes, he was," said David excitedly. "Did you know him?"

"Well, I certainly knew of him," said the man. "I guess everyone knew of him. He did so many wonderful things. I believe you lived in the schloss on a large hill at the edge of town, is that correct?"

David was so excited to meet someone who knew his family. Maybe this would be the answer. "Yes, on the Strassen Strasse, he answered excitedly.

"It is so wonderful to meet someone from the Fatherland," said the man. "How is your father doing? Did he come through the war okay?"

"No, he didn't," said David. "He and my mother were killed when an allied bomber crashed into our home after bombing Hanover."

"So sad," said the old man. "The war hurt so many people. It was bad enough that the Nazis took our young men to war, but so many homes were destroyed and so much heartache on both sides. So, how about you, what are you doing in America?"

"I'm a doctor," said David. "My wife and I were at a medical convention in New York and I thought I would show her a little of America while we were here."

"A doctor," exclaimed the man. "My son is also a doctor. He was at a convention in New York this week past. Perhaps you met him there. His name is David Strauss."

Suddenly the man looked a little embarrassed. "Please excuse me; I just realized that I haven't introduced myself. I'm Karl Strauss. I own this shop. I guess I was so excited to meet someone from home that I forgot myself."

"I am so pleased to meet you, Herr Strauss. Let me introduce my wife Jillian," said David.

"I know that it is a bit forward of me," said Karl, "but we are having a few friends and family over tonight and I was wondering if you would accept an invitation for dinner. My wife gets so homesick for Germany. She would be delighted to talk with someone from home."

Looking at Jillian for her approval, David said, "We would be delighted Herr Strauss."

"Thank you so much," said Karl. "We will look forward to visiting with you. Where are you staying?"

"We are just down the street at the Bismarck Hotel," said David.

"A nice place," said Karl. "I will send a car around for you. About seven o'clock?"

"Seven o'clock it is," David said as he reached out and shook the man's hand.

That evening as they waited for the car, Jillian was feeling nervous. Things were happening so fast. Just two weeks ago, life was normal. Heinrich had not thought about the past for many years. He had a good practice, not that he needed it. The construction company was doing well, and their home had been completely restored. She really didn't need nor want this in her life. In the back of her mind she had always hoped for a restoration of Heinrich's memory, but never without fear. Now, every new revelation added to her dismay. Who was this man she was living with? Never in her wildest dreams had she thought that they would wind up in a small town in Middle America uncovering his past. What could he have been doing here? Suddenly a black Cadillac was outside the door. A cold wind whipped at them as they stepped out of the hotel. Jillian pulled her wrap closer as she and David got in the back.

The Strauss home was large by American standards. The lower floor was well lit with only a few lights on in the upper two floors. A curved driveway ran across the front with an extension on one side that led to a portico. The driveway extended around to the back with a bank of garages that were visible as their car drove to the front.

The first thing David saw upon entering the Strauss home was a large portrait of a young soldier in dress uniform. David recognized him as the man he had met at the convention in New York. Strangely enough, the Strauss home was exactly where he wished to be when he decided to come to Roquefort. The other strange thing was the familiarity he felt. He didn't remember ever being here, but he felt comfortable.

He was also was shocked at the number of people in attendance. It this represented a few friends and family, he wondered what a 'real' dinner party was like in America. As he and Jillian were escorted in, Herr Strauss and his wife walked over. "Doctor Müller let me introduce my wife Hilde."

David in turn introduced Jillian to Mrs. Strauss. The Strausses then took them each by the arm and began to introduce them to their friends. David felt a wave of emotion as he saw the Strausses together. He didn't know what was happening to him. He didn't normally feel these emotions, only with Jillian. As a doctor, he'd learned to keep them in check. He always felt care and concern for his patients, but reality required him to keep a thin barrier between them. Then it happened. Karl said, "Herr Müller, I would like to introduce you to my son David and his wife Catherine."

David felt as if his heart had stopped. Here she was, and the feelings were the same. She was absolutely stunning in her beauty and poise, at least until she saw him. The color left her face and she became flustered.

David reached out, took her hand and said, "I believe we have met before." He couldn't believe how calm he was. "I think I owe you an apology. Too many memories, too little to eat, and too much to drink can be a lethal combination."

With that he turned to Karl Strauss and said, "I guess I did meet your son and his wife at the convention in New York. I just did not know their names."

Heinrich couldn't believe it. *What was this man doing? He had nerve, that's for sure.* Heinrich wanted to drag him outside and beat the truth out of him. *How am I going to get out of this? Ten years down the drain. There's no way they will believe that my intentions were honorable. The old tyrant is going to nail my hide to the wall. If I had run for governor and won, he would have backed me to the bitter end. As it is, I have only raised his grandson to be kind and decent, supported his daughter-in-law, and healed the sick. This of course was nothing that Papa would consider important. Well, I guess I might as well ride it out and see how it plays.*

The evening went rather smoothly as David was able to explain to the Strausses the changes that had occurred in Germany after the war. He noticed that their son showed a particular interest when he discussed the renovations they had made to the family home. He was quite surprised when David explained how they had turned a portion of the property into an orphanage for children displaced as a result of the war. When asked why he did this, David said, "First of all, something needed to be done for the sake of the children. The other reason may seem strange, but my father always said, 'Bad things happen because good men do nothing.' I believe we could have done something to stop the war before it happened. As it is, we did nothing. My work with the orphans is an apology to the children for my part in their pain."

When David said, "Bad things happen because good men do nothing," Herr Strauss looked at the man he believed to be his son and said, "That is what I have been saying to you again and again." Looking at David he said, "My son could have been governor or even President of the United States, but no, he just wants to be a doctor. Did you know that he received the Congressional Medal of Honor? He could have written his own ticket, but no, he wanted no part of it!"

David wondered how the junior Strauss had been able to deal with this all these years. I certainly could not have done it. He wished he could remember his own father. He only knew what others had said about him. He was certain though, that his father would have supported him no matter what he had chosen to do. He would certainly have never humiliated him in public the way Herr Strauss had. David decided then that he did not care to have dealings with the man again. He just was not the pleasant shopkeeper they had met earlier this day.

The highlight of David's evening was Catherine. He simply couldn't keep his eyes off her. He only hoped that Jillian hadn't noticed. After his embarrassing introduction to Catherine in New York, he didn't want to seem overly interested. Yet, David did believe that somehow she was connected with his past. He couldn't imagine what... but there was a connection.

As Catherine looked at Dr. Müller, there was something familiar about him. When she looked at his eyes, she felt as if he was someone she knew and he was wearing a disguise. That was it, just like at Halloween when a friend comes over wearing a mask and all you can see of his real identity is his eyes. She knew those eyes. She knew she shouldn't be staring, what would people think? She had to know who he really was. As she studied this stranger, she suddenly turned and looked at her husband. He quickly turned away and began to talk with his mother. That was odd; it was as if he was intentionally avoiding her.

"Catherine, how are you?"

"Fine, Amy and you?"

"Couldn't be better, please forgive me for intruding, but I heard you have a new pool man and I have been frantically searching for someone to help. Carter, our old pool man moved to Columbus. I guess the grass is greener in the big city."

"No problem. I'm sorry to say that I can't help you though, Roberto, the new guy did a terrible job. I paid him what he asked and told him 'don't bother to come back.' I guess..."

David had been idly listening as the ladies talked. When Catherine said, "don't bother to come back..." He lost his breath. That was it, the same voice and the same words locked soundly into his memory. He quickly turned to Catherine to ask her about the phrase he remembered but she was deeply involved in discussing swimming pool workers. David became agitated, wouldn't they ever stop talking? He wanted to interrupt but didn't want a repeat of his New York experience. It wouldn't pay to get tossed out now when he was so close.

The evening drew to a close and he was disappointed. He knew that Catherine was somehow involved, but he didn't get the opportunity to speak with her alone. In the end, the only information he had gained was that somehow Catherine was involved. No new information there. The only thing he knew for sure was that he was glad he was not Herr Strauss' son. The man was almost intolerable! Had he been the man's son, they would have been at one another's throat at the first comment the old man had made and it would have been downhill from there. He made the comment to Jillian on the drive home.

She said, "You shouldn't be so judgmental, he only wants what's best for his son."

David replied, "No, he only wants what he wants. He doesn't care what his son wants. To him his son is only a means to an end. I'll bet he jumped up and cheered when he found that his son had received the Congressional Medal of Honor; not because he was a hero, but because it was his ticket to the White House."

"I noticed that you could not keep your eyes off Catherine Strauss," said Jillian, changing the subject.

Oh great, thought David. *How am I going to deal with this?*

Just then they arrived at the hotel. They thanked the driver and went in. David was quiet as they went up the elevator to the room.

As they began to get undressed David said, "I'm sorry if I embarrassed you, it's just that I am sure I know her and that's the nearest thing to a clue that I have had for a long time."

"Why don't you just drop it," said Jillian pleadingly. "We have had a good life for the last ten years without knowing the past. All you are going to do is stir the water and when it settles you will be exactly where you were. It would not be so bad except you will be depressed for months afterward. Remember when you saw the man you called Rotten? You spent weeks searching for him and nothing. Promise me that if this does not turn out the way you hope that you will drop it altogether. Please?"

"I'm so sorry," said David. "I know how this must look to you and I will try to drop it if it does not work out. I can't make promises though. If you had a child that was lost, and there was a chance you could find her, wouldn't you keep looking?"

"Yes," said Jillian looking at the floor.

"That's what it's like. A part of me is wandering out there, lost, and it's up to me to keep searching. I won't be complete until I find my lost past."

As Heinrich and Catherine arrived at their home, they sat in the car a few minutes before going in.

"Your father was in rare form tonight," said Catherine. "I can't imagine what Dr. and Mrs. Müller must think. I was so embarrassed for them. I was also very proud of you. I know it was hard not to get in an argument with him. His old political cronies were enjoying it though. I believe they loved every minute of it."

"I'm sure that you are right," said Heinrich. "I would have been surprised if he had not brought it up. Let's go on in."

Later as they were preparing for bed, Catherine said, "Are you sure you have never met Dr. Müller? There's something familiar about him. I get the strangest feeling when I'm around him. It's like he has a great secret that he's hiding; and yet, I feel as if he's looking for something. I don't know; I just can't put my finger on it."

"I don't know what the man's up to," said Heinrich. "Yes, there is a chance that I might know him but you wouldn't, it's impossible. I think he's up to no good."

"Really? Where would you have met him?" said Catherine. "Why would it have been impossible?"

"Well, the details are a little fuzzy," said Heinrich. "It was during the last part of the war when I was in the prison camp. I met a German doctor and we became good friends. I have tried over the years to remember his name, but I can't. On the last day of the war, as our camp was being liberated, we came under artillery fire from the Russians. As you know, the hospital received several direct hits, which is how I got beat up so bad. My friend was killed. I know because I personally checked his body and I know he died. There is no way he could have lived," he said with a quiver in his voice. "I know he was dead." Tears began to flow.

Catherine put her arms around him and said, "I'm sorry I brought up such a painful experience. I remember you talking about your friend and I should have known better than ask"

"It's alright," said Heinrich. "That's all in the past. I don't know who this man is or what he has on his mind. He looks a little familiar, but he doesn't seem to know me. I wonder if he's trying to pull some kind of swindle. You see this sort of thing on television all the time. The next thing you know, he'll pretend that he *is* my old friend and try to borrow money. I guess I'm trying to say I don't think the man can be trusted." He wondered if Catherine would believe even a little of this load he was dumping. It could work though; she did watch a lot of TV and was wary of strangers.

Chapter 34

The next morning David snuggled up to Jillian in their warm bed and said, "Catherine, I had the strangest dream last night."

He felt Jillian stiffen before she rose up and said with a loud voice, "What do you mean, Catherine? What are you up to?"

David jumped up and said, "Jillian? What are we doing here?"

He jumped out of bed and began searching for his clothes. *What is going on? What will Catherine do if she finds out I have been sleeping with Jillian?*

"What do you mean what are we doing here?" Jillian said with irritation showing. "This is our hotel room. Are you losing your mind!?"

David didn't say a word; he just walked into the bathroom and began to wash his face with cold water. He saw his reflection and was shocked. *What has happened to me?* As his mind began to clear, he realized he was married to Jillian. But why? He was supposed to be married to Catherine. Who was Catherine with last night? He knew he had to come up with some answers before someone decided he was crazy and had him committed.

He walked back into the bedroom drying his face with a towel, he said, "I'm sorry dear, I just had one of those intense dreams that got me disoriented. When I woke up, I had absolutely no idea where I was."

"Why were you talking about Catherine?" asked Jillian.

"I have no idea," said David. "To be honest, I can't remember what the dream was about. It just seemed to fade away after I awakened. Let's order up some breakfast while I shave."

This time when he went into the bathroom he switched on the light. He almost passed out when he looked into the mirror. *What's happened to my face?* The man he looked at in the mirror was a total stranger. He reached up and began to rub his face to see if it was real or if someone was playing a joke on him with makeup. His hands told him that it was real enough. *If I go back into the bedroom and ask what happened to my face, she is going to think that I am a total idiot.* He reached under his jaw and pinched just in case this was some face putty. *Ouch! No, it wasn't face putty.* He quickly shaved and went into the bedroom.

"I think I am going out for a walk," he said casually. "There are some nice little stores around, why don't you go out and see if you can spend a little money. Let's meet back here at noon and we'll have some lunch and then go sightseeing."

"It won't take a minute to get dressed," she said. "I'll go with you."

"No, I would like to just go for a walk and see where my mind takes me," he said. "If you are around, I'll spend all my time looking at you and thinking what a lucky guy I am and I won't get a thing done."

"You do have a way with words," she said. "I'll see you at noon."

As David left the hotel, he turned to the left this time to avoid the jewelry store. He began to walk and everything looked almost as if he had just left it. Maybe some fresh paint here or there, or new awnings, but just as he remembered it. He turned right two blocks down the street and before he knew it, he was passing the high school. Across the street was the drug store. He stepped in and walked to the back booth and sat down. Memories of high

210

school, basketball games, and laughter crowded his mind. He was back! He was not sure where he had been, but he was back. Tears welled up in his eyes as he remembered Catherine sitting across from him with blue and white ribbons in her hair.

He was brought back to reality when the waitress said, "What can I get you?"

He ordered a cherry vanilla Coke. The waitress looked at him and said, "Have we... never mind," and then turned away.

A few minutes later David was enjoying something he had forgotten existed. He thought he could drink this forever. There are times in your life when even the most insignificant things can take on new meaning. Just then the bell on the door rang and in came Julie Anderson, the biggest gossip in town. She was a little older than when he last saw her, but it was her.

Here I am, not knowing if I am left handed or right, but I can remember Julie Anderson. Must be one of life's ironies.

She sat at the next booth facing him. *That's her style. Doesn't want anything to get past her.*

"Hi Julie," he said.

Startled, she said, "Excuse me? Have we met?"

He remembered then that he had a new face. Apparently he was the only one that knew. Thinking quickly he said, "No, I'm afraid not. Someone told me that if I met a stunning redhead in Parker's Drug Store, it would likely be Julie Anderson, so I took a chance."

With a slight blush she got up and moved to his booth and sat across from him.

"Would you be Heinrich Müller, the German guy that visited the Strausses last night? You don't sound German," she said.

"You're very perceptive," he said, "How did you come up with the name?"

211

"You're in small town America now," she returned. "Not much happens here that everyone doesn't know about. You're sitting in her booth you know."

"Whose booth?" he asked.

"Catherine's of course," she answered.

"Catherine's?" he queried.

"Yes, Catherine Strauss," she said. "That's her place you are sitting in."

David pretended to be looking around. "I did not know that people owned booths in drug stores," he said.

"No, silly," she said, "She doesn't actually own it, that's just where she always sits when she comes in here."

David quickly finished his drink and said, "I must be going now, Mrs. Strauss may come in and find that I have stolen her booth." With that he stood up and walked out.

As he walked down the street his head was spinning. *Heinrich Müller? How can I be Heinrich Müller and who was that with my wife?*

He soon found the park he played in as a child and settled on a bench with his back to the sun. The sun felt good. It was one of the constants in the world. No matter where you were, it was there, giving peace and stability. He leaned back and tried to relax. So much had happened in the last few hours he needed to make sense of it. One more new revelation and his mind would go into overload. Clearing his thoughts, he let himself go into a half sleep. As his mind drifted back, he remembered those months before he went into the army. He and Catherine were in their little apartment arguing. She was telling him he needed to be a man. He had a family of his own and it was time for him to make his own decisions. How could he love and hate the same person at the same time? He remembered being torn in two directions. If he went one way he would disrespect his father. If he went the other way, his wife would have no respect for him. There was no way to win. *If I go in the army, maybe I'll get blown up and I won't have to deal with it.* She was such a beautiful girl and yet the loathing in her eyes made him want to walk away.

His next recollections were working in a hospital. People saluted him and said "sir." That was a good feeling. He was helping wounded soldiers. There was a feeling of love and respect. He was happy at last.

Now he smelled death all around. It was hopeless; he was pretending to help the wounded when he knew there was no hope. Oh yes, the death train. Tears drifted down his cheeks as he remembered the faces. Faces without names, no wait, there was Hall, Rocky, Johnson, and all the others. He could see them now, dying without hope. There was the unmarked grave in the misty darkness. Did their parents know?

The lights of the prison camp burned brightly as they arrived. Fear gripped his heart. Now all the wishes to be blown up vanished. He wanted to live. He did not want to wind up, as a body in an unmarked grave like so many of the others. He wanted his family to know what happened. He could see the hospital now with the remaining wounded being cared for by him and Heinrich. Yes, Heinrich... Heinrich Müller. He became my mentor. He was German, but he was the best doctor that I ever worked with. He could do more with less than any man I have ever known. There were the talks and the laughter. There they were - sitting on the porch in those old chairs that some of the men had made from scraps. Then there were the explosions. Got to get to the wounded... then blackness.

The next scenes that crossed his mind were he and Jillian loading bricks in a wheelbarrow. They were at the schloss. So much work to do, Uncle Hans and Erik were there helping. It was such a feeling of accomplishment to see everything come together. There were vacations at Mallorca with the kids. How he loved those rascals. He wished they were with him now.

Suddenly he came out of his reverie. How did he wind up married to Jillian? Why were people calling him Heinrich Müller and who was this person calling himself David Strauss and living with his wife?

It seemed to him that he had concatenated two lives, the first half was his and the second half was that of his friend

Heinrich. *What now? I guess the next step is to confront this guy calling himself David Strauss.* He checked his watch and realized that he needed to meet Jillian. He didn't know what happened to his first marriage, but he didn't want to screw this one up.

After talking with the concierge, David was able to secure a rental car. He also had the hotel dining room make and pack a picnic basket.

When Jillian arrived back at the hotel, she had very few packages, but was smiling. "What a quaint little town," she said. "I didn't find any new clothes, but I still did not waste my time. Did you know that everyone in this town knows everyone else's business and they are not shy about sharing it?"

"Why don't you put those things away and let's go for a drive and a picnic. You can share all the gossip while we eat," he said.

As they drove through the countryside, David's mind wandered through the beautiful fields he he'd seen as a young boy. The trees were wearing their fall clothes and it was indeed breathtaking. Suddenly David turned the car on a narrow road that wound between the fields and through a small forest. They came to a clearing and he pulled over and switched off the engine. They were near a small lake surrounded by trees. A large oak next to the clearing had a limb sticking out over the water. Hanging from the limb was a well-worn rope with the end tossed through a fork in the tree about four feet from the base. A picnic table with green peeling paint stood about twenty feet from the lake and well clear of the rope. Judging from the vegetation on the ground surrounding the table, this place had not been used for some time.

"This is a lovely place," said Jillian. "How did you ever find it?"

"Just lucky, I guess," said David.

"You'll have to do better than that," said Jillian.

"To be honest with you, I don't know how I knew of this place," he lied. "I just seemed to remember that it was here."

214

"Something has happened," said Jillian. "You seem to be different today, a little calmer, more self-assured. Do you want to tell me about it?"

"I am not sure that I know myself," said David. "Suddenly this morning I remembered this town. I don't know why or how, but I do. As far as being self-assured, it's just an illusion. This is the one thing I do know, for the first time in ten years I have a memory that's my own. This is not one that Uncle Hans has told me about or one that I have read about. This one is mine and mine alone and it is wonderful."

"Don't you think that the memories we have together are wonderful?" she asked with an impish smile.

"You know what I mean, now don't start acting like one of those women," he laughed.

"What kind of women would that be?"

"You know - jealous. The kind that don't want a man to have had a life before they met."

"I'm sorry, I was just teasing. I'm glad you have a memory of your very own."

"Enough of that!" he said. "Let's eat and you can become a small town American and spread the local gossip."

They took a checked tablecloth out of the basket and spread it on the table. *Why do we always have checked tablecloths on picnics?* Inside the basket were fried chicken, little sandwiches with the crust cut off, potato salad and, of course, apple pie. There were also two wine glasses and a thermos of milk.

When Jillian asked about the milk he said, "The cook said, 'You'll never find wine that tastes as good as a glass of cold milk on a picnic.' So I toast to you my love, and old memories, and new ones."

With that they clinked their glasses and proceeded to have the best meal they had eaten in weeks.

As they were eating their apple pie, David said, "You have been wined and dined, now for the scoop. What's this gossip you've been holding back on me?"

"Well," said Jillian leaning across the table as though someone might hear. "This comes straight from Margie Johansson who works for Marcel's Jewelry down the street from Herr Strauss. She could tell us this since we really don't know the Strausses. (Jillian tried to imitate Margie) 'It seems that something happened to David in the war. Nobody is sure if something happened to his private parts in that explosion or not, but the word is that David would not sleep with Catherine for months after he came home.'"

"Now how would anyone know that?" asked David with a disgusted tone in his voice.

"Interesting that you should ask," said Jillian sounding like Margie. "She heard it from Janis Copeland who got it from Marjean Kelly their housekeeper. Now Marjean said they stayed in the old man's house when David first got home because he was still recovering from his injuries from the explosion."

"What explosion?" interrupted David.

"Who's telling this, me or you?" said Jillian with a mock frown.

"You," said David.

"Okay, that will come in due time," said Jillian. "Now, where was I? Oh yes, now she said, trying to sound like Margie, 'that he claimed to have amnesia. That's where you can't remember anything.'" She smiled. 'Have you heard of that before? Most likely he didn't want to remember her... everyone knows they were having family trouble before he left for the war. Some say that he joined the army just to get away from her. The old man had political connections and could have gotten him deferred if he wanted to. Well, he claimed that he could not remember her so he just didn't feel right sleeping with a stranger!'"

Then she tilted her head, lowered her voice a little and said out of the side of her mouth, still imitating Margie, "If it had been me, I'd have introduced myself and hopped in bed with him in a New York minute. He is one good-looking hunk of man if you know what I mean. Anyway, nobody believed that tale, 'cause if he could remember how to cut people up he would certainly remember his own wife. It turned out that he is the best surgeon that this area has ever had. People come from all over to get him to operate. They say he learned everything in that prison camp."

"Prison camp?" asked David.

Jillian waved her hand like she was swooshing a fly and continued, "He just lost his ambition though, says he's not interested in going to some big hospital, just wants to stay home. You can hardly blame him though, being off to war all those years. Well, to make a long story short, the only way she could get him in the sack was to marry him. Have you ever heard anything so ridiculous? She had to marry her own husband. Anyway, they had Judge Chandler come to the house and had a full blown wedding. Not like the first time they were married, but a full wedding just the same. It was at the old man's house, just family and thirty or forty of the old man's political cronies. They called it renewing their vows. I can't imagine what their boy thought, his parents just getting married."

"They had a son?" said David.

"Oh yes," said Jillian slipping back into character. "He was born while David was overseas. Everyone had to count up months, but he is legitimate." shaking her head in the affirmative.

"How was that for shopping?" she said. "My ears hurt."

"It sounds like you had a busy morning," said David. "Now tell me about the prison camp and his injuries."

"Oh yes," she said. "It seems like the last year and a half of the war he was in a German prison camp. It seems that he was blown up... when... the... camp... was freed."

Suddenly tears welled up in her eyes. She put her hands over her face and her body began to tremble. David came around the table and put his arms around her.

"No, no," she said, pushing his arms off. "This can't be happening. I don't want to know any more. Let's leave Heinrich, let's go home."

"I can't," said David. "We've come this far and I've got to know."

As they repacked the picnic basket Jillian was quiet. It seemed as if the wind was colder. The color on the trees was no longer spectacular and the song of the birds died out. It was as if the whole world around them knew something had happened and was going into mourning.

They remained in their rooms that evening and had supper sent up. Jillian's face was strained and her eyes were red from the tears that would involuntarily appear from time to time. She had a book before her, but never turned the pages. David remained quiet. He couldn't look Jillian in the eyes. He wasn't sure why he felt guilty when he hadn't done anything. *Was it wrong to find the truth even if the truth carried pain? Would it be better to live a lie and never know?* The only thing he wanted was for bedtime to come so that tomorrow would arrive more quickly. For better or worse, tomorrow would change his life forever and he was not going to run.

Chapter 35

The next morning David left Jillian in bed. She had turned away and lay facing the wall. Before he left, he went to kiss her. He could see from her eyes that she had been crying. She turned and gave him a listless kiss, then turned away. He felt sick inside.

He turned to the right as he left the hotel, this would take him past Strauss and Son's Jewelry. He stopped in at the Shoppe and asked to see Mr. Strauss. When he came out, David thanked him once again for inviting Jillian and him to dinner. "Jillian enjoyed seeing an American home and thoroughly enjoyed visiting with your family and getting to know them. In fact, that is why I stopped by. I believe your son and I may have some friends in common. I would like another opportunity to speak to him. Can you tell me how I can reach him?"

"I really don't know. Perhaps you could call Catherine; she would know his schedule at the hospital."

David tried to keep the excitement out of his voice. "Would you give me her number, please?"

"Certainly." With that the older man took a pad from his desk and wrote the number.

"Would you like to use the office phone?"

"Thanks that would be nice." David then dialed the number with the old man watching on. This made him a

219

little uncomfortable. Catherine answered after what seemed an eternity.

"Yes?"

"Mrs. Strauss? This is Heinrich Müller. It was a real pleasure meeting you and your husband the other night. Jillian so much enjoyed meeting you. She said you were the wonderful American woman she has heard so much about."

"That was so nice of her. I enjoyed meeting her as well. She seems so genuine and down to earth, a no nonsense woman."

"That's nice of you to say. I think she is special too. Now, the reason I called. I was wondering if you could tell me how to get in touch with your husband. I have remembered some people I met during the war, and thought we could discuss them before Jillian and I leave."

Catherine hesitated for a moment. "I don't think that should be a problem. He told me that he would have a light schedule today. He was going to make his rounds this morning and then would have the rest of the day free. Do you have something to write on?"

"Yes."

"His number is TE-3-9883. Ask for Dr. Strauss in surgery. He should be nearby."

"Thanks, you've been a big help. In case we don't meet again, it's been a pleasure."

"No problem."

With that David hung up. He thanked Mr. Strauss and left. He decided to call from a phone booth. He didn't want his conversation to be overheard by Mr. Strauss or anyone else in the Shoppe.

There was a phone booth at the end of the block and around the corner. It was a few steps from the door of the bank. David was glad that it was around the corner; it could not be seen from Mr. Strauss' store or the jewelry store that housed the world's busiest busybody. He tried to think what to say when he talked with the person calling himself David Strauss, but nothing came to mind.

David's hand shook as he dialed the number...
"Roquefort Hospital."

"I would like to talk with Dr. Strauss in surgery please, tell him it is Dr. Müller calling."

"Just a minute Dr. Müller, I'll see if I can reach him."

When Heinrich heard the message, his blood ran cold. *I guess the other shoe is about to drop.*

"Dr. Müller, it is good to hear from you. How can I help you?"

"I have been remembering some common friends we might have. I was wondering if we could have lunch together and discuss old times."

"I guess that could be arranged, I had some other plans, but they can be changed. It will be a pleasure visiting with you. Do you like hamburgers?"

"Yes, I do as a matter of fact. It's been a long time."

"Okay, there is a small café called Franks, about a half block down on Willow Street, just south of third. There is a park across the street. I believe it's still warm enough to eat in the pavilion. Will that do for you?"

"Yes, that will be fine. Is that west of Echols?"

"It is, three blocks. You're getting to know your way around."

"Surprisingly so."

"How about 11:30? That will give us a little extra time."

"Perfect, I'll see you then."

David wasn't sure what to do with his time until 11:30, but he didn't want to go back to the hotel and face Jillian. He decided give her a call on the phone. "I am going to meet with Dr. Strauss for lunch and see if we can uncover more of my past. Will you be okay?"

"I'm not sure what I'll do since I already know all the gossip, but I guess I'll manage."

As David hung up the phone, he felt guilty. He knew though that having her around would stop him from asking questions that needed to be addressed. Since he had some time to spare, he decided to get in the car and drive around and see if he could remember more about the town.

Heinrich called Catherine and told her that he would not be taking her to lunch. "Dr. Müller called and wanted to visit so I thought I would treat him to some good American hamburgers at Frank's diner and eat in the park"

"Do you think he's up to something?"

"There's only one way to find out."

"That sounds like a good idea. At least you are prepared. I love you."

As soon as he hung up, Catherine sat down and stared out the window. As she did, she remembered the day she went to the hospital ship in New York to see David. How happy she had been that day... Now this man was coming in and stirring up the past; she remembered David's tears last night. What could she do to help? Suddenly she got a determined look on her face, walked over and picked up the telephone. She called the hotel and asked to be connected to Mrs. Müller's room. "Jillian? This is Catherine Strauss, I was wondering if we could have lunch together today?"

"Mrs. Strauss? Well, I guess we could." There was a tremor in her voice. "What is this about?"

"I just got a call from David and he said he and your husband were getting together to talk over old times in Germany. It seemed to me that you and I were getting left out. I thought that we could take this opportunity to visit. I can have Helen make us a light lunch and we could talk. Is everything okay, you sound upset?"

"It's okay. I am just a little out of sorts. Yes, I would enjoy having lunch with you. What time would you like to get together?"

"Suppose I pick you up in about forty-five minutes and I could show you a little of our town. We could go to my house for lunch and wait for our boys to finish up. Who knows how long they will be and there is no point in you spending the day alone."

"That would be fine."

"Super! I'll see you shortly."

Jillian hung up and sat down. How could life change so quickly? Two weeks ago, she had everything a woman could want. Her husband was a doctor; she had three wonderful children, and a beautiful home. Now she knew that it could all be gone by the end of the day.

Catherine picked up the phone and dialed David's private number at the hospital.

He answered on the first ring. "David? Since you and Dr. Müller are meeting for lunch, I decided to invite Jillian over for lunch here. Maybe I can learn something from her. I will show her the town and we can visit for the afternoon. This will be a legitimate way to get information. Besides I feel so bad for her being left out and in a strange town. After you and Dr. Müller finish visiting, why not bring him here and maybe we could all do something together this evening?"

"I am not sure that's such a good idea. I really am tired and may be coming down with something."

"I'm sorry, I was so sure that you would agree that I have already invited her. I was getting ready to pick her up when I thought to call. It really would be rude not to invite them over so they could see how 'real Americans' live. If they are up to something, we can send them packing."

"You are right, as usual. See you then."

Heinrich hung up the phone and put his face in his hands. *How am I going to get out of this? I don't want to lose Catherine. If she ever finds out what happened, it will be over. No forgiveness!*

As David drove, he decided to see where Catherine and her husband lived. It was easy enough to find. He drove past the house and turned around. Driving back, he parked across the street a few houses down.

What he saw was a two-story red brick home with white shutters. The home was on a large lot, probably a half-acre. The lawn was well manicured with fall leaves blowing across. Parked in the drive in front of the house was a new Buick convertible. It was a long way from the black

223

Mercedes he drove at home. There seemed to be an unwritten rule that doctors had to drive something black and sophisticated. As he sat there he saw Catherine Strauss come out of the front door. She got in the car and drove out. As she passed by he dropped down in the seat to avoid being seen. He didn't want to explain what he was doing here.

When Catherine stopped at the front door of the hotel, Jillian was waiting, a look of apprehension on her face. Catherine smiled, "It's good to see you Jillian. I'm glad you wanted to visit. I know that it can be lonesome to be alone in a strange place."

"Yes, it is. Heinrich has been distracted these last two days. It is like being alone."

"Let's just drive around look at the neighborhoods and see if any of it looks familiar to you. Did you know that half of the people in Roquefort emigrated or descended from German immigrants?"

"No, I did not realize that. I see that many of the homes in the older areas have the same look as the houses in Stadthagen. But the houses in the newer areas are a different style. Even though they are a different style, they are all similar."

"That's David's doing. The Strauss Construction Company builds homes for low-income families. He started it with some of the local veterans that were out of work. They had spent the previous four years building airstrips and bridges with people shooting at them. David felt that if they could do that, they could build homes. Using the same building techniques they had in the army, they set up six or eight different floor plans using common sizes for walls and partitions. This allowed them to reduce material costs and the time it takes to build a home. Now returning veterans can purchase quality homes at a lower price."

"How wonderful!" Jillian said excitedly. "Heinrich's cousin and I run the Müller Construction Company. We build hospitals and orphanages. There is so much satisfaction is helping those in need."

"You run a construction company?"

224

"I do the sales and marketing. Heinrich's cousin Erik runs the construction end. Together we do the designs. I make them beautiful, he makes them functional."

"That is amazing Jillian. I can see from being around you that you have energy. I like that."

As they drove around looking at the homes and scenery Jillian began to relax. She began to feel that Catherine could be a friend and would understand her concerns. She looked over at Catherine. "My Heinrich appears to know a lot about this village. I'm not sure what to think."

Catherine's breath caught. "What do you mean?"

"We have been married for about nine years. During that time his mind has been blank on his life before the war. I feel so bad for him, he has struggled so much, now he is having memories that leave me worried."

"Tell me about it if you don't mind. What kind of memories is he having?"

"Well, to start with, the man in New York said his English was from Ohio. How could this be? Yesterday he drove us to a place to picnic by a lake. He had not asked for directions. How did he know where it was? What life has he had before we met? He said he went to medical school at Harvard, but that is so far away."

Catherine was silent for a minute. "Why don't we go to my house so that we can quietly sit and discuss this?"

Jillian was impressed when she went into Catherine's home. While it was not nearly the size of the Müller estate, there was an uplifting feeling as they went inside. The floors were hardwood with area carpets. The furniture was not so large and heavy as she had in her home. It had a light airy look that was not found in the old traditional furniture. There was a large piano in the living room and flowers everywhere. "What a lovely home. I had not pictured American homes like this. I had thought they would look like Mr. Strauss's home."

"Thank you. Papa Strauss's home is different because he brought his memories with him from Germany. He really never left home."

"What a beautiful piano, do you play?"

Catherine looked at it with a sad smile on her face. "No, David plays, at least he used to. I bought it for him on his second Christmas home from the war. It was a little disappointing. Before he left for the war, he played constantly. In fact, he would have been a musician if not for his father. He plays several instruments. I thought he would be so excited, but one of the only skills he lost from his injuries was his love for music. I don't think he has ever attempted to play it since Christmas morning. He just sat there looking at it and said he could not remember how to play."

Jillian sat on the couch across from Catherine. "How sad, music has been such a part of our lives. Heinrich loves to play. He can play almost anything. He even composed a song for each of our children after they were born. He says music is God's gift and it would be a sin not to use it."

Catherine's eyes became moist and she struggled with herself to maintain her composure. She had heard David say that many times after fussing with his father about his playing. "Oh? How many children do you have?"

Jillian smiled. "We have three, a son and two daughters. Gretchen Marlene is six and is called after Heinrich's daughter and his mother who both died in the war. Our Heinrich is four. Then our little surprise came along. Phoebe is three." She had a faraway look in her eyes.

"How nice." Catherine's smile was genuine. "We also have something in common. Our daughter is called Gretchen."

"Really? That is quite a coincidence."

"Yes, David wanted to call her Catherine after me. We searched for something to go with it to avoid two Catherine's in the same home. I hate the name Cathy, so we couldn't call her that. Anyway, we came up with Gretchen Catherine. It seemed to have a nice ring to it."

"It does," said Jillian.

Catherine took a sip from her Coke. "Who is watching after your children while you are gone?"

"Who isn't?" Jillian laughed. "They have so many mothers and fathers. Uncle Hans and Erik and his family are caring for them, but we have an orphanage on the north side of our property. The workers love them and look after them as though they were their own."

Catherine was shocked. "You have an orphanage as part of your property? Tell me more. It must be a large estate."

Jillian relaxed and settled more comfortably on the couch. "The Müllers have lived on their estate for over two hundred years. The total acreage is about one hundred acres. There are barns and riding stables. At the back, there is a small lake where Heinrich used to fish and ice skate as a young boy. The house is huge. As a young girl I dreamed of living in a castle with a knight in shinning armor, but I never thought it would happen to me. I was so shocked when Heinie took me to his home. I knew he had money, but I had no idea that he was *that* wealthy. His first wife Ursula and his daughter Gretchen were the light of his life. They were killed along with his parents when an American bomber crashed into the north wing of the house after being damaged during a bombing run. When I looked at it, it was still as they left it. Uncle Hans and Erik were living in the caretaker's cottage. They didn't know what to do. I still remember the look in Heinie's eyes as he stood there. He said, 'Let's rebuild it, and build an orphanage on the north side to care for the children left homeless by this terrible war. If we had taken a stand at the beginning, the war may have never taken place. The least we can do is to care for the children.' I was in love before, but that - that sealed the deal. I knew that I was looking at the finest man I have ever met."

"He does sound wonderful.

"Ursula... That is what your husband called me the night we 'met' in New York."

"Yes, we talked about it later and he has no idea what happened. He had memory loss during the war and has these flashes occasionally."

Catherine did not know what was going on with Jillian's husband and David, but she knew that Jillian was the real thing. The love in her voice and the way her eyes shinned when she was talking about her husband could not be faked. What's more, she liked Jillian and would not believe anything bad about her!

A woman in a maid's uniform stepped in and said, "Excuse me Mrs. Strauss, the sandwiches are ready. Would you like them on the patio or shall I bring them here?"

Looking at Jillian, Catherine said, "Why don't we eat on the patio? It's such a beautiful day."

Jillian smiled and said, "That sounds wonderful."

Looking at the maid, Catherine said, "We'll have it on the patio. Thank you, Helen."

The patio was enclosed on three sides and opened onto a spacious yard with a swimming pool and an adjoining tennis court.

Jillian had noticed that Catherine was well toned. Now she knew why.

"You play tennis?"

"Oh yes," said Catherine. "You?"

"Yes, I love it, that and horseback riding. I took up riding after Heinrich and I were married. We had the stables, so I decided why not?"

Catherine laughed. "I agree.

"I'll tell you what, why don't I invite my friend Ann Marie over and let you two meet. She told me that I would be in trouble if I let you get away without letting her meet you. I think you will hit it off. She thinks like you do."

Jillian smiled. "That would be a capital idea!"

Chapter 36

David arrived at Frank's Café just a few minutes before Heinrich. Heinrich walked in with a smile and shook hands. "Have you ordered yet?"

"No, I thought I would wait in case you were late. I know that hospitals can get hectic at times."

"Fortunately, today has been routine." Heinrich turned to the waiter at the counter. "Two hamburgers all the way and a Coke." Turning to David he said, "What would you like?"

"I'll have the same."

Heinrich looked at the waiter. "Bag those would you?"

"Right, they'll be right out."

The two of them sat at a table and made small talk while they waited for their burgers. "I should be big as a horse the way I eat these things. The hospital's right around the corner and this place is really convenient."

After they got their lunches, they walked across the street to the park. They found a spot where they would have some privacy. As they began to eat Heinrich lay his burger down after the first bite. He took a long drink from his Coke. "Let's cut the small talk and tell me what you really have on your mind."

David, startled, put his hamburger down. Suddenly, a look of fury crossed his face. "I want to know who you are and what are you doing with my wife!"

Heinrich face reddened. His body became tense as if he were ready to spring. "I am not sure what you mean. I never met your wife before two weeks ago. Even then it was casual."

David was exasperated. "You know good and well she's not the one I'm talking about! Catherine! Catherine's MY wife!"

Heinrich's face reddened even more. His voice became aggressive. "Are you out of your mind? You should hear yourself!"

Suddenly the tension seemed to leave David. Despair covered his face. Throwing both hands in the air, he shook his head from side to side. "I know what I sound like. I sound like a crazy man. I probably **am** crazy as a loon. I've been living in a dark room for ten years. Suddenly the doors are thrown open and I'm blinded by the light. The world I knew is gone and I'm trying to find my way back."

Heinrich relaxed a little. "Okay, that sounds reasonable enough. Tell me your story and if I can help in some way, I will."

David put his hands down. He smiled a little. His hands shook as he took a drink of his Coke and shook his head. "Thanks. You can't imagine what I have been through. All of these things jumping out at me and I have no one to talk to. Jillian just cries if I say anything." He started laughing. "Isn't this a mess...? The only one to talk to is the person I perceive as my enemy."

Heinrich looked intently at him. "I'm not your enemy. You can't imagine how badly I want to clear this up. So please, go on with your story."

"Now this is going to sound really strange, but these are my memories as they have come back to me. First of all, I am an American. During the war with Germany, I was held prisoner in a German POW camp: Stalag 21. It's still not all clear to me yet, but I became friends with the German doctor in charge whose name amazingly was..." pointing to himself "Heinrich Müller." My last memories were talking with Heinrich. An artillery barrage started falling around us. When I woke up yesterday morning with Jillian, it was like waking up with a hangover. I knew where I was and I knew Jillian, but I couldn't remember why I was sleeping with Jillian and not Catherine."

Suddenly he laughed and started eating his hamburger. "I'm hungry. You can't imagine what a relief it is to tell the story aloud. What do you think?"

Heinrich wondered for a moment if he should try to keep David in the dark. "You're right; it does sound crazy, but tell me more. Maybe we can clear up some of your memories. How do you feel about all of this?"

"How do I feel? I am not sure at this point. Some of my memories are tangled. It's like I led parallel lives. They are both becoming clear as time goes on. But I remember waking in an American hospital. I was in the American sector of Germany and there were American doctors attending. I didn't know who I was or what happened. They told me I was a German doctor from Stalag 21. My name was Heinrich Müller. I would have been turned over to the Russians except for my record at the POW camp. It appears that I was a big help to the Americans and protected them from the kommandant and his henchmen many times. In fact, they got into a tussle with the Russians who wanted me returned because I was a doctor with special skills. It seems that they told the Russians I was dead in order to protect me. They tried to rebuild me as best they could. Uncle Hans found me there and he and my cousin Erik took me out and entered me into a hospital in Switzerland. I spent nearly a year there. I had no memory of my past and could not walk. On a respite from the hospital I met Jillian and she became my therapist. She taught me to walk again but I have had no memory of my past for the last ten years." A look of tenderness fell over his countenance. "I have never met anyone who has such a kind heart as Jillian. This whole thing has hurt me because it has hurt Jillian. I know what they say about patients falling in love with their nurses, but this was different. Well, anyway we got married and have three children." David's anger flared.

"Now suddenly I find myself here and wondering why you are here with my wife!"

Heinrich just sat and stared dumfounded. Then he quietly stood up and stepped around the table. "David, mein bruder!"

David stood up and turned with a startled look on his face. "Heinie?"

"Yes!" The two men threw their arms around each other with tears flowing.

Heinrich stepped back looking at David. "I thought you were dead!"

David sat back down relieved. "Well, I'm not! Now tell me how you wound up with my wife!"

Heinrich sat on the table with his feet on the seat. He looked at David and shook his head with a disbelieving look on his face. "How did you live through all that? I checked and you were dead!"

"I believe the correct quote is 'The reports of my death were greatly exaggerated.' Now tell me your side of what happened."

"You and I were in the infirmary having a last drink. Tell me if I go too fast for you. Anyway, we were there talking about the end of the war. I was worried about being taken by the Russians. You were talking with me about coming to the States. I want you to remember that part. That was when a private, I can't remember his name, came running in telling us that Corporal Rothenberger was having the men shot. We jumped up and were running for the door when the Russians started shelling the camp. Do you remember any of this?"

"Rotten! I may have met him a few years ago. Other than him, I can vaguely remember some of our experiences at the camp. I remember our talks, but the rest hasn't come back yet. Go on though."

Heinrich shifted a little to a better position on the bench. "Major Rothenberger, the new kommandant, had left the camp with a detachment of solders to make a last fight

232

and perhaps to die honorably. The Russians began firing artillery. If they had been aiming for the hospital, they could not have done any better. The second shell hit the office where we had been sitting. It blew us both to the porch. I have thought about this many times and believe that I have pretty well reconstructed the events as I saw them. My head was ringing and I was barely functional. You got back up and started for the yard. The next blast hit the porch and it came crashing down on us both. I was barely conscious at this time. I crawled over to you and began pulling debris off. I got you clear enough to see most of the damage. You were burned pretty severely and had been crushed by the debris. I didn't have much hope for you when I checked for a pulse. I didn't find one. As I think about it now, I wasn't in much condition myself to be checking on anyone. As I was leaving, a brilliant but misguided idea came to mind. I knew that if the Russians got me, I would be lost forever. I switched dog tags with you thinking I would use them to get to the American lines. After I was clear of the Russians, I would turn myself in to be a prisoner of war. I thought it was a good plan. It would have been too if another shell had not hit as I was leaving. That's the last I remember until I regained consciousness a long time later. Apparently I had been in and out of consciousness for some months but I don't remember any of it. That's when I found out that they had already begun reconstructive surgery on my face. I didn't want them to stop halfway through when they discovered I wasn't you. So I decided that you weren't that ugly. My plan was to get all the medical attention I could and then disappear.

David's mouth opened and a look of disbelief came over his face.

"Honest! Anyway, getting lost is easier said than done. I was afraid that if I admitted my guilt, I would be in real trouble. I could not, however, find an easy way to disappear. If you had not been so much of a hero, it would have been a lot easier. Your life really started getting in the way when I met this beautiful English nurse."

David was startled. "Those English nurses are everywhere aren't they?"

"She was kind and beautiful and just about anything a guy could look for. I didn't think I could ever fall in love again until I met her. She became the light of my life." Heinrich stopped and stared at nothing as though he was looking at another time and place. "I loved her dearly but she would not have anything to do with me because I... YOU... were married. I won't bore you with all the details, but suffice it to say that your life screwed that up too."

"Heh, heh, I may owe you an apology. Keep on. This is getting interesting. I'm still wondering how you conned my wife."

"Wait a minute! Before we go any further let's get something straight. I am not sleeping with your wife. I married her. Besides that, don't look at me with that self-righteous glare. It seems to me that you're tagging along with a pretty stunning little number yourself."

"That's different!"

"Oh? Try to explain that to Catherine. I'm sure she will be very understanding. Heinrich took another drink of his Coke. "Anyway, I developed a plan. As soon as I got to the States I was going to disappear. I figured as large as New York is, it wouldn't be hard to drop out of sight. There was some paperwork to be done and I needed more therapy but I thought as soon as it clears, I will take off. Who do you think was waiting at the bottom of the gangplank as I was getting off the ship?"

David smiled. "Catherine?"

"You're right again. My problem is that I have too soft a heart. When Florence Nightingale left she told me that too many women had lost their husbands and she would not contribute to one more loss. Couple that with your talks about worrying what would happen to Catherine and Davy and I was in a real pickle. I was in love with my nurse, but I couldn't break the heart of my best friend's wife. Now that sounds strange, doesn't it? At this point, I really didn't know what to do. Here's one that'll make you laugh, I felt an obligation to you. We had talked so much about our hopes and dreams and you had talked about your concerns to see that your wife and son were taken care of that I did the only thing a man could do under those circumstances. I lied. I faked amnesia. I hoped that Catherine would cut me some slack until I could learn the lay of the land. She did. The problem was that I was getting pressure to take over and be a real husband. Then one night she came to my room and proposed. You will note that I said 'my room'. I was stunned to say the least. Being the gentleman I am, I didn't tell anyone she did the proposing. We called it renewing our vows, but it solved my problem."

"So I hear."

"What?

"You live in a small town. Everyone in town knew of your theoretical proposal before you got off your theoretical knees. Go on."

"The rest is history. We have been married for ten years and have two children, your David and my Gretchen."

David smiled, "We seem to be copy cats, I also have a Gretchen. Gretchen Marlene."

"Marlene... mother would have liked that. Before we go any further, would you mind telling me how Uncle Hans and Erik are doing? One of my greatest regrets is losing them."

David smiled. "Don't worry about them, Uncle Hans and Aunt Adele are happy and doing well. We have finally got him to somewhat retire. He still keeps an eye on the orphanage and watches over the property. Erik was my savior though. I have never met a more loyal friend in my life. When I was in Switzerland, he never left my side. He checked and approved or disapproved every procedure the hospital implemented. After a year, he urged me to take a holiday to the south of France. That's where I met Jillian. Jillian helped me learn to walk again. I hired her as a physical therapist and in three months she did what they could never have done in Switzerland. She is so creative. She would come up with an idea for a new piece of exercise equipment and Erik would purchase or design and build it. He is a most brilliant engineer. I love them both with all my heart. It took real dedication to do the things they did. Right now, Erik is president of the Müller Construction

Company. He and Jillian have made it one of the largest construction companies in Germany. We specialize in hospitals and orphanages. That sounds like a radio commercial, doesn't it?"

"Thank you for caring for them. I have worried these past years but had no way to check."

David said, "Just a minute, before we go any further I have something I believe belongs to you."

David reached into the side pocket of his coat and pulled out a set of German dog tags. He handed them to Heinrich. At the top of them was the name 'Heinrich Müller'.

Heinrich sat and looked at them for a long time. "That was a lifetime ago. Can you forgive me?"

"What is there to forgive? You did what you had to do."

They spent the rest of the afternoon reliving their past lives, remembering Stalag 21 strangely enough with a bit of nostalgia thrown in. It was probably fair to have some good feelings about the place they became friends. They discussed the good times and the bad. They laughed and became somber as they remembered those that never made it home. Most of all, they were amazed at how their lives had paralleled since the war. They both had daughters named Gretchen, they were both surgeons, and they both had construction companies although David admitted his was not of his own making. "Your family started it; I just helped it to grow with Jillian's help. She is an amazing woman. She and Erik are really the driving force."

"It sounds like you have more than love going for Jillian. I am hearing a lot of admiration and respect for her as a person."

"She **is** a formidable person in and of herself. I guess I do have more than love for her. Now back to business. I don't see how we can come out of this cleanly. What are we going to do about this mess?"

Heinrich sat quietly for a moment. "First of all, what do you want to happen? Do you want my wife or do you want yours. You can't have both."

236

"As I have been remembering the life I presently have, I know that I can't leave Jillian or give my children up. I still love Catherine, but my last memories of our life together are not so pleasant. Then there's Jillian... how can I say it, so much has happened. Jillian and I have built so much together. Do you understand?"

"Yes, I do. I have much the same feeling about Catherine. Now that that is settled, the afternoon is gone and we haven't addressed the most important part of the problem. What are our options? I see two obvious ones. We could do nothing or we could make a clean sweep and tell everything. If we do nothing, we might survive this dilemma. If we tell all, we are likely to lose everything or at least come out with scars. Catherine has a very narrow viewpoint of things."

David stood up. "Let's talk while we drive. It's getting kind of late."

As they were driving, David looked over at Heinrich. "Logic would dictate that the right thing to do is to keep our mouths shut. We could possibly survive this whole thing."

"So we should lie, right?" Heinrich looked relieved. "We'll just pretend that we met during a time you visited Stalag 21 where I was assigned. I have not discussed the war with Catherine that much. She probably won't know the difference."

Chapter 37

David and Heinrich were both apprehensive as they pulled into the driveway of Heinrich's home. David started laughing. When Heinrich looked over David said, "This would be funny if it was happening to someone else."

Heinrich gave a nervous smile. "You're right, you know."

"Here we are two war heroes who have faced death on a daily basis, both owners of very successful construction companies, doctors who save lives every day, and we are scared to tell the truth to our wives."

Heinrich looked at David. "You're still with me aren't you?"

"You bet!" said David smiling nervously. "I don't want to lose what I have, and I certainly don't want to mess up your life. After seeing Papa in true form the other night, I don't envy you one bit."

As they entered the house, Catherine and Jillian were waiting in the library. It had always been Catherine's favorite room. Between two windows on one wall was a large fireplace with couches and chairs surrounding it. A small fire was burning to warm against the chill in the air. Two other walls held bookshelves filled with books of every kind. "A room for knowledge" she had called it. *Well,* Heinrich thought, *some knowledge should remain hidden.* "What have you girls been up to this afternoon?" He walked over to the bar. "Anyone for a drink?"

"I would like a Coke," Catherine said, smiling. "How about you Jillian?"

"Yes, a Coke would be fine for me, too."

The men settled for beer as everyone sat down.

After sipping her coke, Catherine said, "Ann Marie came over and we spent the afternoon with girl talk. She just left. I'm surprised that you didn't see her as you came in."

"No, I guess we were so busy trying to remember who was who that we completely missed her," said Heinrich.

Catherine smiled. She was in her element. Turning to David she said, "Oh well, no big deal. What would you like to do with your final evening in town?"

David looked at the others for approval, "I wouldn't mind taking the ten cent tour of town. It is such a beautiful place."

Catherine looked disappointed, "I'm afraid that I took Jillian over town already this afternoon."

"It's okay," Jillian said. "I won't mind at all. I find America so unique, each family having his own house. In Southampton, where I was raised, we shared our home with three other apartments. Each apartment got a small portion of the front or back garden to do with as they would. Everything was alike. I wouldn't mind at all seeing more of this town."

"Wonderful then." Catherine stood up. "If you boys will give us girls a few minutes for touch up we will be ready in a jiffy."

Heinrich laughed, "I've never seen a girl do a touch up in a few minutes. We might as well relax."

Later that evening as David and Jillian were getting ready for bed he took Jillian's hand and sat on the edge of the bed. "During my meeting this afternoon, I discovered some things about myself that I should probably share with you."

"Heinrich, unless it affects our marriage I don't want to know. You had a life before we met and it was gone until this week. Maybe some things happened that would have upset me if we had been married, but we weren't. We have created a life and memories of our own and that's the way I would like for it to stay. I love you for the man you are - not the man you were. Can you understand that?"

"Yes, I do. You don't know how much that means to me. You don't know how much I love you."

"I think I do my love."

She leaned over and kissed him.

As David lay in bed that night, memories began to flood over him. He could see Catherine in her cheerleading outfit sitting in their booth in Parker's Drugstore. Her beautiful eyes were pulling him in again as they had so long ago. He remembered their walks in the park and picnics at the lake. He could see her as she leaned against the tree while they had lunch in the schoolyard. He leaned against her and kissed her once again. Her lips were soft as she put her arms around him. It was wonderful until Mr. Lively stepped up and shouted, "What are you doing!" He felt Mr. Lively shaking him. He wanted to push back.

"What are you doing?" Jillian was shaking him.

"Huh?" David opened his eyes and realized he had been asleep.

"You grabbed me and started shaking me. Are you okay?" Jillian had a concerned look on her face.

"I'm sorry; I was having a bad dream about the war. I guess now that I can remember it, I'll have that to deal with too!"

"I'm sorry, love. I wish I could help."

She put her arms around him and began to kiss and nuzzle him around the neck. David gently pushed her away and said, "I'm sorry, but I have a lot on my mind." He knew he could not dream about Catherine and make love to Jillian. It just didn't seem right. Life had certainly gotten complicated...

The next day as Heinrich went to work, he began to think of David and their friendship. He remembered the times they had together, both good and bad. This led to

240

Catherine and the lie he was living with her. He told himself it was okay and it wouldn't hurt her if she never knew. He also knew that he was lying to himself. The deception was okay when David was dead, but somehow it seemed wrong now. It didn't make sense, but it still seemed wrong. For the next week, his sleep was restless. He tossed and turned and woke up as tired as he was when he went to bed. "I need to put it out of my mind," he told himself, but it did no good.

One night he and Catherine were undressing for bed when she commented, "You look exhausted, is there anything wrong?"

"I just haven't been sleeping well," was his reply.

"I noticed that this started shortly after your German friend was here. What did he do that bothered you so much?"

Before he could reply, the phone began to ring. The call was from the hospital. "Dr. Strauss, there has been an accident on Highway 5 and three people have been brought in. One of them is in very serious condition."

"Can Dr. Blair handle it?"

"He is the one that requested we call you. After we got the man in the most serious condition stabilized, Dr. Blair said that you were the best one for the job. He is working on the other two now."

"Okay, I will be there shortly."

Turning to Catherine, he put his hands over his face and rubbed his eyes. "I guess you know what that's all about. Don't wait up. I may be there all night."

Catherine kissed him. "I understand. That's one of the things a doctor's wife has to deal with. I want you to know how proud I am that you are such a wonderful doctor. You will always be the one they call."

Heinrich finished in the early morning hours. Knowing he would be making rounds in a few hours, he decided to sleep at the hospital. Anyway, he wanted to close by his injury patient in case a problem arose, so it fit his plans.

The next day he ran his normal schedule and took time in the afternoon to meet with Frank Boris and Ed Rodenburger on a new building project they were planning. After the meeting, he changed into evening clothes and went to a cocktail party hosted by large contributors to the hospital.

Arriving home late, he went straight up to bed. He was so tired he thought he would fall asleep walking up the stairs. Catherine had just arrived home as well. She had been attending a meeting of the Daughters of the American Revolution. He walked into the bedroom and pulled his tie loose as he sat on the edge of the bed. "Please sit in the chair. If you continue to sit on the bed, the mattress will sag and it will have to be replaced."

"Sorry. So how was your day?"

Catherine smiled. "A lot better than yours I believe. You look terrible! Have you gotten any rest since last night?" Heinrich looked at her and thought he really didn't care if the bed did sag.

He moved over to the chair, pulled off his shoes and began to rub his feet. "Not a lot. If you add up all the naps, maybe three hours."

"Did your accident patient come out all right?"

"Yes, it was not as bad as it looked, just tedious. I thought we would never get all the glass and gravel out."

"That's all I want to know. You don't want to be picking me up off the floor."

Heinrich smiled as he finished getting undressed. Catherine had always been squeamish about blood and surgery.

Catherine was sitting at her dressing table and rubbing cold cream on her face to remove her makeup. "I have been thinking about our discussion last night.

"Discussion? About what?"

"About you not being able to sleep after your visit with your friend Heinrich Müller. I think that he is kind of strange. Don't you?"

"No not really."

"Well, you didn't see the way he stared at me? It gave me the creeps. I can just see him sneaking around the house at night looking in the windows. Oooh!" She shook her head and shoulders.

"You have him all wrong. He's as fine a guy as you'll ever meet."

"You haven't seen him in ten years, how would you know what kind of person he is?"

"I just do, that's all. We had a long talk the afternoon we visited and he's the same man he was when we were in the camp together."

"I just don't know how you can trust him. He was a Nazi, you know!"

"He was not a Nazi! He was a member of the German army. There's a big difference!"

His head was starting to hurt. He didn't need this now. He was just too tired!

"How do you know he wasn't a Nazi? Maybe he was a spy and trying to get your confidence."

"He was not a spy. I'm going to bed." He threw back the covers and slid between the sheets.

Catherine was getting agitated. She turned to look at Heinrich in bed. "Well, what was he doing showing up here out of the blue? Why did he grab me that night at the convention?"

Heinrich closed his eyes for a second. Catherine was like a bulldog when she got something on her mind. She just would - not - let - go. "He has been sick. He was trying to get his memory back. I tried to help, that's all!"

"What do you mean; get his memory back?"

"He has had amnesia for the last ten years. I helped him clear things up."

"Amnesia? That's a lot of bunk! If he had amnesia how did he find his way here? He must have been trailing us. How did he know me? There is something really fishy here. I think you need to do something."

Heinrich was exasperated. "Catherine, there is nothing to do something about. He is just a friend that needed help. I gave him some help and that's that! I'm going to sleep."

Catherine walked to the bed and sat on the edge next to Heinrich. "There's something you are not telling me. I can see it in your eyes. Did he ask for money?"

"No Catherine! He did not ask for money."

"Is he a communist? Maybe the Russians captured him and turned him into a spy. Didn't you see the McCarthy Hearings? There are communists everywhere."

He was so tired. "Catherine, please give it up. He is not a communist, spy, or anything else but a nice guy. He needed some help and I gave it to him. End of story."

"What are you hiding? I know you are hiding something. It shows in your face. We are going to talk this out until we get to the bottom of it. You will feel a lot better when you quit hiding the truth from me."

Chapter 38

Heinrich pushed himself up until he was in a sitting position. He really didn't want to tell her like this, but no more lies! "Okay... I will tell you. Just don't interrupt until I have finished. I am going to tell you the story of two friends in a German prison camp."

"What are you doing?"

"I asked you not to interrupt. Do you want to know what's going on or not? I really think you don't want to know. You just don't know it yet."

"Okay, I'll keep quiet."

"Alright, there were two friends in a German prison camp. We'll call them David and Heinrich. All through the time they were there, David continued to tell Heinrich how much he worried about what would happen to his family if he didn't come out alive. Heinrich's family was dead. They were killed in the war. Now, on their last day in the prison camp, it was shelled by Russian artillery. The infirmary they worked in received several direct hits. Both men were seriously injured."

Catherine had a strange look on her face, wondering where this was leading.

"Heinrich saw his friend David under some rubble and crawled over to help him. On checking his pulse, Heinrich decided his friend was dead. As a German, Heinrich didn't want to be captured by the Russians so he decided to switch dog tags with his dead friend."

Catherine's face was losing some of its color.

"As Heinrich was crawling away, another shell hit and he was knocked unconscious and in a coma for a number of weeks. When he finally regained consciousness, he discovered they had started making repairs to his face and were mistakenly making him look like his friend David. There was nothing for him to do at that point except let them continue."

"Wait a minute are you saying..."

"I asked you not to interrupt me until I was finished. Heinrich's plan was escape as soon as the repairs were made to his body and he had healed. No matter how he tried, he could not escape the hospital. It seemed as though David's family had pull with the powers that be and they were taking special care of him. Plan after plan to escape failed until he was shipped to the States. Once again before he could escape, David's wife was there to greet him. He was in a quandary. How could he walk away and leave her standing there, lost and alone? This continued for several months until he realized he had fallen in love with her. What now, he asked himself? David's wife solved the problem by proposing marriage to him. They called it renewing their vows. Ten years have passed and here we are."

Catherine sat quietly with her eyebrows together for several minutes. Heinrich was wondering what was going on in her mind.

"I'm not understanding everything. What happened to Heinrich and how did you make it back?"

"David did not make it back."

"What do you mean? You're here now."

"Yes, I am. But David, your David, did not make it back."

"Then who are you?"

"I am Heinrich Müller."

Catherine jumped up. "WHAT??? No, you're David. I know you too well. I'm not sure what you're up to, but it's not funny and I don't appreciate it one bit!"

She walked to the bathroom and got a cup of water and swallowed it in one gulp. Walking back in she stopped beside the bed, folded her arms and stood looking at Heinrich. "I don't understand."

Heinrich sat there feeling stupid. He had never visualized this discussion going like this. He wasn't sure why he had told her in the first place. "Okay, let me tell you again. The man we had dinner with last week was David Strauss. My original name was Heinrich Müller."

"But you can't be Heinrich Müller; you're David, my husband." Her head was shaking from side to side.

Heinrich stood and attempted to put his arms around her, but she looked down and brushed him away. Tears were rolling down her cheeks.

Calmly Heinrich said, "More than anything I wish I was David, that is, your David that left so many years ago. But I'm not, I'm Heinrich Müller, your husband and I love you."

In a voice so quiet Heinrich could barely hear, Catherine said, "If he was David, why didn't he say something?"

"He only discovered his identity that day. He had had amnesia for the last ten years. We spent the afternoon helping him regain his memories."

"Why didn't he talk to me?"

"We decided it was best to let things go as they were. He was married to Jillian and I was married to you. We felt there would be nothing to gain by rocking the boat."

Catherine's face began to turn red. She turned away for a moment then turned back. A Jekyll and Hyde transformation had taken place. With hands balled into fists she said, "WHO ARE YOU TO DECIDE WHAT IS BEST FOR ME???" in a voice that was anything but quiet.

Heinrich took a step back as though he may need to defend himself. "I'm sorry; it seemed to be the best thing to do at the time." He stammered.

247

"SORRY? Sorry doesn't cut it mister!" She was mad now. She turned and walked into the bathroom again. Heinrich took the opportunity to pull on a pair of pants over his pajamas as though that would somehow protect him.

Catherine came from the bathroom with tears running down her face. "You mean he didn't care enough about me to want to talk to me? After all we were to one another?"

Heinrich was quiet for a moment. "Well, he couldn't very well come up and say 'Hi, I'm David, your long lost husband. Oh yes, meet my new wife Jillian.'"

Catherine looked at Heinrich with rage on her face. "This means our entire life together is a lie!"

"Well, I wouldn't say it was a lie. We are married, remember?" His voice squeaked like a teenager's.

"I married someone I thought was David. Now I discover I married a complete stranger."

"We weren't strangers. I lived here for months before we were married." He said defensively.

Catherine walked away from Heinrich then turned to face him. Taking a step in his direction between each sentence she said, "We lived together because you lied to me. We got married because you lied to me. You didn't use your own name, so that was a lie. Our whole life together is a lie." She threw her hands up in disgust.

Heinrich began to walk to Catherine as though to embrace her but she put her hands up to stop him. "Catherine, I don't think our life has been a lie. We have loved one another and built a good life."

Catherine looked at him coldly. "I want you out of here tomorrow."

"You can't mean that. Doesn't our home mean more to you than that?"

"It's not open for discussion. I don't ever want to see you again!" She turned and walked into the bathroom and closed the door. Briefly a thought came to her that she had done something like this before, but she quickly pushed it away.

Heinrich stood there, dumfounded. How had this happened? Why had he been so stupid as to tell her? Slowly, he turned and walked out the door and went to the guest room to sleep. Maybe tomorrow.

Sleep didn't come to Heinrich that night. Thoughts of Ursula and Gretchen and a funeral on a cold day with the wind blowing out of the north traveled back and forth through his mind. This was mixed with scenes of little David and his Gretchen Catherine at the good times, always laughing, always happy. Surely he couldn't lose everything again. What great sin had he committed that God was going to punish him forever?

The next morning, exhausted, he went down to breakfast and found Catherine eating. "Can we talk about this now that we have had a chance to rest and calm down?"

Catherine got up and walked out without acknowledging his existence.

Heinrich got a cup of coffee and set at the bar, not knowing what to do. A few minutes later Catherine came in and said in a voice devoid of emotion, "I am going to go over to Ann Marie's this morning. When I get back I would like your things to be out of here." She turned to leave the room.

"Please listen!"

Catherine stopped with her back to him.

"Doesn't the past ten years mean anything to you? They were good years and I love you."

Catherine started walking again without a reply and left the room.

He sat and sipped his coffee. He felt numb all over. Once again he felt the same pain as the day he was told of the airplane crash into his home. A few minutes later he heard the door close and Catherine's car start. Like a zombie he walked to the bedroom, took his suitcase out of the closet and began to pack. The last time he had used it was when he and Catherine went to the conference in New York. So much had happened in a short time. His sins, whatever they were, were catching up with him. He had lost all he valued once again.

Why didn't I just let the Russians take me? It would have been far better than this.

Leaving the bedroom, he went next door to his office. Opening the safe, he reached in and took out two large stacks of cash and placed them in his briefcase. Prior to the war, his father had advised him to always have cash available for emergencies. Going into Catherine's office, he sat at her desk and wrote a short note. Going through the motions, he put it in an envelope, wrote her name across the front, and placed it in the center of the desk.

His next task was to take care of business. Stopping at his attorney's office he had a power of attorney made out giving Catherine his seat on the board of Strauss Construction. He had another signed to give Dr. Blair the right to manage the office they shared together. He knew Dr. Blair had always thought he could do a better job as office manager. Well, he had his chance now. What surprised him was that he really didn't care about any of it anyway. His only concern was to make sure Catherine and the kids would be financially taken care of without having to ask Papa for anything.

With the details taken care of, he drove to the train station. Sitting in the car, he gazed at the scene around him. This was his first view of Roquefort the day he arrived. There had been a band playing, and the mayor had a key to the city. He loved this town and the people in it, but they were no longer his friends. He had no friends. They were David's friends. One word from Catherine and he would be in jail, a despised imposter. Putting the car keys on top of the sun visor he left the car parked next to the station and went inside and bought a ticket to Columbus. Twenty minutes later, he left Roquefort and all that he held dear in his life. Once again, he was a fugitive and alone.

When Ann Marie answered the door she knew immediately that something was wrong. "Catherine! You look terrible, what's wrong?"

Catherine tried to maintain her composure. As soon as she tried to talk however, tears started to flow. "He's gone." She started to sob uncontrollably.

"Who's gone?"

"David that's who, it was all a big lie."

"Catherine, you're not making sense. What's a big lie?"

"David, that's what! You've got to promise me that you won't tell anyone, not even Scott."

"Tell them what?"

"Promise!"

"You know I won't tell anyone. Now tell me what's going on!"

Catherine's hands were shaking as she wiped her nose on the back of her hand. "Last night David and I had a big argument..." She started crying again.

Ann Marie picked up a box of tissue and handed it to Catherine. "Argument about what? You two never argue."

"The German guy Heinrich and his wife, he told me who they really were!"

"You're not making any sense. What could they have to do with anything?"

Catherine was crying again. Ann Marie was exasperated. "We're never going to get anywhere if you don't stop crying. Let me fix you one of Scott's special drinks."

"You know that I don't drink."

"Yes I know, but this is for medicinal purposes. It doesn't count."

As Ann Marie was at the bar clinking glasses and bottles she said, "I want you to just sit for a few minutes and not talk. Just breathe deeply and try to relax."

She came over carrying two glasses of amber liquid. "Here now, drink it fast and don't try to breathe. It'll make it easier to keep down."

"What's the other glass for?"

251

"That's for me. As much as you have been crying, I think I may need one too."

Catherine did as she was told and swallowed the entire thing in one gulp. Tears came to her eyes and she tried to breathe. "How can you drink this stuff? It's horrible!"

"At least it's gotten your mind off crying. Now start at the beginning and tell me what happened."

"Well, it started last night when I was asking David about his friend Heinrich. I know that I should have left it alone, David was dead tired from working all night." She went on to tell the events as she remembered them.

"I can't believe that! David's not David??? No! You had to have gotten confused. I don't know what's going on, but I have known David most of my life and I would swear that he's the real thing."

"I don't know what to do. How can I be married to two men at the same time?"

Ann Marie gave a sly smile. "Lot's of women would envy your position."

"Don't be silly at a time like this! What am I going to do? Our whole life together is based on a lie!"

"Catherine, honey, welcome to reality! Don't you know that everyone's life is based on lies? Every girl who has ever dated has pretended to be something she isn't. If we didn't lie, no one in her right mind would ever get married. He pretends to be one thing; she pretends to be another. Then they get married and find out. What did you say to him?"

"I told him to pack up and get out. I said I never wanted to see him again."

"That was last night, what did you say this morning?"

"Pretty much the same thing, I told him when I got back he should be out." Catherine had calmed down by now. Perhaps the 'medication' had taken effect.

Ann Marie looked at her with a stunned expression on her face. "Are you out of your mind? Don't you know that every woman in town would like to have her hooks in him? He will be the catch of the season!"

252

Catherine was quiet now. "I hadn't thought of that. Maybe when I get home I should call his office and ask him to come back and talk." Sniff, sniff.

"I would think so. Let him simmer for a couple of hours. When you call him, he will do anything you want."

"He already does that."

Ann Marie shook her head. "What could you have been thinking? You had the best man in town and you threw him out."

Catherine's eyes started to tear up again. Ann Marie stood up "Don't start that again. Let's go shopping. That always makes me feel better."

They decided to drive in to Columbus. Catherine wanted a new winter coat and all the best stores were there. She did find the coat she was looking for, but there was no satisfaction. Instead she had the nagging feeling she should be home taking care of what mattered most.

When she did get home, she walked through the house. It had an empty eerie feeling about it. Helen was there as usual, but Catherine knew something was not right. She checked in the bedroom and found David's suitcase missing. She knew then that she should call the office right away and get this straightened out. When she stepped into her office she found the letter in the middle of her desk. Her heart ached and her fingers trembled as she carefully opened it.

> *Dear Catherine,*
>
> *I really don't know what to say. I guess we said it all last night. I can only tell you I love you and would not have hurt you for anything in the world. I never intended for the last ten years to happen, but they did and they were the best ten years of my life. Give the children my love and tell them Papa is out of town.*
>
> *I left papers with our attorney giving you my spot on the board of directors of the*

construction company. Listen to Frank Boris and you won't go wrong. He has a good head on his shoulders. I left Dr. Blair in charge of the office. I have told everyone that Dr. Müller has given me the chance to do research on new techniques at a hospital in Bern, Switzerland and I will be gone quite a while. After a while everyone will forget me, and your life can go on. If you want a divorce, just send the papers to Heinrich Müller in Stadthagen since he is the real David.

Ten years ago I was going to pass through and try to make my way back home to Germany. I guess I will resume my trip now. The sad thing is that I don't have a home in Germany anymore. It looks like David is the only winner here. He took my home in Germany and now he has taken back his home in Ohio.

I love you with all my heart and soul,

David

Oh yes, I will leave the car in the parking lot by the train station. The keys will be on the sun visor.

Catherine sat with tears running down her face. Her eyes burned from being rubbed so much today. What had she done? She never dreamed he would leave town. What was she doing going shopping when she should have been home taking care of her husband? She laid her head on her arms as she sat at her desk. Her body shook as she silently cried. *Will I ever get the chance to tell him I do love him?*

Chapter 39

In Columbus, Heinrich took a taxi to the airport and purchased a ticket to London with a change of planes in New York. He was operating mechanically now, giving no thought to home or his past. His only objective was to get as far, as fast as he could. Perhaps if he could put distance between his source of pain and himself it would not be so acute.

He had a four hour layover in New York City and it lasted an eternity. He purchased some medical journals at a bookstore but found they did not interest him. In fact, nothing seemed to interest him. He walked from one end of the terminal to the other. It seemed the more he tried not to think of Catherine, the more he did think about her. Finally the call came and he was able to board his flight.

The trip across the Atlantic was long and noisy, but he was glad to be on it. Soon the pulsating drone of the engines lulled him to sleep. He had hardly slept for three days and when he did sleep, it was deep. He did not dream and he was grateful. He jerked awake when a voice over the PA system began to give instructions in preparation for landing at London Heathrow Airport. His mind was foggy but he felt better than he had in days.

He took the train in to Paddington Station. As he got off and walked to the surface level the chill of the London fog hit him. He remembered the morning he boarded the hospital ship. How uncertain he had felt at that time when

255

his main worry was being discovered. Here he was again. It had been a good ten years, better than he would have dreamed. Was this to be his life - finding happiness only to have it snatched away? Enough of that! He had to find a place he belonged. This time he would not let his heart get involved. He had to learn to be tough.

He inquired at the station and found a small bed and breakfast just around the corner at Norfolk Square. After he had settled in, he changed clothes to something more adapted to London weather and began his walk. He wasn't sure where it was because things had changed so much during the intervening years. He knew he was in the neighborhood though. He just walked and let his mind drift. As he turned a corner, there it was. It was now called Bayswater Hospital. That was all that seemed to have changed. The hospital grounds looked the same. He walked up the paths where Lila had strolled with him in his wheelchair. He sat down on a bench and closed his eyes. He could smell the scent of her soap and feel the soft touch of her hands once again.

"You alright mate?"

Heinrich opened his eyes without as much as a movement. He must have been asleep. "Yes, I'm alright. I must have been daydreaming."

An older gentleman in a seaman's cap and blue dungarees was standing in front of his bench.

"Don't feel bad mate. There's a lot of that goes on here."

Heinrich stood up and smiled. "I guess I better get on with it."

"I hope I didn't spoil your dream, sir."

Sighing, Heinrich turned toward the door. "No, but thanks for your concern."

He walked through the front door. It had not changed a bit. Stopping at the desk, he inquired of the nurse on duty. "I'm trying to get some information on one of your nurses that worked here just over ten years ago, a Lila Turnbull."

"I haven't been here so long sir; you will probably have to inquire at the records office down the hall to the right."

"Major Strauss! Is that you?" came a voice from the side. A middle-aged nurse with a huge smile came hurrying over. She stuck out both hands. "It is you, isn't it?"

He smiled in return. "People don't call me Major anymore. Just call me David."

"It is so wonderful to see you again. Most of our patients haven't returned, but occasionally one does." She beamed. "It is so good to see you." She hadn't released his hands yet. Looking down, she seemed embarrassed and turned them loose. "Are you still in medicine?" She turned to the duty nurse. "Rebecca, this is the doctor that saved the boy out in the front garden area. He was sitting in his wheelchair and pulled out his knife and cut the boy's throat. Saved his life, he did."

Rebecca looked at him incredulously. "Then the story was true!" She looked Heinrich up and down as though she was appraising a large piece of chocolate. "He **is** as good looking as you said, too!"

He was starting to feel self-conscious now. He may have been this bold with girls when he was younger, but it had never happened to him. He just stood and smiled, looking from one to the other. It did feel kind of good though.

The second nurse's face became red. "I'm sorry for being so rude; you just caught me off guard. I'm Mary McConnell. I'm afraid I was one of your distant admirers when you were a patient here. All the girls were in love with you. We couldn't believe it when Lila transferred to Southampton. Now what can we do for you, love?"

"I was actually here to ask about Nurse Turnbull. She took care of me most of the time I was here, and I wanted to say 'Thank you' while I was in town."

"Well, it's good that I was here, love, because she and I still keep in touch. She'll not be in Southampton anymore. She married Drake Barrington, the son of an Earl! Can you believe it? They raise horses on a farm near Wetherby. My husband and I do the races so we see her and the children during the season. Would you like her address? I was invited to her wedding, such a beautiful affair." Suddenly

257

she stopped. "Here I am rambling on and I have not let you get a word in edgewise."

"Her address won't be necessary. I had just wanted to tell her how much I appreciate all she did. Perhaps you can pass that on?"

"Oh yes, I will be sure and do that. She will be so sorry she missed you. Are you sure you wouldn't like her address?"

"I am sure. You cannot imagine how good it has made me feel to see you once again and to stand in this hallway."

"Would you like a tour? I'm sure Dr. Barnhill would be glad to meet you. He is the administrator in charge now."

Heinrich was ready to leave now. There was only one reason he had stopped by. Lila Turnbull. He wasn't even sure what he expected to accomplish. Right now he felt sick inside and the only thing he wanted was to get out of here.

"Are you alright, Doctor?"

Heinrich glanced at his watch. "Oh yes, but I should run now, I have meetings to prepare for. It was so nice to see you again." He took her hand as she walked around the counter and gave her a quick peck on the cheek. With that he turned and left.

He began to walk at a rapid pace, not sure where he was going, anything to keep his mind distracted. Finally he stopped in Hyde Park and sat on one of the benches. For a while he just sat and stared, not really seeing anything. He was not sure what he expected when he stopped at the hospital. It had been ten years and of course Lila was married. He was glad that she had found happiness, but he was sick inside. Would he ever find the unconditional love he and Ursula had found? He thought that Catherine truly loved him. He couldn't blame her. Thoughts flashed in his mind. *I should never have turned loose of my heart. I am a fugitive, I simply forgot for a while and I'll never make that mistake again. What could I have been thinking? At least the kids love me, but then I'll never see them again. Why would God do this to me? First He took Ursula and Gretchen, then Lila, and now Catherine and the kids. Why? Am I destined to be a wanderer all my life? Haven't I tried to do the right*

*thing? What does He have against me? Well, no more! I've
had it! I'm going to live for me from now on.*

Heinrich stood and began to walk again. This time he
walked with resolve. He forced the darkness out of his
mind. He wasn't sure why he felt better, but at least now he
had a plan. He wasn't sure where to go from here, but felt
that something would be waiting around the corner.

As he exited the park, he began walking down
Bayswater Street. Across Bayswater he saw a sign for the
Eastgate Travel Agency. He crossed over and looked in the
window. Inside was a large poster of Mallorca, Spain. *Why
not?* He stepped in and found the place empty. There was a
bell on the counter and he tapped it two times. A woman
appeared in the door from the adjoining room. Her hair was
red and he read 'Mallory' on her nametag.

"May I help you sir?"

Smiling, Heinrich said, "I would like to arrange a holiday
in Mallorca."

"For two?"

"No just me."

She grinned, "Could you use some company?"

Smiling, Heinrich said, "I certainly could, but I better
pass this time."

"Too bad."

She turned pages in a large book. "You are in luck love.
We have a villa available near the seashore. Another
fortnight and it will be booked solid. As soon as the rain
and cold are upon us, people will be flocking to Mallorca
like gulls. It is a bit large for one?" She looked pleadingly.

Heinrich laughed. "At Eastgate Travel you certainly aim
to please."

"Service with a smile is our motto." Mallory placed a
large book with pictures of a beautiful villa situated on a
hill overlooking the beach in front of him.

"What do you think, will this be suitable?"

"Perfect."

"Would you like to hire a car or prefer a limousine?"

"Hire a car, please."

If you will relax over here, I will get you a cup of tea and some biscuits while I make the arrangements or would you prefer coffee? You Yanks prefer coffee don't you?"

"A cup of coffee would be wonderful."

He relaxed while Mallory made the arrangements. Preferring to remain in the background for the last ten years, he had avoided traveling first class. He had forgotten how nice it was. A half hour later, he walked out with tickets in hand. As he walked out he remembered the joy he had felt as a young lad traveling with his parents to Mallorca. He was as excited now as he had been then. Living in Ohio as he had, he missed the seashore and all that it brought. With his own place away from the crowds, he could relax and decide what to do next.

Chapter 40

Traveling alone is much easier than with a family, though not as rewarding. It felt good to have everything 'arranged' in advance when he arrived. After unpacking, he drove into town and purchased a few clothes and swimming apparel. Having packed for English weather, he was not prepared for the warmth and sun of Mallorca.

He spent the next week doing just as he had planned. He sunned on the patio, went swimming several times a day and read more books than he had in the past ten years. All of his reading in the past had been in medical journals or new ideas in construction and architecture. It was relaxing not to have any responsibilities. It was empty, too. He grew restless. Exactly what was he doing? Wasn't he supposed to be having a good time, or was he just putting in time until he died? The counter side of responsibility was purpose. Right now it didn't matter if he lived or died, because no one cared. That was it! Tonight he would go out with a purpose. Tonight he would get some action.

He dressed carefully that evening as he prepared to go out. Off came the wedding ring. If Catherine didn't consider them married, so be it. He put on a fine Italian Suit he had purchased, upon arriving, and a silk dress shirt. As he left for dinner he was single, rich, and available!

Putting the top down on his Alfa Romeo he sped along the shoreline highway. In honor of his beautiful Italian car, he would be Italian tonight. As long as he was a liar anyway, he would do it right. He stopped at a dinner club he knew was frequented by the English.

Walking in, he surveyed the area and asked for a booth to the side not far from a large table of English patrons. They were loud and boisterous, as the English abroad tend to be. He noticed that there were three of the ladies who did not appear to be part of the main group. To the dismay of his wife, one of the men kept leaning over and making comments in a loud whisper to the girl sitting next to him. She responded with an embarrassed smile and turned to talk with her two friends.

Seizing the opportunity, Heinrich walked over and touched her arm. Leaning over he said with his finest Italian accent, "Signornia, would you honor me with a dance?"

Startled, she stood almost tipping her chair and said, "Yes, thank you."

They walked to the dance floor and began softly gliding around the room.

"I hope you will pardon my intrusion, but you looked to be in distress."

"How can I thank you? They invited us to sit with them and then just took over. I thought I was going to have to take my shoe off and hit the man next to me. His wife was getting upset with me, as though I had a choice."

"You are American." It was said as a statement more than a question. "What are you and your friends doing so far from home?"

She smiled. "The three of us just graduated from Briarcliff College for Women. We thought we would have some fun before we got jobs as responsible adults."

"Good for you. Responsibility is not nearly as much fun as you may think. I have tried to avoid it most of my life."

"Really? Where are you from?"

"Scusa me. I have been so rude. I am Sergio Rossetti. Call me Serge, please. I am from Roma. When I have to work, I race cars. What will you do when you become a responsible adult?"

"I have a degree in nursing. I want to be a surgeon's assistant. Oh, and my name is Susan, Susan Jones. Have you ever heard of any name so plain?"

His heart jumped. "You have a beautiful name, Susan Jones the nurse. I am so glad to have met you; I have hurt my finger. Perhaps you can come to my table and nurse me back to health."

"Ha ha ha." She gave a nervous laugh. "I think you do more than race cars. I would loovve to nurse you back to health."

When the song was over she walked to her table and picked up her drink. "Excuse me girls. I have to nurse this poor man back to health." With that she walked over to his booth and slid in beside him. They ordered food and talked as they ate. She told him the perils of being a nurse and he lied about anything that came to mind.

As it got late he kissed her ear and whispered, "The moon looks so beautiful over the water from the patio of my villa. Would you like to see it?"

Her eyebrows went up. "Villa? You bet I would like to see it."

As he paid the bill and ordered his car brought around, she went to her friends and told them she would not be coming straight home tonight. Her friends giggled as she walked away. The car was waiting as they stepped out into the cool air.

Heinrich slipped his coat off and placed it over her shoulders. "The night has cooled down. Perhaps this will keep you warm." The wind blew through their hair as they drove along the seashore. The waves shone brilliant white as they crested and rolled ashore. It was a perfect evening. Soon they dropped down from the highway and came to the villa. The white exterior seemed to glow in the moonlight

As they stepped inside, Heinrich turned on the hi-fi and soft piano music began to play. He opened a bottle of wine and poured two glasses. They walked through the double glass doors onto the patio and stood at the rail looking at the waves coming in. Heinrich leaned over and kissed her.

As they kissed, he could feel her tense up. When their lips parted she said, "This is such a beautiful place. How many rooms does it have?"

"It has three bedrooms, three and a half baths, a living room, a kitchen, and a library. Would you like to see it?"

She breathed a sigh of relief. "I sure would. I have never actually seen a villa before."

They took a tour of the house and as he showed her his bedroom, he gently kissed her. When they parted, she nervously looked up at him and said, "I guess this is where I have to 'pay the piper'."

"Pay the piper?"

"Yes, you know, I let you bring me all the way out here thinking that we were going to do something and I guess I should hold up my end of the bargain."

Heinrich felt horrible for what he had considered doing. He smiled. "There is no 'Piper to pay'. You are a wonderful signornia and I have enjoyed your company. I will be glad to take you back to your hotel if you like or you can use the guest room and I can take you back in the morning. You friends can believe what they wish."

"Would you? That would be so great. I thought I could be a woman of the world, but I guess I'm just an old fashioned girl at heart."

They were back to the living room. "Would you sit with me for a moment? I would like to talk to you like, what do you say, a Dutch uncle."

They sat on a love seat that faced the doors overlooking the seashore. Susan was looking uncomfortable. "You are a nice and beautiful signornia. You left the comfort and security of your friends to go away with a perfect stranger."

"You weren't a stranger..." She defended. "We talked and I think I know you well."

"Not at all my darling. You know only what I allowed you to know. Please, hear me out. I think you are a wonderful girl. I, on the other hand am..." He looked thoughtful. "A cad; I prey on beautiful young women. You do not really know me and you should not ever put yourself in this position again." He smiled. "Enough of Dutch uncle; let us

264

enjoy the music and the ocean. Tell me about America. Where in America do you come from?"

They sat and talked for hours. Heinrich enjoyed this young American's company. This was the first time since leaving home that he felt relaxed. This evening he did not have to think about what he had lost.

The next morning his maid brought them an assortment of baked rolls, jellies of every kind, a pitcher of orange juice, a pot of coffee and a pot of steamed milk. They sat on the patio and enjoyed the morning breeze.

Heinrich looked thoughtful for a few minutes. "I love the seaside in the morning. When I was a young boy, my parents would bring my brother and me here and we would play in the sand. Those were such happy times."

"You have a brother? Does he race too?"

"No, like so many of the others, he and my parents were killed in that horrible war."

"I am so sorry, Serge."

"It is okay. Life goes on. Now, I seem to be wasting mine."

"I am sure your life is not a waste. Racing must be a very exciting sport."

"See what you do to me, Susan Jones, you have made me become serious. Enough of that! I promise not to be serious for the rest of the day. Now, what would you like to do today?"

She had a disappointed look on her face. "We have to leave today. Why did I have to meet such a handsome gentleman on my last night?"

"Don't be calling me a gentleman now." He teased. "You may get me confused. Suppose I take you back to your hotel and we can complete your little charade."

They drove the winding road in silence, each with his thoughts. Unlike last night, the trip was over too quickly. As they reached the door of her room, she turned the knob and began opening it. He pulled her to him and kissed her long and hard. As he released her she staggered slightly.

"Now the illusion is complete." He smiled.

She whispered in his ear, "I was right, here I am safe and sound with my virtue intact. You are a gentleman." She kissed his cheek and smiled as she closed the door.

What am I doing here? I cannot be this kind of a man. He smiled as he realized he was still thinking with an Italian accent. *I have no home with Catherine; Ursula is dead. I am lost. I have no home.*

When he reached the villa, he made a call and arranged a flight to Rome and on to Zurich. He packed his bags and left a large tip for the maid.

Driving to town he said goodbye to his childhood. He had learned something about himself. No matter what Catherine thought, he was David Strauss, husband and father. He could never be the kind of man Sergio Rossetti was. *I love Catherine and can love no other.* He laughed to himself. *I guess I will always be a boy scout.*

Stopping at the rental service he dropped the keys to the car and the villa.

"You were not happy here at the Villa Sereno?"

"I was very happy, graciás. I must leave early to attend business in Roma. Would you arrange transportation for me to the airport?"

"Certainly, Señor Strauss. Please come see us again."

Turning to the young boy in the back of the room he said, "Julio, a taxi for the señor."

The boy jumped up and ran out of the door. Shortly a taxi skidded to a stop at the front door and the lad jumped out. He grabbed Heinrich's suitcase and began dragging it to the door. "Your taxi is here señor."

Chapter 41

On to Rome, then to Zurich, Heinrich had a plan. He caught a taxi straight from the airport to BSI Bank.

As he stood before the bank he remembered the day he and his father stood on these same steps.

"We will set up a special account for you and you alone. If you are ever in trouble, always know that this money will remain here for you. I will tell no one else about it. It will be our secret."

I guess I am in trouble, Papa. Thank you so much for caring for me enough to give me this protection.

He went in and got a bank draft on his account and went out where his taxi was still waiting.

"Please take me to the train station."

The trip to Stadthagen was long, but he got to see his beloved Germany once again. How he had missed the cobblestone streets and stone homes. He had never thought he would see his home again. At last he would visit his Ursula and Gretchen again. They would love him for eternity. They would never throw him out.

Arriving in Stadthagen, he checked in at a hotel near the train station. As soon as he was settled, he called Heinrich Müller.

"Dr. Müller? This is David Strauss from America. Do you remember me?"

"David? Yes! Where are you?"

"I'm at the Altera, near the train station. Can we meet? Preferably alone."

"Yes. Is everything okay? What's wrong?"

"I'm not here to cause you any trouble. Things have not gone so well with me, but we can talk when you get here. Can you come right away?"

"You bet I can. What is your room number?"

"I will be waiting in the lobby. Thanks."

He hung up.

Fifteen minutes later David was walking through the front door of the hotel. He spotted Heinrich in the lobby. Heinrich stood up as David walked in. They had a quick embrace. David was concerned. "What is wrong?"

They sat down on sofas.

"A few days after you left, I found it necessary to tell Catherine our story. She was not as understanding as I hoped she would be. In fact she was not understanding at all."

"What happened?"

"Basically she called me a liar and a cheat and asked me to leave. I tried to explain to her, but she would have none of it."

David looked pained. "That is so Catherine. It sounds as if she hasn't changed a lot over the years. I'm so sorry. I didn't know. I wouldn't have hurt you for anything in the world."

Heinrich smiled a sad smile. "It's not your fault, old friend. I guess I must have forgotten, Catherine has a strong sense of what's right and what's wrong and no in between."

David looked Heinrich straight in the eye. "Oooh yes, I remember. It would take more than amnesia to make me forget that. I've been in trouble with her more times than you can imagine."

"Well anyway, there was no talking with her. 'It was wrong... there can be no excuse... you are a liar... the last ten years doesn't count for anything...' I'm sorry; I am beginning to sound like a sore loser. Speaking of amnesia, how are you doing?"

"Great, I guess. Large patches of memory just appear. When I remember something, it's like I haven't thought about it for a while. The biggest problem I have is the timeline. My last memories as David were the four years in the army. They seem like yesterday. Now, tucked into my memory gap are the nine years as Heinrich married to Jillian. It gets very confusing sometimes. The worst part is that I feel there is something very important that I was supposed to do. I just can't remember what it is. Well, enough about me, what can I do to help?"

"Strangely enough, I am looking for a job and a place to live."

"Neither of those should be hard to take care of. You have a house already. Why don't you move back in?"

"No, that's your home now. There can only be one Heinrich Müller, that's you!"

"This is awkward. I do understand though. What are you looking for in the way of work?"

"I would like to work at the hospital as a staff surgeon. This is the only place I want to stay. If I had a small salary and a place to live in near the hospital and cemetery, I think my needs would be met."

"Well, 'David' neither of those will be hard to fill. Let me pick you up tomorrow and I will take you to the hospital and introduce you. They are always in need of staff. With my recommendation the job will be yours. Besides that, the first time they see you in the operating room, they will never allow you to leave.

"Before we do that though, we will get you situated in a home. I, no, you have a piece of property three blocks from the hospital that we have been setting up to rent. It's not far from the cemetery either. I will take you over the first

269

thing. If you don't like it, there are some others that might fill the bill."

"What do you mean; I have a piece of property?"

"What I mean is that everything I have is yours. It was all started with your money, I live in your house, and we run your construction company. Need I say more?"

"Now let me tell you a few things. I have nothing. I am not here to make any claims or cause any problems. I am here to be near Ursula and Gretchen. As long as I am here, I might as well work and help people. At this point in my life, that's all I need."

"You don't understand, Heinrich, you saved my life. Because of you I have Jillian and the children. That and my work make my life complete."

"First of all, call me David. That's been my name for the past ten years and I've grown accustomed to it. That is, if you don't mind. Now, let's get this straight. It's you that saved my life. For one thing I am not speaking Russian. The second thing you did for me was to give me the happiest ten years of my life. I guess that's not entirely true. I took the happiest ten years of my life from you. I had thought that true happiness had passed me by and died with Ursula and Gretchen, yet I found it again. If I have lost it, it's because it was never mine in the first place. It was yours. I'm sorry, but thank you."

"We are getting into a real complicated area. I love Jillian. My memories of Catherine are still somewhat confused. I don't know how to reconcile my love for Jillian with my love for Catherine. My memories of Jillian are the newest. My love for Catherine is somewhat vague. I think we should wait and see if this will sort itself out. I have just talked a lot and said absolutely nothing. To be honest with you, I have no idea what to do, so I vote we wait."

"Catherine voted for me, so I have no options," Heinrich said.

"Okay, now back to the problem at hand. In the morning we'll find you a place to live. Then we'll go to the hospital and get you a job."

270

They both sat quiet for a moment then David looked at Heinrich. "I am so sorry that I messed things up for you. When I was trying to recover my past, I had no idea I would be destroying someone else's future. I wouldn't have done it for the world."

Heinrich stood up. "Please, don't worry about it. I've lived for the past ten years with the nagging feeling in the back of my mind that this would happen someday. Maybe that's really why I had true confessions that night. I was tired and just didn't want to deal with it any longer. What's done is done. It didn't work out and I'm going to go forward with my life. It may not be at the breakneck speed that I once had; but I'm going to make a difference in someone's life before I die."

David had stood up as well. He extended his hand. "You have made a difference in mine and in all those I've been able to help as a result of your actions."

They shook hands and parted. Heinrich walked up the stairs to his room feeling good. This was the best he had felt since he and Catherine had parted. Once again he had a purpose in life.

That night David dreamed about Catherine again. This was the first time since he had returned to Germany. He saw her when they were growing up together. He relived the first time he kissed her and how Scott teased him so much. His life flashed past in a blur as they went on church picnics and swimming parties. He remembered once again how much he loved her. It ended in the drugstore at their booth when he gave her an engagement ring. Even though his father was a jeweler, he'd bought it with his own money. The stone was tiny, but she didn't care. There were tears running down her cheeks and he could still taste the salt in the kiss. He held both her hands in his and began to talk. That was when he awakened soaked in sweat. There was something he was supposed to do or remember but his mind was a blank.

The next morning Heinrich and David did as planned and looked at the home. It was much nicer than Heinrich had expected. When Heinrich asked what the rent would be, David shook his head. "You still don't get it do you? There is no rent. You can stay here as long as you like, rent free. If you decide you want to stay permanently, I will sign it over to you. I can't do enough for you so you might as well get used to it. I have my best friend back and words can't express what I feel. If you like the house, we can go over to the hospital now. I made a ten o'clock appointment with Dr. Klaus, but we can be early if we wish."

Heinrich laughed. Excitement coursed through his entire body. He wondered if he was glowing. "I love the house! I remember riding my bicycle past here when I was a lad. You have kept it in immaculate condition. I am amazed that it is available."

David beamed. "For some strange reason I haven't put it on the market. I had no reason that I know of, but I just didn't do it. Now I know why."

Dr. Klaus was very cordial when the two men came into his office. It was very obvious that David was respected and carried quite a bit of influence in this community; however, when Heinrich presented a letter of recommendation from the Chief of Staff at Roquefort Hospital he began to smile.

"I don't think we need to go any further with this. I could put you to work today, but I am sure you need a few days to get settled. Where will you be staying?"

"I have a small home on Buschingstrasse only about three blocks from here."

"Excellent. Suppose you start next Monday."

Dr. Klaus picked up his telephone and pressed a button. "Frau Schwartz, will you come into my office, please?"

The office door opened and his secretary came in. "This is Dr. Strauss..." pointing to Heinrich. "He will be on our surgical staff starting Monday. Please take care of any paperwork. That will be all." Turning to Heinrich he said, "I would like to give you a tour of our facility. You will find it is one of the better equipped ones in this part of Germany due to the generosity of Dr. Müller here."

David walked to the door to leave. "I need to be taking care of some appointments, if you need anything just call."

As Heinrich and Dr. Klaus were touring the hospital, he asked Heinrich. "You're an American, how did you and Dr. Müller meet?"

"During the war we were in Stalag 21 together. He was the camp physician, and I was a prisoner. We learned from one another and became close friends. I had not seen him since the end of the war until we happened to meet again at a conference in New York City. We visited and renewed our acquaintance. When he saw the work I was doing with Ohio State University Medical School, he suggested I come here and trade techniques. I needed a break and thought it would be good."

"Wunderbar! This is an exciting time for us. I am looking forward to working with you."

After he completed the tour, Heinrich walked to his new home. Instead of stopping, he continued past until he came to the cemetery. He was able to go straight to the family plot where he visited with Ursula and Gretchen. He talked with Ursula about his new job and how exciting it was. "I took a tour of the hospital with Dr. Klaus and he showed me the changes that have taken place. It looked good. What he didn't know is that I was working in that hospital while he was still in medical school. It is good to be home."

He left, promising to return soon. His next job was to furnish his new home. After visiting several furniture stores, he came to the conclusion that he was not going to find the furniture he had in Ohio. He had enjoyed the lighter airy atmosphere of his home in Roquefort but would have to be satisfied with the traditional look.

When Jillian returned from her business trip to Munich, David suggested they talk.

Jillian was worried. "You look serious. What is wrong?"

He took a deep breath and released it slowly. "Remember when we were in America and visited with David and Catherine Strauss?"

Jillian stopped unpacking and stared uncomfortably at him. "Yes..."

"Do you remember that I told you there were things in my past that you might want to hear about?"

"Yes, and I also remember that I told you I was not interested as long as they did not affect our lives together."

"That's right. While you were out of town, David Strauss arrived in Stadthagen."

"He did? Why?"

"He told Catherine his story and she asked him to leave. He had nowhere to go, so he came here. He has started working at Stadthagen Hospital."

She straightened up. "But why would he come here?"

David spoke slowly. "...because this was his home."

Jillian had a quizzical look on her face. She folded and unfolded her arms in front of her after sitting down. "Perhaps now is a good time to tell me your story."

"This is what I learned while we were in Roquefort. David and I talked that afternoon and verified what I thought I knew. I just couldn't figure out how it happened."

"Don't beat around the bush, get on with it!" She was on the edge of her chair now, her hands gripping the armrests.

"It seems that when the attack on the camp occurred, the hospital received several direct hits."

Jillian was agitated. "We already knew that."

"Please, relax. If I am going to tell you the story, I have to set it up."

"Okay, I'm sorry. I'm all ears, now get on with it."

"We were both injured and he came over to check on me. He checked my pulse and weak as it was, he thought I was dead. As he told me, he was in such bad shape he probably wouldn't have felt it if it was a bass drum.

274

Anyway, he was worried that the Russians would take him prisoner."

"Why would they do that?" she interrupted.

David put his hand up. "Let me tell it please. The reason he was worried was that he was German."

"German? I thought he was from Ohio!"

David stopped talking and just looked at Jillian. He smiled and shook his head. Still, he didn't say a word.

"Okay, I'm sorry. I just couldn't help myself. You are the slowest story teller on the planet!"

David continued to look at her.

"Alright, I'll be quiet."

David started again. "He was German, believe me. In his dazed state he came up with what appeared to be a brilliant solution to his problem. He traded dog tags with me."

Jillian looked exasperated. "Now how would that help? You were German too!"

"No, I wasn't. That is what I have been trying to tell you. My name is actually David Strauss and the David Strauss you met in Ohio is...was Heinrich Müller."

Jillian looked as if she had been struck dumb. She kept trying to say something but no words came out. Finally she stopped and just sat there. She looked up at him. "You mean Catherine is your wife! How can that be? It's been too long. What about our children? Is he claiming his home? Are we going to have to move..."

Putting up his hands with the palms forward, David said, "Stop! Nothing is going to change for us. Just relax and your questions will get answered."

"How do you expect me to relax? Suddenly everything is different."

"Nothing is different." He explained. "We settled that at the park in Roquefort. He told me he was not interested in coming here. He loved his home in Ohio. I was happy with the only life I had remembered before that trip. I had a beautiful wife, wonderful children and a purpose in life."

"Then why is he here?"

"He unwisely told Catherine. She went crazy. She did not want to know more, he was a liar that had stolen her life and she wanted him out!"

"Why didn't he just go to a hotel?"

"Think about it. He was a German soldier that sneaked into the country pretending to be an American war hero. If she decided to call the police, he would likely spend years in jail. The only sensible thing for him to do was leave. He traveled a while, but had nowhere to go, so he came home."

Jillian just sat a while. "Poor Catherine, I feel so bad for her."

David was stunned. "Poor Catherine? How about poor David?"

"Do you mean you or him? This could get confusing you know."

"Him. Let's keep the names the way they were. It makes life easier. Besides that, he is not interested in our home or our business. Calling him Heinrich would only confuse people. Now, why poor Catherine? David is the one who spent ten years loving and caring for her. Now she ups and tosses him away on a technicality."

"Technicality? She lost the man she loved. HE stepped in and deceived her. She had dedicated her life to you, not him. Suddenly she finds out that you have come to town and the two of you decided not to let her in on your secret. Now she is living with a stranger and the man she loved is dead to her."

"Didn't she love HIM for ten years?"

"That's not the point. She was in love with the man she thought he was. Now she discovers it was all an illusion."

"Oh." David looked dejected. Jillian was finding holes in an argument that seemed perfectly logical when he and Heinrich discussed it. While the basic setup wasn't his fault, his decision to go along with it made him guilty.

"I think he was the man she thought he was, just not the person. Besides that, his intentions were honorable."

"My father used to say 'the road to hell is paved with good intentions.' Now what are you going to do about it?"

"Do about it? Nothing! I didn't start it and it's not my fault. In fact, I'm glad he did it. If he hadn't, I would have never met you and I might still be in a wheel chair as well."

"All very good reasons that you owe him."

I walked right into that one. "I see now why you do so well in sales. I think at this time we should back off and just see what happens. Trying to fix things is what got us in this mess in the first place."

Jillian put her arms around his neck and gave him a peck on the lips. "Okay, let's wait."

As he quickly left the room, a thought crossed his mind. *That was too easy. I wonder what she's up to.*

Chapter 42

Jillian walked into David's office and leaned against the doorframe with her arms folded.

He looked up from the papers on his desk and noted her position. "What can I do for you, fair maiden?"

She smiled and he got a funny feeling in his stomach. "It has been two months since David arrived and nothing has changed. All he does is work and carry flowers to the cemetery. It's time for you to do something."

David leaned back in his chair and studied her face. Immediately he knew he should be on guard. "I don't know of anything to do. I've talked with him a number of times and it's always the same answer. Catherine asked him to leave and was quite adamant about it. He says he's happy with his life as it is and would appreciate it if I would not bring it up again."

Jillian walked around his desk to his side and leaned against the edge. "I don't care what he says; he's too nice a person to live that way. Something has been running through my mind for some time. Tell me what you think. I believe you need to go to Catherine and straighten this whole mess out. He did it out of loyalty to you. It's up to you to try everything you can."

"I'd rather not do that. I think the best thing I can do is let them live their lives and solve their own problems." David hadn't mentioned that he had been having dreams of Catherine again and didn't want to take any more chances. "The more I remember about Catherine, the more I remember the arguments we had. No matter how she remembers it, we didn't get along that well. Maybe that's why I had amnesia. I didn't want to go back."

"I can't believe that a grown man like you would let a little thing like her intimidate you."

"Please, Jillian let it lie," he said dejectedly.

"No, I think this is something you should do. Heinrich is your friend and Catherine will only listen to you."

He knew there was no point in arguing. "Okay, I give. You win. Now what?" He felt sick inside.

Jillian smiled, slid into his lap and put her arms around his neck. "You are so wonderful. I don't know how I could be so lucky to have found my little lost puppy that day on the seashore."

David kissed her and stood up, almost dumping her on the floor. "You have already won; you don't have to butter me up anymore." He was smiling, but his stomach was in knots.

Catching herself and standing she smiled her smile. "All right then, your bags are packed and I have you booked on a five-thirty flight to London, then to New York and on to Columbus, Ohio, USA. You should be able to take it from there."

After David left, Jillian sat in her office chair looking out the window at the beautiful scene before her. Children were playing hide and seek in the wooded area. Others were jumping rope and of course, the constant soccer game was going with the boys who would play anywhere. It was a beautiful sight. She wondered if it would continue or if this part of her life was over. Why did happiness seem so elusive? Given the chance, it would slip away and hide, much like the children playing hide and seek in the woods. She was heartsick. Over the past weeks she had heard Heinrich tossing in his sleep and calling Catherine's name. She knew him well enough to know that given the chance he would never return to America, but this would fester inside and would bother him until he did what he called the 'honorable' thing. She also knew that he was now trapped between two allegiances; she was his wife and the mother of his children, Catherine was his first love and the mother of the son he had never met. He was honor bound to two families. There was no right answer. She prayed that she wouldn't lose her happiness. Thinking about it though, she knew that she would do it all over again even it ended today. The quality that made him so special was also the quality that might take him away.

Chapter 43

David had been dreaming of Catherine since Heinrich had returned and was exhausted when he boarded the plane for New York. After takeoff, he laid his seat back and almost immediately fell into a deep sleep. He had hoped the dream would go away, but it was back. Catherine was sitting across from him in 'their booth.' She had the red, white, and blue ribbons in her hair. He had just given her the engagement ring and kissed her across the table. This time it was different. As he took both her hands in his he said, "Catherine, I love you with all my heart. I pledge my love for you through this life and all eternity." He leaned over and sealed it with a kiss. As his lips touched hers, he awakened. A feeling of dread coursed through his body until it engulfed him completely. This was the same pledge he had given to Jillian the day they arrived at the schloss. He had left home with the hope of solving Heinrich's problem. Now he realized that Heinrich might have to solve his own problems. His were far greater. He knew he still loved Catherine after all these years and had made the same commitment to her as he made to Jillian. He didn't sleep for the rest of the trip. He would close his eyes and immediately the smiling face of Catherine would appear, ribbons and all, as he leaned over to seal his covenant with a kiss.

Instead of taking the train to Roquefort, he rented a car at Columbus Airport. He wanted to drive and have a chance to see the countryside at leisure. It would also delay the problem.

Most of the snow had melted and the bravest of the trees had sent test shoots of green out. He loved this time of year. Spring always brought out thoughts of new beginnings. Perhaps this would carry on with Catherine.

Arriving in town, he checked in at the Bismarck Hotel, the same place he had stayed with Jillian. There was a certain comfort with being in familiar surroundings. After settling in, he checked the phone book and dialed the number of Dr. David Strauss. The voice that answered was not one David knew. "This is Heinrich Müller calling, is Mrs. Strauss in?"

"Just a moment please."

Memories flooded as he heard Catherine's voice. "Dr. Müller? Or should I say Strauss? Where are you calling from?"

"Either name works for me," David answered. "Actually I am in town. Can we talk?"

"Why?" she said with an edge to her voice.

David could feel the blood rushing to his head. "You know Cathy, I have just flown five thousand miles to have this conversation and I don't need a smart answer. Last time I was here I made some startling discoveries that I wasn't prepared to deal with. I don't know how you feel about things, and I certainly don't know what I feel, but I believe that we need to face them and get our lives in order."

Catherine answered with ice in her voice, "When?"

"How about now," David answered hotly. This wasn't going as he had envisioned. How did she get him riled up so quickly? After all these years and it was if time had not passed. There were some things he had not remembered.

"Come on over then. Do you remember how to get here?"

"I believe I can find it. See you shortly." He hung up the phone before she could answer.

He used the drive out to calm down. It was wonderful to drive in the States. The roads were so modern when compared with those in Germany. Some of the roads in Stadthagen were still waiting for repair from damage over ten years ago in the war. The war had certainly not touched this town. At least not in the physical way it had in Europe. Broken hearts and broken lives were not as obvious as potholed streets.

He pulled into the drive and stopped in front of the door of the immaculate house with the immaculate yard and, he was sure, the immaculate mistress.

He was surprised when Catherine answered the door herself. He guessed that she gave the maid the rest of the day off in order to keep the town from knowing what was going on.

"Catherine, I'm sorry I was short with you over the phone. It wasn't my intention to cause trouble. I am probably tired from the trip."

She had a strained look on her face. She waved her hand for him to come in. "Don't worry about it. Come in." She stood and looked at him before tears came to her eyes. "Is it really you David?"

Memories of the good years together flooded to the surface of his mind once again. This was the girl he had dated through high school. This was the companion that he had spent hours with making plans for the future. "Yes it's me, Cathy."

He stood there with his arms hanging, not knowing what to do.

Crying, Catherine threw her arms around him. She gave him a kiss full on the lips. "What have they done to you?" Her body shook as she cried and continued to hold him. "What have they done to you?"

She had turned her head and laid it against his chest. He put his arms around her and pulled her close. Once again they were together. How he had missed her. This was the girl of his dreams. She seemed to fit perfectly, as though she belonged in his arms. He didn't want to let go... but slowly he did.

Placing his hands on her shoulders he gently pushed until he could backup a step. Smiling he said, "What do you think of my new face? It takes a little getting used to, but I've gotten to like it."

Catherine had a horrified look on her face. "How can you be so glib about it? My beautiful David is gone!"

The reality of the situation struck him once again. "If it's the face you want, you sent him away. If it is the heart and soul of the man you loved and who loved you, I'm here."

"Are you here David...? I just don't know what to think anymore." She turned and walked into the library. A fire burned in the fireplace. She sat on the couch and warmed her hands.

David followed and sat beside her.

"Please sit over in that chair," she said, pointing to a loveseat across from her. "I can think a lot better if you're not beside me."

"I can't," he said.

He sat beside her, took her in his arms and kissed her. As he held her close, his heart raced and his head swirled, what was he doing?

"I thought I was over you," he said. "I had my mind made up how this was going to go and I then would leave."

"What made you change your mind?" she said.

"You weren't supposed to kiss me. I had a wall built up around my heart. Suddenly it's you again... red, white & blue ribbons in your hair... Do you remember?"

"How could I forget? I have dreamed it over and over these past months. We were sitting in our booth and you were holding my hand. You had just given me my ring; your hand was sweaty..." Smiling with a tear running down her cheek she said, "How am I doing?" Then without waiting for an answer she said, "You looked me straight in the eye and said, 'Catherine, I love you with all my heart. I pledge my love for you through this life and all eternity.'"

His eyes were on the floor. Taking a deep breath and raising his eyes to meet hers he said, "I believe that's the way I have remembered it every night for the last three months."

Tilting her head to the side she wiped a tear from her eye. "What a mess. I have missed you so much these past years."

With a look of surprise he said, "How could you have missed me? In a way, until a few months ago, I was here."

Her voice cracked a little, "You're right, but it was not entirely the same. He was the perfect version of what I thought I wanted. But it wasn't the same."

"I don't understand," he said.

"Little things, music for instance. Our little home was once filled with music. I could listen to you for hours."

He looked at the piano for a moment then stood and stepped over to it. Sliding onto the bench he ran his hands lightly over the keys without making a sound. Suddenly sounds began to come from the piano. He began to quietly sing... "I'll be loving you always, with a love that's true always..." and it went on... "not for just an hour, not for just a day, not for just a year, but always..."

"Stop!" she said. "I can't take it. You're killing me."

Ignoring her comments and shaking his head he said, "That song has been in the back of my mind for years, but I couldn't make it come out."

"You guys are all alike. I believe it's called 'insensitive.' I guess you haven't changed that much. That's one place... 'the other David' had you beat, at least until the end."

She sat quietly for a few minutes. David decided not to interrupt her meditation.

"...and, I don't know," she said as if there had been no interruption in their conversation, "There was always a secret place I could not reach, in... 'Heinrich'. It's hard to call him that. Anyway, I felt it was tied up with painful memories of the war."

Smiling painfully, she said, "I guess it was, I just did not know whose memories they were."

Looking away at the fire she said, "Then there were our growing up times. I realize now that the only memories he had of that time were the ones I told him about. He skillfully replayed them back, just like a record player."

Turning to look at him she said, "Why did you do it? Didn't you still love me?"

Startled back to reality he said, "Do what?"

"Pretend you didn't know me. You cannot imagine how much that hurt me."

"Nobody intended to hurt anyone, Cathy. Put yourself in my shoes for a minute. For ten years I had been Heinrich Muller. I had a wife and children, a schloss in Germany, a successful medical practice, a large construction company and of course a family of uncles and cousins. Now within twenty-four hours I find that it is an illusion and I have a wife and family in America. I was okay with it until we kissed at the door. Now I am torn between my heart, and my honor. How can I be true to everyone? You cannot imagine how much I love you and yet I have a responsibility to Jillian and the kids."

"What about me? Don't you have a responsibility to me? How about Davy?"

"As far as I can see, you and Davy, and the rest of your children have been loved and cared for by someone who loved them and loved you as well."

Anger rose in Catherine's voice. "How can you talk so glibly about Heinrich, or whatever his name is? He ruined our lives."

"He didn't ruin anyone's life. He was just trying to survive. On top of that, he was kind enough to watch over the family of his best friend."

"You have got to be out of your mind!" she shouted. "He moved in and stole your life."

Once again, David was brought back to reality.

286

"Stole my life," he asked incredulously. "I didn't have a life to steal. Do you know what I remembered of my previous life?"

Continuing he said, "There was only one memory of my past that I kept. It was a woman's voice saying, 'Don't bother to come back at all.'"

Catherine flushed as she looked at the floor.

"I never knew where it came from, but it flashed into my mind over and over during those past years. Then I heard it for real the night Jillian and I came to Papa's party. It was your voice." He had calmed down until he spoke in a whisper.

She looked up with tears in her eyes and said, "Oh David, I'm so sorry."

He shook his head. "I'm sorry too. I shouldn't have brought it up. That was the past."

Standing and walking over to the love seat he looked her square in the face as he sat. "Let me start over and tell the story from the beginning from my point of view. Please don't interrupt. One day my memory begins to come back."

"Just a minute!" she said.

He raised his hand palm up and looked at her indicating the conversation they had just had. "When it does, I discover I have a wife and son in Ohio. At the same time I have a wife and three children in Germany. That is a lot to soak up in a matter of hours. You appeared to be happy with your life, and I was happy with mine. The only thing I could think of was 'why take a chance on messing up both our lives.' It seems that my efforts were futile, here we are, not knowing which way to turn."

She looked toward the fire and crossed her arms to regain her composure. A little of her hostility had returned. "How can you take this so calmly? Like a thief, Heinrich Müller stole your face and your life! He is nothing but a thief and a liar!"

David shook his head. He knew now what he must do. "I think you have it all wrong Catherine. Heinrich Müller saved my life, both physically and emotionally!"

"Well, he has a strange way of doing it." She said more calmly. "I don't know how you can sit there and defend him after what he did to you." She was becoming agitated again.

"Perhaps if you will listen for a minute - with an open mind, I can tell you!" Anger was edging into his voice again.

"What do you mean? I have an open mind!"

"Right! Let me tell you about the day the camp was liberated."

Catherine interrupted. "I have heard this story before."

"This is what I was talking about! You are so sure of yourself... You have life put into little boxed marked right - wrong - good - bad - truth -lie! You don't know what to do if something happens that you can't sort out. You just close your mind to it."

"There is nothing wrong with knowing the difference between right and wrong, or the truth and a lie!"

"What is the worst thing that has ever happened to you?"

"What do you mean?" Catherine sounded unsure.

"I mean what is the worst thing that has ever happen to you?"

"It must have been learning that you were missing in action." She looked at the floor and cleared her throat.

"That really didn't happen to you - it happened to me. I will tell you the worst thing that has ever happened to you. I remember it well. Sandra Jorgenson got put on the cheerleading squad and she was captain over you. You came home from school devastated. You said your life was over. How am I doing?"

"That's not fair," she said angrily.

"It may not be fair, but it is still the truth. Life is not fair. Everything does not fit in little boxes labeled right and wrong. When that airplane crashed into Heinrich's home,

288

from an American point of view, it was just a few more Krauts getting what they deserved for starting the war. From little Gretchen's point of view, she was an innocent child who did not know what the war was about."

Catherine's voice shook as she quietly said, "Little Gretchen?"

"You remember her. She was the daughter he lost during the war; the same name as your daughter. Ironic isn't it, now he has lost her twice."

In a calmer voice David said, "The only thing I am asking of you is to give him a chance. If the worst thing he has done is to pretend to be me, then he must be a pretty good man on his own. I think so. That's why I flew five thousand miles to have this conversation; that and one other thing... I'm sorry the way things turned out Catherine. I did love you and still do. I don't know why things happened the way they did, but they did and I am prepared to live with it. It's just another of those things that don't fit into the neat little boxes. Jillian lost a father at Dunkirk and a fiancé at Anzio. She has done no wrong. Should I add more pain to her by doing what is 'right' according to someone's definition? As I see it, there is no way out of this without either someone being hurt or deciding to deal with the situation as it is. You've done nothing wrong Catherine, but like the rest of us you got caught in the trap we call 'life'. The question is, is the life you had with Heinrich worth saving?"

Catherine sat with her hands folded in her lap. She looked very tired. Raising her hand to her brow, she shook her head from side to side. "I don't know, David. Suddenly everything, every value I have held dear has been challenged and I don't know if I am capable of dealing with it."

She looked up at David. "Why do you say that Heinrich Müller saved your life?"

"In a round about way he did just that. I have certainly had plenty of time to think about it and this is the conclusion I have come up with. When Uncle Hans and

Erik found me, they took me to the finest hospital in Switzerland. Because they were extremely wealthy, I was able to receive individual attention there that I could not have received anywhere else. When they could do no more, I met Jillian. Now I am not saying that you could not have helped me, but she was an expert at physical therapy. Between her and Erik, they created any equipment they needed to help me. After all that, she drove me until I thought I would die. It was painful but she recreated me as a man who could literally and emotionally stand on his own.

"I remember our first night here when we met Papa. I did not know then who he was, I only knew I did not like being around him. If I had returned straight home from the war, he would have taken over my life just as he had before. Very likely you and I would have divorced. Because I had no past, my only loyalty was to my German family. They had no agenda. Their only concern was for my welfare."

Catherine stood and walked to the fire and began to warm her hands. She turned back to David with a look of concern on her face. "Doing the right thing for the wrong reason doesn't make it okay."

David stood and gave Catherine a slight smile. "I guess it doesn't according to your standards." He laughed and shook his head. "I would have never survived here." He turned to leave then turned back. "Do you still go to church?"

Catherine was startled at the question. "Yes, why do you ask?"

"As you probably remember, I am not much of a scriptorian but doesn't it say in the Bible, 'I the Lord will forgive whom I will forgive, but for you it is to forgive all men.' Or something like that."

"That's a switch, you quoting the Bible to me."

"There are a lot of things you don't know about me. People do change."

Catherine took a few steps closer. "One thing before you go. I am guessing you know where Heinrich is."

"He is called David Strauss now and he is living in a small house in Stadthagen. He works at the hospital and visits the graves of his parents, his wife Ursula and his daughter Gretchen every day. That is pretty much his life. Jillian and I try to get him to come over, but he will not come into the house. When we do meet, we go to a small restaurant nearby.

"I'm staying at the Bismarck. I'll be checking out tomorrow morning at eleven. If you would like to talk again before I leave, please call."

Catherine hugged David. "Thanks for being who you are. I wish I could be what you need. I am sorry for who I am, but I don't know if I can change. I'll call you in the morning after the kids have left for school."

Chapter 44

It had been a hard day at the hospital. Heinrich had been on his feet since early in the morning. He considered not going to the cemetery just this one time but as he came to the flower shop he automatically turned in.

"Good afternoon Dr. Strauss. I have your flowers waiting."

He paid for them and began his walk. *I will have to be tired some other day.* The afternoon was beautiful. The sun was shinning through the trees and the breeze was still cool. He enjoyed this walk. It reminded him of earlier days before the war and before he had to grow up. He and Erik would ride their bicycles down this street past the cemetery to the edge of town. They would put their bicycles in the trees and go for a hike or rock climbing. They would skip rocks or fish in the stream. Life had no demands, only that they be home in time for supper. He turned into the cemetery and walked toward the area where his family was buried. As he did, he noticed children playing and thought it odd since school was still in session. Drawing nearer he saw something familiar about them. Of course, they were David's children, but who was with them? Gretchen? David? He started running. He dropped the flowers along the way. How could this be?

"Gretchen, Davy! Is it you?"

"Daddy!" The children ran to meet him. Tears were streaming down his face as he dropped to his knees and wrapped his arms around them.

"How? What are you doing here?"

"We got tired of waiting for you to come home," said a voice from the trees.

He looked to his left. "Catherine!" Letting go of the kids he stood as she ran to his arms.

She threw her arms around him and kissed him. As they kissed, her body began to tremble and tears ran down her cheeks. She leaned back in his arms and looked at him. "Can you ever forgive me?" she said through her tears.

"Forgive? There is nothing to forgive... I should have never deceived you."

She put her finger over his lips and said, "If you hadn't, we wouldn't have Gretchen and she is worth everything."

With tears in her eyes she said, "With you I had the best ten years of my life and then I almost broke up our family with my stubbornness."

Heinrich kissed her again. "You come as a complete package and I love everything about you."

The children had gathered up the flowers he had dropped and were placing them on the graves. "How is this Daddy?"

"Absolutely beautiful!"

Catherine stepped back and surveyed the scene before her, David was down with the children arranging flowers over his lost family... and she knew it was right. The thought flashed in her mind, *what God has joined together let no 'woman' put asunder.*

The End

17807118R00160

Made in the USA
Charleston, SC
01 March 2013